THE
IRON WAY

ALSO BY TIM LEACH

THE SARMATIAN TRILOGY
A Winter War

OTHER HISTORICAL NOVELS
The Last King of Lydia
The King and the Slave
Smile of the Wolf

THE
IRON WAY

TIM LEACH

An Aries Book

First published in the UK in 2022 by Head of Zeus
This paperback edition first published in 2023 by Head of Zeus,
part of Bloomsbury Publishing Plc

975312468

A catalogue record for this book is available from the British Library.

ISBN (PB): 9781800242913
ISBN (E): 9781800242968

Typeset by Siliconchips Services Ltd UK

Map design by Jeff Edwards

Printed and bound in Great Britain by
CPI Group (UK) Ltd, Croydon CR0 4YY

Head of Zeus Ltd
5–8 Hardwick Street
London EC1R 4RG

WWW.HEADOFZEUS.COM

For Sara

AD 175

Antonine Wall (disused)

DAMNONII

R. Clyde

VO

DAMNONII

S o u t h e r n

U p l

R. Nithe

SELGOVAE

NOVANTAE

Maia

Conca

Solway Firth

Bibra □

Legend
□ Roman forts

Alauna

□ Magis
□ Gabrosentum

0 — 25 miles

0 — 50 km

Part 1

THE WALL

1

In the unforgiving land at the northern edge of the Empire, a monstrous shadow loomed upon the horizon.

It was not the jagged edge of a cliff or a towering forest, for this was a shadow that men had made. Rising tall and impossible above the rolling hills and scattered trees was a great wall of stone, cutting across the landscape straight as the stroke of a sword.

Once, in this place that the Romans knew as Britannia and the local tribes called by half a hundred different names, the border of the Empire had been but a thing of thought and dreams. A cold feeling that danced across the skin as a man crossed through a field of heather, a question that local chieftains argued over in cattle raids and bloodfeuds, a mystery marked in the position of the stars and signs read in the land itself. Some claimed to find it by where a single white stone was found amid a pile of grey pebbles, others in the dried-up passage of an old river, or the place where a hazel tree had been split by a bolt of lightning when the Romans first set foot upon this land. Every man and woman had to mark their own border in their minds, between the last far reaches of the Empire and the wild lands beyond.

But one day it was said the great Emperor from across the sea had grown tired of borders made from thoughts and dreams. He had craved a legacy of stone that marked the land as his, and so the Wall had been raised from the earth at his command, done so quickly that some local tribes insisted it had been done at the whim of a vengeful god.

From afar, it looked invincible. It was said that a man could walk upon it from one sea to another and never lay his feet upon the earth. A little fort at every mile, every inch of the ground surveilled, and all throughout the night there were torches burning on the ramparts, unsleeping guardians who watched the darkness with spear and bow in hand.

Yet every border has its weaknesses, if one looks close enough.

There was a milecastle near the centre of the Wall that had once possessed some sense of Imperial grandeur. Proud pale stone, an iron-studded gate of dark oak that seemed fit to stand against the blows of a giant. But it had been lazily built by some Legion used to warmer climes, and lacking the wit or the care to adapt their work to a different world. For now the wooden boards on the ramparts were rotten and warped, the mortar of the stonework worn away by rain and wind, and there was rust upon the iron of the gates.

Even so, the sentries were still and steady upon the battlements, and below them the gate guard stood alone and faced the wild north beyond. All held themselves tall, did not flinch at the cutting wind or shirk their duty as the hours drew on. Even here, at the very edge of the Empire, in the deepest part of the night, it seemed that the spirit of Rome was watchful.

There was little enough for them to see in the day – mist rolling across distant hills, a herdsman coaxing worm-ridden sheep through the bog, a lone trader and his mule come to sell heather beer and dubious potions to the soldiers of the Wall. At night they would see even less, for the native people of this land considered it ill luck to be abroad after sunset. A sentry might pass his entire night watch and count himself lucky to espy something to break the monotony – the ghostly sight of a white owl quartering the fields, perhaps, or the flash of distant lightning in the valley beyond.

But not this night. For in the darkness, there were shadows crawling through the bracken.

They were crouched low, and moved only when the wind blew to cover the sound of their passage. A dull-eyed sentry might have mistaken them for a breeze shaking the undergrowth, or for a pack of wolves following the scent of a herd. But, careful as they were, the raiders could only move quiet and unseen for so long. The scrape and rustle of leaves turning aside threatened to give them away, as did the rattle of a spearhead poorly socketed in the haft and singing in the wind. And the clouds that had covered their approach played the traitor now, thinning and scattering, and one could see the glimmer of moonlight on a broad leaf blade of a spear, and shining upon white teeth, upon faces painted for war.

Yet still no alarm was sounding, no whisper of arrows stitching through the interlopers, no horns or signal fires warning the next milecastle along. Up on the battlements, one sentry's head began to nod up and down – half asleep at his post, or so it seemed. Witchcraft, a charm of luck, or the favour of the gods kept the raiders unnoticed as they drew closer and closer to the Wall.

But all luck runs out eventually. For the gods are fickle, and jealous of good fortune.

Open ground lay before the raiders, for the undergrowth had been cut back from road and fort long before. It was creeping back now after many years of neglect, but still left bare terrain that no raiding party could hope to cross unseen.

The shadows crouched there and waited for a time, trying to decide. For their choice was to slink back through the heather to their steadings in shame, or to make a rush across the open ground and die beneath the Wall. Hands flexed upon spears, eyes darted around to their companions. None wished to be the first to flee, or the first to chance their lives upon the open ground.

But then, at last, they chose a third way. As the moon tilted through the sky and the clouds broke open, the raiders stood up, stepped forward, and waited.

Now was the time – for the challenge to be called, the horns to sound, for the volley of javelins and arrows and sling stones to cut the raiders down where they stood, for the might of Imperial Rome to destroy those who dared come to her borders with weapons in hand.

There was nothing.

Laughter, then, from the figures in the darkness, little hoots and cries of victory, blessings called to the gods of war and the hunt. They strolled forward unhurriedly, spears and shields carried low, and made their way to the gates of the milecastle. One of the raiders gave a little push to the sentry who stood before the gate – he swung gently on the spot, pivoting and swinging like a scarecrow. The light of the moon was upon him now, his cut throat shining black in the light and his body raised upon a spear. Another of the raiders gave a mocking wave towards the battlements, where two men had been propped against the corners of the fort. For only the dead watched in that place, and they made for poor guardians.

The gate was unlocked, and swung open, creaking, at the push of an open palm. The rolling countryside beyond stretched out before the raiders, and suddenly there was a hesitance to cross that threshold. Like children going to a forbidden place, children who, even if they are unwatched by their mother and father, still feel watchful eyes upon them and fear the judgment that was sure to follow. They looked to one another, and found themselves afraid.

But then, from the bracken behind them, came the steady tread of hooves falling upon earth.

Like something from a nightmare the figure seemed at first – a tall man, cloaked and cowled, who rode upon a towering horse and might have been one of the deathly spirits that were said to wander those lands in the night, snatching away the travellers unlucky enough to be away from the safety of their steadings. But the raiders greeted him with soft calls of welcome, reached up to touch him in the saddle as though seeking a blessing.

That rider did not slow as he approached. He rode through the gate, hawked and spat on the Roman ground, and the others followed soon after, sniffing the air like wolves. For there was the soft smoke of cooking fires upon the air, the tang of manure in the fields. The farms were close, and unprotected, and they whistled back through to their companions, urging them forwards.

Only one sight gave them pause. An ocean of fire, a sprawling campground that lay to the south. Not the squared shape of a Roman Legion on the march, but something different, and alien to that land. Distant shadows moving there, men and horses in their thousands. An army that had no place there, in the shadow of the Wall.

But their leader gave the great campground in the distance but a single glance. He whispered his orders, and set them on a wide circle away from the fires in the night. It was time for them to hunt.

Behind them, upon the Wall, the impaled sentries twisted and nodded in the wind, as the first of the torches on the rampart began to flicker, gutter, and burn down to nothing.

2

The campground ringed the Roman fort of Vindolanda, there in the shadow of the Wall. A wandering traveller who stumbled upon that place might have thought it a besieging army, a horde of barbarians come to make war upon the Empire. For the flickering light of the campfires fell upon the sharp, cold eyes of practiced killers, upon tattoos that showed wolves and dragons and eagles, predators on the hunt. These were no soldiers of the Roman Legion – they were Sarmatians, the nomad warriors who had beaten upon the borders of the Empire for centuries, hungering for iron and gold and blood. Five thousand of them gathered in the shadow of the Wall, a force that few could hope to stand against.

But when one looked closer, one might see the marks of shame and defeat that hung heavy upon them – the weary stillness with which they sat upon the grass, the hunch of the shoulders and slackened jaws. No weapons did the Sarmatians carry, though some had fashioned pieces of wood into the shape of daggers and swords, the way a child might whittle a toy to play with. Shadows of weapons that might give them some comfort, for it was a disgraceful thing for them to be disarmed. And always before there had been great songs about the fires, songs of lovers and heroes, laughter and poetry. Now they sat near silent, tongues thickly bound by shame.

Only here and there, a few men whispered to one another. The same words spoken over and over again, like a prayer to the gods. 'Twenty-five years,' they said to each other. 'Twenty-five years, and we shall go home.' For that, it seemed, was all that was left to those men. None of the freedom of the steppe, the reckless cycle of feud and raid to earn them honour. Only the slow scratching away of one year after another, until they could go home once more.

About the fires they huddled in great ragged bands, sharing warmth and companionship. For the Sarmatians did nothing alone, kept no secrets from one another. All was done with clan and kin, men and women drawn together by blood or the sacred oaths that they swore upon their swords. Yet around one fire, only two men gathered.

One was marked with reddish gold hair, touched here and there with silver, with his beard cut in the fashion of the Emperor – the very picture of a Roman soldier. The other dressed in the leather trousers and belted jacket of the steppe, copper skinned and dark haired, with fresh ragged scars upon his cheeks, the fractured lines of old tattoos still visible beneath them. Some twisting scaled beast, now cut through by the fresh white lines of a blade.

The conquered and the conqueror sat together about the fire, and passed a flask of wine back and forth as brothers might have done. Here and there about them came the sound of horn and drum, quiet and subdued, and the two men kept a companionable silence for a long time, taking it in turns to feed the flames.

At last the Roman spoke.

'Is there any more talk of mutiny, Kai?' he said.

'None that I hear,' Kai answered. He held his hand close to the fire, testing the heat. 'They are calmer, now that we are close to the end of the journey.'

'I thought there would be trouble when the new rations arrived. Rotten meat and spoiled grain.'

Kai shrugged. 'The horses feed well. That is all that matters to my people. Why should shamed men care if they starve?'

Silence again, and by the light of the fire Kai watched the man to whom his fate was now bound. The Roman had one of those endless-seeming names that their people favoured, but he was simply Lucius to the Sarmatians, or, as he was sometimes called, their Great Captain. A man who had been Kai's prisoner in the wars upon the eastern steppe, had earned his freedom through courage with the sword. A man who had bargained with his Emperor for a peace between their peoples, who had saved the Sarmatians from extinction. But at such a high price, for both of them.

'It has been a long road,' said Lucius, as though answering Kai's thoughts, 'and a hard one for your people, I know. But tomorrow, your weapons will be returned to you. You shall be warriors once again.'

'You speak as a man trying to convince himself,' Kai answered.

'You think that I lie to you?'

'I think that warriors need an enemy to fight.' He shaded

his brow, looked about in mockery. 'And yet I see nothing here.'

Lucius pointed towards the Wall, the black line painted against the sky. 'You think that they built that for nothing?'

'Oh yes,' Kai said, a sour twist to his mouth. 'No doubt a race of giants lies beyond it. That is why this land is half abandoned, and they send starving men to guard their little pile of stones. What heroes we shall be.'

Lucius made no answer.

'We all hear the rumours,' said Kai, 'and you have never had the heart to lie well. They did not send us here to fight. They sent us here to rot, and be forgotten. We were promised a war.'

The Roman's face twisted, then – the expression of a man angry at himself, or so Kai thought. 'Some would be grateful for peace,' said Lucius, 'rather than war. I know plenty of Legionaries who would choose the Wall over the Danubius.'

'It is not what was promised to us.'

Lucius shook his head. 'Like a child you are sometimes, with how you speak of these promises.'

'Like a man who expects an oath to be kept, when it is sworn upon a sword.'

Silence again, save for the crackling of the fire.

They both knew the truth of what Kai had said. A promise had been made, far to the east. As a Roman general rose up in Egypt and declared himself a new Emperor, the Sarmatians were to have fought against him, a war to end all wars. But the rebellion was over as soon as it had begun, the traitor's head hacked off by one of his own centurions, salted and wrapped like some piece of rare meat and presented as a gift to the Emperor of Rome. There was no war for the Sarmatians to fight, and so they had been sent to north and west instead, beyond the water and the white cliffs to the farthest reaches of the Empire.

'I do not mean to be ungrateful,' said Kai. 'You gave up much to bring us here, I know. I only ask that you do not lie to me.'

'I know. I am sorry.'

Kai grinned, a flash of teeth in the darkness. 'Perhaps I am wrong,' he said. 'It must be a fearsome people that live beyond that Wall, if Rome needs such a thing to guard it. And such mighty warriors as us.'

'Now it is you, I think, who does not believe what he is saying.'

'I merely practise what I shall tell the others.' Kai turned his gaze to the great shadow upon the horizon. He wondered if he would ever grow used to the sight of the Wall. The Sarmatians came from a place where one might ride for months and find no barrier to their passage, no buildings upon the earth or borders marked save those found in the minds of men. They were a people who built nothing more grand than huts to shelter in during the worst of winters, and it seemed an ill-omened thing to him to block and cut the land apart in such a way. An act against nature and the gods. 'What do you think truly waits for us here?' Kai said.

'The soldier's life. Watching, waiting. Taking taxes from the land. Keeping the peace.' Lucius pointed to the buildings scattered outside of the fort, as a canny tout might have pointed out the wonders of Rome to a traveller. 'Wine and women in the *vicus* – that's the town outside the walls. Good hunting too, I would have thought, in the woods and the hills. It is not such a bad life.' But his voice was half-hearted as he spoke.

'Where would you be, if not here?'

'Back upon the Danubius, fighting one war after another. Oh, I would have the rank of *primus pilus*, a crown of valour on my head. And a tombstone soon enough, outside one fort or another. On the Danubius, centurions lead from the front, and do not live long.'

Kai smiled once more, and voiced the start of an old Sarmatian proverb: 'Though our lives be short—'

'—Let our fame be great,' Lucius said, finishing the saying. 'Yes, we would both have had a warrior's death, out in the east. Brave, and futile. We will have to give your people a new motto to live by here.'

'Aye. To live long, and see our homes again.' A pause. 'I do hope for that, more than anything.'

'I know,' Lucius said.

Kai drank from the wineskin, wincing at the sharpness of the *posca*. 'There is one thing I am grateful for. That I serve such a captain as you.'

The Roman flushed then – such a simple thing to embarrass him, Kai had found. For they were a plain-spoken people, the Sarmatians, who spoke of their love and hate for one another as matter-of-factly as they spoke of the health of their horses or the changing of the weather. Lucius, it seemed, was not one who was used to being spoken of kindly.

Once more, the Roman pointed to the shadow in the sky. 'See that milecastle?' he said, and Kai followed the line of his hand to a place on the Wall where no light shone. 'The torches have burned out. Some lazy sentries sleeping, or drunk.'

'What will happen to them?'

'Flogged, if they are lucky. Beaten to death by their fellow soldiers, if they are not.' He looked solemn then. 'I will have to do the same, and so shall the others who will command you. Make sure the others know that.'

'I will. They do not fear hard commands.'

Yet even as he said it, Kai wondered if it were true. If here, his people were to be given a command that they could not follow – that he could not follow. For even in the open air, Kai could feel the bars of a cage closing about him. They were a people that had always wandered free across the steppe, now bound to a single place for twenty-five years. And he stood then, suddenly restless, hungry for the one thing that might bring him a little peace. A dangerous kind of peace, as a man wounded in the gut might beg for the drink of water that shall kill him, but a peace nonetheless.

He heard Lucius speak again: 'Where are you going?'

Kai made no answer.

Lucius stared at the fire, and said nothing for a time. Then: 'You should not go to look for her,' he said softly.

'You speak as my captain?'

'As your friend.'

'Then you know that I must.' And without waiting to hear any more, Kai set off into the darkness, feeling the wet grass beneath the wraps on his feet, the scars on his cheeks aching at the soft touch of the wind.

Often, on their long journey to the north and to the west, he had found himself awake and wandering at night. It was the time that favoured him the most, a time of dream and forgetting; for looking upon the fires about which the Sarmatians gathered and seeing the shadows of their horses, one might almost think they were back upon the Sea of Grass. If only he chose not to look at the brutal straightness of the road nearby, the squat buildings that broke the horizon like boils upon the flesh; if he let the darkness turn the fields of crops into the tall wild grass of the steppe. And he himself – in the night he might be mistaken for someone else, the kind of man he had once been, a man who still belonged among his people.

He drifted through the camp, passing those few who, soaked in enough wine to forget their shame, had begun to caper and dance, seeking to forget where they were. He went past the men who sat and stared into the fires and mourned for the life they had once had, and wandered by those others who clutched at one another for comfort in the darkness.

He did not join any of them, for he did not seek to sing or brood or make love. He joined a ragged line of other men who made the same journey as he. Together, they made their way to the eastern edge of the camp, to look upon the women.

For a second campground was out there, little more than a bowshot away, picketed by sentries and a tenth of the size of the first. That was where the women stayed, for the Romans had insisted that the men and women camp apart on the journey – an imperial distrust, perhaps, thinking that the barbarians would be undone by lust. Or perhaps they thought to keep the women as hostages to the men, not trusting the sword oaths that bound them. Kai had once spoken of it with another Sarmatian, and the man laughed and said: 'They do not know our women, then. It would be safer to keep us as hostages against *them*.'

Every night, there were those who came to the fringes of the camp, the way heroes of the old stories peered through enchanted waters into the Otherlands to see a shadow of a lost love. Perhaps a hundred men were there that night, yet by some unspoken courtesy they did not acknowledge one another. Each man might pretend himself alone, and left to his own private dreaming. And so Kai looked upon the distant shadows, searching for one in particular. A woman named Arite.

It was a chance in a thousand that she had come with them from the steppe. Five hundred women had joined the five thousand men sent to the west, chosen by lot, the pulling of a black stone from a jar. And for all that Kai had hoped that Arite would be one of the chosen, looking for her there in the darkness he felt as much regret as longing.

He thought he saw her then, the flare of a fire casting light upon gold and silver hair. A tall figure, striding restlessly from one fire to the next as a captain will make the rounds of his sentries. And perhaps it was true what the storytellers said, that desire might still speak in silence and from afar, for he saw that shadow go still and seem to look towards him. And other things he remembered then, from the winter before. Eyes shining in the darkness, the rough skin of her hands clasped about his back, his head resting against the soft hollow of her neck and shoulder.

But something was wrong. There was someone else drawing near to Kai, another shadow in the night who broke that unspoken code between the men. A man made faceless by the darkness, yet Kai would have known him anywhere.

Once that man, Bahadur, had been one of those fortunate and ever joyful men whom the gods seemed to favour, his face marked more by laughter than age. But capture by the Romans had stilled that laughter, taken his songs from him. And there were wounds to the heart that the Romans had not given to Bahadur. For Kai and Bahadur were bonded together by only one thing, that night. They were both looking for the same woman.

A tilt of the head to the side – an ache about Kai's heart, to see Bahadur's shadow move so. It was a gesture he knew so well, when Bahadur sought some solution to a problem that seemed impossible. He had always found one, too, for that had been his gift. Before Kai had done the only thing that Bahadur could not forgive, and the bond between them had been broken.

A wave of a hand – not the greeting that one might offer to a friend, but of the sort to drive a stray dog away from the herd. The kind of gesture often followed soon enough by a thrown rock, or a spear. Kai knew that Bahadur would stand there watching him until the sun rose if necessary, until the Roman whips were falling upon his shoulders. And still he would not go, until he saw Kai driven before him first.

Kai took stumbling steps, suddenly clumsy in the darkness, the way grief seems to unbalance the world. Back towards the camp, towards the safety of the fire with Lucius and the company of men. To sleep, and dream, and try to forget.

But as he did, he saw another fire rising on the horizon. A great blossom of yellow and orange uncurling towards the sky, the thick black smoke rising high. At first he thought it some ritual of this country, a festival to ward off spirits in the night, or seek a blessing upon the crops. Who knew what strange customs people kept here, at the edge of the world?

But then he saw signal fires catching flame, points of light dancing across the great Wall in both directions. And the horns were calling all across the valley, sounding and echoing from the stone, a kind of music that Kai had heard before, far to the east. It had sounded through years of war and raid across the border, a sound that Kai and his people had learned to fear and now would have to learn to answer.

The alarm of the Legions, calling the Sarmatians to stand and fight. To die for their new master, to die for Rome.

3

Blood in the air, the call of the hunt – Kai felt it keenly, though there was no sign of the enemy that he could see, only the sounding of the horns and the fire on the horizon.

Weaponless they were, but all about him Kai could see men snatching up flaming brands and mounting their horses, seeking to guard the borders of the camp. No fear among any of them, only a wolfish joy that they might at last have the battle that had been promised to them. There was but one place for Kai then, at Lucius's side, and even in the dark it was but the work of a moment to find his commander. For Lucius was the one who stood still, an island in the river of men who flowed to him and beyond him, giving orders to all those who passed.

'An alarm?' Kai said, when he reached the Roman's side.

'It is,' said Lucius. 'I do not know what has caused it.'

Kai pointed at the great fire to the east. 'A signal fire?'

'Too large,' Lucius said, as he looked towards the flame and smoke that rose into the sky. 'Must be a building going up. Could be a drunk blacksmith who left his forge untended. Or raiders, south of the Wall.'

'What do we do?'

'Picket sentries, mount half the riders and circle the camp.'

'No weapons?'

'I cannot arm five thousand men in the darkness,' said Lucius. 'And we shall not need them, unless these raiders have come to fight an army.'

'What of those on the Wall? They shall come and fight?'

Lucius shook his head. 'They will protect their posts above all else. They will not come out until morning.'

'Hiding behind walls, that is your way,' Kai said, and lifted his chin proudly. 'My people, we go hunting.'

'I told you, I cannot arm five thousand Sarmatians in the dark.'

'Then let twenty of us go.'

Lucius shook his head. 'We do not know the country, and there is no time to arm properly.'

Kai felt a ghost of a smile upon his lips. 'It may be an even fight for them, then.'

Lucius stood for a moment, irresolute – perhaps he sought to judge whether Kai was answering the hunter's call, or a lonely man's wish for death. In that moment, Kai found that he did not know himself.

'Very well,' said Lucius. 'Take twenty men.' He hesitated. 'But take no foolish chances. I shall see you back to Sarmatia, to your daughter. Do not make me break my promise.'

Kai clasped his commander's arm, the warrior's farewell. Then he was back among the shadows of his people, searching for those who would go with him.

No time to pick out the men he knew – he would have to trust to fate and the luck of the gods. He cast himself back into the sea of his people, letting himself be carried by the waves and currents of the men who flowed about him, searching for something that he could not name. He saw a warband mounted together and singing songs of war, but when he drew close he could smell the reek of wine that rolled from them and he did not call them out. Elsewhere, another group had the look of seasoned fighters, but the light of the fire shone on eyes that were blank and death mad – men seeking spears to throw themselves upon.

At last, he came to a band of Sarmatians who stood still and quiet in the darkness. And in that silence, he found what he was looking for.

'I need twenty riders,' said Kai when he was among them. 'Only those fit to ride and fight. Do not lie if you are sick, you shall merely slow us down.'

All at once they were around him, hands reaching forward, eyes rolling wild with desire. He asked them to pledge themselves to a battle in the darkness, against an unknown enemy and uncertain numbers, yet they did not hesitate. From his people, he would have expected nothing less.

He clasped each of those hands in turn, counted to twenty, and that was it. No time to mark if they were friends or strangers he was to ride with, proven men or boys newly come to the warband, before he led them to the horses, who tossed their heads and stamped in the corral, as hungry to fight as the men. Monstrous warhorses of a breed that had never been seen in that land before, thickset as wrestlers, the muscles dancing beneath their skin at every step, horses bred to fight and kill. Eyes bright and heads held high, for they did not know themselves defeated. It was not they who had surrendered to Rome.

Lucius was ahead of them at the supply wagons,

commanding in the hard Latin tongue with the men who guarded them. And the Sarmatians Kai had chosen mounted and gathered patiently, waited for their honour to be restored. For the long road of shame to be finished, and to bear weapons once more.

They watched the long bundles lifted from the wagons, close-bound in waxed skins to protect them from the rain as though they were priceless silks. Then they were unwrapped and laid out beneath the stars, the great long spears of their people, the two-handed lance of the steppe. With it, they had broken Roman Legions and driven the Dacians before them, fought proudly for their freedom. Now, they might win something else back instead. Kai closed his hands about the lance that was passed to him, and was complete once more.

'Ride soft,' he said to the others, 'and watch your footing. If you lame your horse, turn back on your own and be sure to return here by morning. They shall kill you as a deserter if you are any later than that. Do you understand?'

Twenty riders nodded back at him, the spears dipping with them in a warrior's salute.

Out into the night – rougher ground than the steppe they were used to, rolling hillside marked with heather and bracken that might snare the unwary horse, pocked with bog and mire. The air was alive with strange scents – wildflowers and birch bark, the rich perfume of the heather after rain and sun. Sounds as well: a hooting bird whose call he did not know, the familiar, beautiful sound of hooves falling against earth softened by the rain.

They spread wide, moved steady and careful in the darkness, cutting north of where the great fire burned and searching for a trail. A hopeless thing it seemed, for though the ground lay mostly open they only had half a moon to guide them, and the rain fell in veils that twisted in the wind and obscured the land around them. They might have passed within a few bowshots of their quarry and not seen them, hunted for hours for a trail long gone cold. But Kai felt the whisper of a god in his ear, and levelled his spear to a particular place upon the horizon.

'There, on the Wall, at that fort where no fire burns. That is where they will go.'

Moving faster now, the horses growing confident in the feel of the land, the riders eager in their saddles. They were in a strange country, hunting enemies they did not know in number or kind. But in that moment he would have traded all the years of a slave's life for one night as a master of the hunt.

They stumbled across it then, by fortune or fate – furrows left by carts, flanked by the prints of horse hooves. An innocent-seeming trail, in any other time, but they could see the rain still pooling in the fresh tracks that cut north towards the Wall. When Kai looked to the others he saw them grinning, the teeth shining white under the stars.

A man he did not know spoke: 'Perhaps their farmers hold their markets under moonlight in this land.'

'Perhaps,' Kai answered, and tapped the haft of his weapon. 'Let us find them, then, and see what we may barter for our spears.'

Quicker still, the horses tossing their heads in excitement. Perhaps they tasted a scent upon the air, or perhaps it was that they saw what the men could not. For all Sarmatians knew that a horse could see the dead, and this was a land that seemed likely to be thick with ghosts.

A shape in the darkness – a farmer's cart, one wheel cracked and tilted to the side. As they drew close, they saw it was piled high with bags of grain and butchered pigs.

'They abandoned their haul,' one of the Sarmatians said. 'They are running.'

'Then let us catch them,' Kai answered.

The pace quickening, the rider at the front leaning so low it seemed he would fall from the saddle, following the tracks on the ground, whistling and clicking his tongue to let them know where to turn. The Wall looming high on the ridge line above them, like a bleak monument to a vengeful god.

And Kai saw them then, silhouetted upon the hillside – horses and riders, hurrying northwards, though he could not tell how many. And from those shadows, Kai marked one in particular, for it seemed there was a giant among those raiders, sat upon a horse that was half again as high as those gathered about him.

That tall thin man called an order to his raiders. Only some broken fragment of it came to Kai through the wind and the rain, sounding more like the howl of a beast than anything of speech. And yet to Kai it sounded strangely familiar – he could almost understand, if not the words, then the meaning behind them. Then there were screams sounding in the air, figures tumbling from the saddles of the raiders, blood spilling black beneath the moonlight.

No time to make sense of or understand what had come to pass, no time for anything at all. The battle fever was on him, and there was no thinking or remembering. Only a shivering cry that broke from him as he let loose the call of the hunt. And as if in answer to that call, he saw that tall man, the leader of the raiders, turn his great horse away from them. Towards the north, and the Wall.

The feel of an omen across the skin to see him flee, the knowledge that nothing mattered more than the killing of that man. But then a whisper in the air, as javelins flew from the raiders and fell around the Sarmatians, and Kai heard the high-pitched screams from close by, the wet and sharp sound of horses and riders tumbling to the ground.

Not time to think of the fallen, nor of that strange tall man fleeing to the north. He could only think of the living in front of him, the men that he had to kill. Both hands on the spear, guiding it towards the shadows in the darkness, then the terrible shudder of the spear striking flesh, the wrench and twist as the man before him was lifted, suspended in the air as if in flight, and then sent tumbling and rolling to the ground, broken and screaming.

On their great warhorses the Sarmatians must have seemed as monsters in the dark, giants with outsized weapons in their hands, as they tore the raiders to pieces in a single charge. A moment of strange shame at how easy the killing was, and already Kai could see those raiders that were left casting down their spears, holding their hands in the air, the wordless war cries suddenly twisting into a language that Kai did not know, but he knew to be cries of surrender.

And he was calling then to his own riders, to the killers he had brought halfway across the world – calling them off, ordering them to show mercy. But it seemed they did not hear him. A year of shame that the Sarmatians sought to wash away with blood, the long spears thrusting down over and over again, and the horses killing as eagerly as the men, sharp hooves stamping down until the last of the raiders lay unmoving upon the ground.

A stillness, then. The wind and the rain rolling across them, as the battle fever faded away, the men and the horses shivering with the strange coldness that always followed the killing, the last ghostly touch of the dead as they departed this world and struck out for the next. Kai slid down from his horse, to look upon those that they had slain.

Their horses were more like ponies, small squat creatures well suited to the rough countryside, but no match for the warhorses that the Sarmatians rode. The men had soot-blackened faces, pale skin visible where it had been worn away. Kai could see the whorls and twists of tattoos, quite unlike his own, knots and patterns rather than the animals with which the Sarmatians marked their skin. No armour upon them, save for the little square shields that a few of them bore. Kai picked up one of their beautiful spears – half the size of those that the Sarmatians used, but a lovingly polished weapon of ash and iron, dressed with feathers and war charms where the wood met the broad iron blade. He saw others of his people note this too, hurrying to take the spears as prizes from the men that they had killed, kneeling beside them with knives drawn to take other trophies, trophies of flesh. And it was then that they saw there were women and children among the dead.

No warrior women, for they wore the simple clothes of farmers and their hands were bound by rope. Kai remembered the shouted order, the bodies tumbling from the saddles before the battle had begun.

'They must have been captives,' he said, half to himself, 'taken to be slaves beyond the Wall.'

And it was then, as he looked among the dead, that he found one looking back at him.

A boy, lying still on the ground, and still wrapped in a raider's arms as though in a father's embrace. The child lay so still, his face painted in blood, that Kai thought that he was dead at first, the life in his eyes a trick of the light. Until those eyes blinked at him, once and slowly.

Kai unwrapped the raider's arms, lifted the boy free. A child of eight summers, perhaps, his gaze dull and empty. Many times before had Kai seen those eyes on the face of a child, for there were many on the steppe who had lost their families to sickness or feud, captives ransomed back after they had been used for sport, bloodied survivors of ambushes that had cut their clans to pieces. Broken survivors. Sometimes they mended, sometimes they did not.

Kai lifted his head, looked towards the others who were with him. For an uncanny silence had settled about him, a silence that he did not like. And Kai saw his companions were prayer solemn, all looking the same way. And they did not look towards him, or the child. They were staring north towards the Wall.

An evil-looking thing, seen this close. From east to west, one could not see the ending of it. Perhaps it stretched on forever, encompassing the whole world, binding the earth in a chain of stone. And when he followed their gaze, he saw they looked at one particular point on the Wall. The little milecastle in front of them, the one point on the Wall where the torches were dark. No sign of the tall rider who had fled northwards, but no doubt as to where he had gone. For the gate there was open, and through it he could see the sky and stars and the plains that stretched beyond. The end of the Roman Empire. A free land.

One of the Sarmatians, a man whom Kai did not know, looked at him and grinned. 'Shall we?'

A madman's plan. To flee north in the dark to unknown lands, no doubt to meet kin of the men they had just slain while their spears were still wet with blood. Yet still, Kai felt it just as they did, the calling of the open country like the whisper of a lover. The longing to be free.

A tightening around his hand, as the child clasped at his fingers. And Kai reached down, pulled the boy close to him. 'Remember your oaths,' said Kai. 'Remember that you swore them upon your swords. Remember the twenty-five years. Remember the home that you shall see again.'

Another voice spoke from the darkness: 'Oaths did not always mean so much to you.' And Kai shivered, the first touch of fear that he had felt that night. For it was a woman's voice that had spoken, a voice that he knew all too well.

She was no towering figure like those of the champions of legend. Just another shadow in the darkness like any other, easy enough to miss, and yet still he should have known her. For there were none who fought the way that she did.

Most knew her by her war name – the Cruel Spear. But he had known her long before she took the champion's mantle, known her by her true name. Laimei – his sister.

'You did not think to hunt without me, brother?' she said.

'The Romans forbade our women from fighting,' Kai answered.

'You asked for twenty riders, and twenty came. No true Sarmatian would begrudge me a place here.' She shrugged.

'But you are right, a Roman would. Do you think yourself one of them now, with the marks of your clan cut from your cheeks? You are certainly not one of us.'

The others were moving about her, then, and gathering at her back. Hands reaching to her spear, lifting the blood and marking their foreheads with it. For she had been a great champion of their people, back in the east, one favoured by the gods. And he heard them whispering the same words over and over again. *The Cruel Spear.*

Kai pointed towards the fort and the gate, the open way north. 'Do you mean to go over the Wall, and break an oath?'

'Oh, they asked no oath of me,' she said. 'They did not think to make the women swear such a thing.'

'Should we go north, then?' one of others asked. 'We follow your command.'

She paused for a time, cocked her head to the side and listened to the wind, as though she wished to hear an omen on it.

'No,' she said at last. 'I shall not have you break your promises. You are not men like my brother.'

'We return, then.' Kai said. 'With trophies of victory, and blood upon our spears.'

'Perhaps,' she answered. 'Or perhaps there is more blood still to be spilled out here.'

'Shall we kill him?' one of the others said to Laimei. 'Say it, and it shall be done. None shall know of it. Our spears are yours to command.'

She did not answer, and so Kai waited, as they gathered about him in the darkness, his hands slack upon his spear. He felt the boy he had rescued clutching his leg, and Kai worked his hand through the tangles of the child's hair. No fear upon his heart – not from bravery, or a certainty that he would be spared. But Kai had faced such a judgement before, during the long and bitter feud between him and his sister that had begun far to the east. Once before he had stood before his sister and waited for her to decide if he were to live or die. And he had spent his fear for it then.

The shadow of his sister shook her head. 'No need to kill one already dead,' she said. 'For what is a man without a clan, but a corpse still breathing?' She looked away then, to some shadows that lay upon the ground. 'Besides, we have seen enough Sarmatians dead tonight.'

A spell broken, the killing mood gone as quickly as it had gathered. A man came forward to clasp Kai's arm as though they were brothers, and together, they went to gather their dead.

Two had been killed by javelins, and Kai could hear a mutter of appreciation that the raiders had thrown so well in the dark. Another had been struck by a spear and gone beneath the hooves of his own horse. A lucky death, or so it was called, the way the gods often called their favourites home, unwilling to let them be killed by the hand of man or woman, or be spoiled by the slow rot of age – instead, the gods would let a horse be their executioner.

One of the dead had not passed twenty summers, the other two were little older than that. They had come to serve their years and dream of home, and had not lived a week at their post. And there was a chanting, then, about the bodies. Not any of the old songs or prayers for the dead, for there was some new ritual being born there, in that moment. 'Twenty-five years,' they chanted, over and over again. A prayer not for the dead, but for themselves, and the hope that they would one day go home.

4

'One more day.' The Prefect of Cilurnum leaned forward, and put his head into his hands. 'Why could they not have waited one more day?'

Lucius Artorius Castus, standing at attention before that man, made no answer. He fixed his gaze a little above the Prefect's head and let his eyes drift across the wall, taking in the cracking plaster, frescos painted with gods, heroes, a phallus for good luck. All the usual decorations of a commander's quarters at the heart of a Roman fort. His people ruled half the world now, and everywhere they went, proud of their nation or longing for the trappings of home, they brought their art with them – that same white plaster, those same patterns on the walls. Had he been blindfolded and taken to that place; he could have thought himself anywhere in the Empire, even pretend that they were in Rome itself. Until the hard wind blew, and wormed its way through cracks in the walls – the ever-present reminder that they were on the edge of the Empire, half a world away from home.

Just as Cilurnum was the mirror of every fort scattered across Rome, so was its Prefect, Glaucus Montanus. Lucius had seen his like before – Glaucus might have been a fine soldier once, but now his eyes were sunk deep in his head, his arms thin and movements hesitant. An old proverb of the Legion came to mind – that a fat Prefect was a thief, and a thin one had been stolen from.

At last, the Prefect lifted his head. For the third time since he had entered, Lucius offered him a salute, which was finally returned. 'Where have they sent you from, then?' said Glaucus.

'The Danubius, sir. I lead an *ala* of Sarmatian heavy cavalry. We are to take over the garrison of this fort.'

'That is not right.' The Prefect picked up a wax tablet from his table, held it out at arm's length to peer at it. 'It says here you are from Asturia. That is the name of your regiment.'

'It appears some scribe does not know his Sarmatians from his Spaniards. Sir.'

'Of course,' said Glaucus. 'They cannot get anything right. But the gods do have a sense of humour. You have come from the Danubius, and no doubt that is where they will send me, after this. One day left on the Wall, and the barbarians disgrace me.' He paused, and wiped a hand across his eyes. 'I am never going to see Rome again.'

'Do you wish to hear my report, sir?' said Lucius. The Prefect waved his hand in a gesture that could have meant anything, and Lucius chose to take it as assent. 'They crossed the Wall in the night,' Lucius continued, 'through the twelfth milecastle. They killed the men there, tied them to posts and raised them on spears.'

'Why?'

'At a distance, sir, the milecastle would have seemed occupied.'

The Prefect grunted. 'Clever. But how did they get inside in the first place?'

'We do not know, sir,' said Lucius. 'But once they were through, they went raiding south of the Wall. They butchered the men at three steadings, took the women and children captive, filled carts with food and what riches they could find.' Lucius hesitated, remembering what they had found when they had gone to look for any survivors of the raid. One corpse had held a flail for beating grain, another a little dull knife fit for nothing more than cutting cheese, a third only a thin branch half burned from a cooking fire. 'The farmers fought as best they could. But they had no weapons.'

'Of course not,' said Glaucus. 'We disarmed the local tribes around here, to help us keep the peace.' The Prefect scratched and picked at his head – lice, or an irritable habit, Lucius could not tell which. 'That large fire. A barn that went up?'

'It was.'

'Foolish of the raiders to burn it,' said Glaucus. 'They could have been back over the Wall and we would be none the wiser.'

'They did not burn it.'

'What?'

'We found one of the farmers with a spear in his gut and a torch in his hand. We think he set the fire himself, as he was dying.'

At this, the Prefect gave another little grunt of acknow-ledgement – even he, it seemed, still remembered something of what it was to be brave. And Lucius thought of the blackened corpse they had found, the ground clawed open beside him by splintered fingers, the lips burned away, an agonised grin turned towards the sky. The man had given himself the worst of deaths, in the hope that he might be avenged.

'I will need one of your veterans,' said Lucius, 'to look at the dead. If we can know their clan we shall find who has done this.'

The Prefect rubbed at his eyes. 'I do not understand. The raiders are dead. There is no mystery to solve.'

'Their leader escaped, sir. And he was riding a horse different to the others.' Lucius hesitated. 'From what my men tell me, it might have been a Roman cavalry horse.'

Silence, for a time. A scraping of feet at the entrance, as some messenger arrived, scrolls in hand, but the Prefect waved him away irritably.

'Your men are barbarians,' Glaucus said at last. 'They give you stories to mask their failings. I very much doubt that they have such a horse north of the Wall. Nothing but those little hill ponies.' He tapped the desk in front of him: the reports and messages from across the Wall. 'And if such a horse were stolen, I would know it.'

'Of course, sir,' Lucius said. 'But it will be my command here tomorrow. I shall have to be sure.'

A rapping of fingers against wood, as the Prefect drummed his fingers on the table. 'There is a local chieftain whom you might be able to trust,' he said. 'Mor, of the Votadini. He may be able to tell you what clan these raiders come from. Though I would hold little hope of it. They usually keep silent unless you have something to offer them.'

'Thank you, sir.'

'Do not be too eager.' The Prefect shook his head. 'We do not send soldiers to the Wall, we send sacrifices. It does not matter if they are good men or rotten men. The tribes take their tribute. A raid here, an ambush there. Stay in the fort, and feed them a patrol every so often, and you may serve out your years. Get your piece of swampy farmland out in the provinces. Find some lazy-eyed and slow-witted woman to be your wife. That is what seems to pass for happiness in this place.' The Prefect put his head in his hands once more. 'The best go to the east of the Empire, the lucky to the west, the rich to the south. And to the north…'

'Those who are to be forgotten,' said Lucius, finishing the proverb.

'Indeed. How many do you have to house here?'

'Five hundred cavalry and their horses. The rest of the five thousand have been sent elsewhere along the line. Or south, for more training.'

'We have room for them here. Though the men and the horses are barracked together.'

'They shall not object to that.'

'Of course they will not.' The Prefect stood, and from about his neck he lifted the key to the paychest – of all the symbols of command, the least glamorous, but the most significant, for that paychest was kept beside the shrine and the standards at the heart of the fort, as though it too were sacred. Lucius waited for Glaucus to hand it over, but something kept the other man still for a moment. No doubt he had dreamed long of this time, to be free of the post that he hated. Yet now, perhaps, on the edge of his own journey to a new world, he was afraid.

'What did you do?' the Prefect said.

'What?'

Glaucus hesitated. 'I was drunk and I insulted a senator's

daughter,' he said, the words spoken with the quality of a confession. 'That is what I did, to be sent to this place. Ten years ago. What did you do? You must have made some mistake, or you would not be here.'

Lucius made no answer for a time. He thought of all the choices he had made, of all the mistakes, and wondered when the course had been irreversible. A bitter argument with his father, long before, that had led to him joining the Legion. A reckless act when, heartsick for a wife and child lost to the Antonine plague, he had volunteered for a mission across the Danubius. The strange love for the Sarmatians that had grown when he was captured by them, to be at last among a people who held to a code other than power, who found honour in more than mere victory. And then he remembered that he had a better answer than any of those.

'I argued with the Emperor,' said Lucius. 'And I won.'

'Very well,' Glaucus replied. 'Mock me if you wish. Spend a few years in this place, and see what it does to you.'

'It is no mockery, I promise.' Lucius offered the salute, and then took the key in his hand. 'It is the truth.'

Glaucus's hand drifted to his neck, to the place where the key had once hung. He looked around the room as though seeing it for the first time, the last time. A hand half raised towards a fresco on the wall, a little tremor through the fingers as it fell to his side once more. Lucius wondered what memory lay hidden there in paint and plaster – the face of a lover, perhaps, or a dream of glory and honour that had remained just that, replaced with the weary day to day life of a commander on a forgotten frontier.

'Well,' Glaucus said, 'you are the Prefect of Cilurnum now. I would wish you luck, but if you are here, then you have none. And if you have argued with an Emperor, you shall have no trouble with the Legate who rules these lands. He shall be here within the week, and you had best be ready for him. You and your Sarmatians.'

'What kind of a man is he?' Lucius asked.

A little tight smile answered him. 'The kind that looks after his friends. Until they are no longer his friends. I would find a way to impress him, if I were you.'

An eagle, looking down upon the fort of Cilurnum, would have seen a place of unnatural order – straight lines and perfect squares, barracks and storehouses enclosing the commander's quarters and the baths, white walls and clay roof tiles the colour of ripe oranges. But that sense of order ended at the walls of the fort. Beyond them sprawled the *vicus*, a ramshackle collection of buildings that leaned against one another like drunkards at the end of the night. They had sprung up over time like mushrooms, filled with cobblers stitching leather shoes, tired-eyed owners of wine shops, traders in charms and lucky trinkets. Most of the shops were owned by retired soldiers, sour-eyed men of the Legion who nursed old injuries and older grievances. They had dreamed a soldier's dreams, of the rolling farmland that would be theirs on retirement, a fair price for twenty-five years of watching their friends die. They dreamed of faraway lands, sun-kissed fields, or even the grandeur of Rome itself. Yet more often than not they found themselves a scant mile from the forts they had served in, passing the evenings gambling over dice and knucklebones, ending their lives with the flux in winter, or a knife to the gut after a brawl.

Women were there too. Some were the common law wives of soldiers forbidden to marry, others plied a bleaker trade in the brothels and alleyways. And there, in a little cottage on the edge of the *vicus*, lived a woman who was not like the others. Standing in the doorway of the house, wrinkling her nose against the stench of the town, was a Sarmatian woman, Arite.

She bore scars upon her cheeks and hands from wars fought long ago, a braid of gold and silver hair falling halfway down her back. She wore her long loose dress hitched high so as not drag in the mud, and kicked irritably at the dirt that clung to the wrappings on her feet and the patterned soles of her little leather shoes. They were no dirtier than they would have been at the end of a winter camp upon the steppe, but there was something about confinement that seemed to magnify the filth, that made it scratch and itch and prick against the skin.

Once her home had been the open steppe far to the east, a great Sea of Grass shadowed by mountains where the herds roamed free. Now it was a little house in the part of the town where the sun rarely shone.

Still, the place had its comforts. For when she turned to the south and laid her back against the mud bricks of the house, the hateful Wall and town fell away from her vision. She saw only the rolling hills and forests, broken here and there by the cooking fires that twisted through the air. And before her, another sight that spoke of the freedom of the steppe – horses and riders, dressed for war, as they moved across the parade ground to the south of the *vicus*, riding in the intricate patterns of drill and ceremony.

As she watched the twisting pattern of horses and riders,

she saw a figure break away, turning to ride towards her. An ache about the heart to see that rider approach – for a moment, Arite thought that it might be Kai who came towards her then. But it was a woman not a man who approached and dismounted, a woman whose face was so alike to Kai's, copper skinned and sharp boned, black hair close-cropped against her head, that it had been an easy mistake to make. But looking into Laimei's eyes, the resemblance between the two seemed to vanish. They were grey and blank, like a painted shield. A warrior's eyes – giving nothing away, always testing and measuring, and never satisfied with what they saw.

'How are the horses?' said Arite.

'Well enough,' Laimei answered. 'They shall have to grow used to the rough country. Three of them have come up lame already. Easy to mock the Britons and their ponies, but they do have their uses on this ground.' She scratched at her head, worrying at some dry patch of skin, a place where the helmet caught and chafed. 'We might trade for some of their ponies, breed in a little of that stock to our herd. I shall speak with the others, and see what can be done.'

It was little surprise that Laimei spent most of her time among the horses, training the men of the warband in the arts of killing – the secret grips and movements of a spear, the tricks one could teach a horse. For a champion she had been, back in the east. Out there upon the steppe, a woman had to kill her way to her husband – three men slain before she might put down her spear and take a man as her own. Most hurried their way to their three kills, were aided by their kin, led trembling and shaking to dying men on the ground that they might finish and claim as their own. And yet Laimei had refused to claim a third kill, always gifting those she slew to her companions, or her horse. She had left a trail of the maimed behind her that had earned her name, the Cruel Spear, and there were none who knew why she chose to stay in the warband.

Laimei came beside Arite, leaned back against the wall of the house, one foot kicked back against the clay bricks.

'I hate this place,' she said, matter-of-factly.

Arite said nothing for a time. For she remembered the lottery back upon the steppe, the women all standing in a circle, the long grass dancing about them in the wind, for that was how all great things were decided among their people, those matters of living and dying. The drawing of stones from an amphora on the ground, those who drew the white stones remaining upon the steppe, those who took the black going to the west with their men. And she remembered Laimei, hiding the stone she drew in the palm of her hand, moving restlessly among the other women, whispered conversations with one after another. Entreaties, threats, pleadings. Then something passing from one hand to the next, from a woman that Arite did not know, as they exchanged one stone for another.

'You could still have been a warrior,' said Arite, 'if you had kept the white stone and stayed in the east.'

At last, a smile from Laimei. 'I am still a warrior here,' she said. 'I bloodied my spear the night we came here.' But the smile went as soon as it came. 'This is the place the warband goes, and this is the place I must be. They will let me fight again. They must.'

Arite shook her head. 'You might as well have asked to pluck stars from the sky as ask a Roman to put a woman in the warband.'

A barking laugh. 'I have done many things that they have told me are impossible. This is but another.'

'It is not for Kai that you came, then?' said Arite.

'Not all of us are as enamoured of him as you are,' Laimei answered.

'Twenty-five years shall be a long time to hold a grudge.'

'Oh, it is no time at all. There are gods who have hated each other since the world was born. Why should I aspire to any less than that?' She slung the saddle from her shoulder and to the ground. 'Ask your husband how easy it is to hate Kai. He may teach you, if I cannot.'

There were words on Arite's lips then – killing words that could not have been unspoken, words that might have opened another feud. But there was a hesitant shuffling behind them, a sound that bound them both to silence, as a boy tottered out of the house and blinked at the sunlight.

It was the child from the raids, a little boy of the tribe they called the Brigantes, perhaps eight or nine summers old. Kai had brought him to her the night of the raid across the Wall – she remembered how the boy had looked then, white eyes blinking from a face painted in blood, like an animal that had been flayed. 'For one night alone,' Kai had said. 'We shall find his kin tomorrow.'

But none had claimed the boy, though they had ridden back and forth across the countryside from one steading to another. Some of the farmers almost seemed to recognise the child before their eyes went dull and their faces still, they shook their heads and said he was no kin of theirs. Arite did not know what custom it was of theirs to turn from the child, whether he was considered cursed or a coward or unlucky for having lived when the others had died. But it fell to her to take care of him now.

'Does he speak at all?' Laimei asked.

'No. I have learned a few words of their tongue, from the wine seller and the baker. But he gives no answer to anything I say.'

Laimei shrugged, with as little interest as if Arite had bought a hound that could not hunt. The old hot fire rose again, until Arite breathed it away once more. Again and again she had to remind herself that Laimei was not cruel or heartless, that she inhabited the champion's world of gods and monsters, seeming without a care for anything but war and the hunt. She remembered something Laimei had said to her, long ago: *I have no use for broken things.*

And the child was broken. He had the glassy look of children who have seen what they should not, or who have had terrible things done to them. Arite had seen it many times before, on the faces of children marked by war. Sometimes they healed so well that it was as if they had never been broken, and sometimes they did not, and quickly, quietly, found a way to die – wandering by a river in flood season, or circling behind a troublesome horse that kicked their life away, or taking up a winter fever and refusing to fight it.

'We must name him,' Arite said. 'What child will cling to life if it has no name?'

'*You* must name him,' Laimei answered. 'I shall have no part in that fight.'

A vision came to Arite then – an image of a child of the steppe, smiling and laughing and calling to her from across the open plain. A child long since buried beneath the earth. 'I call him Chodona, then,' Arite said.

A pause. 'Little luck in that name, I think,' said Laimei. 'And I would not speak it so loud in front of your visitor.'

A feeling danced across Arite's skin then – a lover's eyes upon her. And when she turned to look into the shaded street, she did see a man walking towards her.

Tall and rangy, even for their people, with thick dark hair that covered him like a bear. Once he had been strong in voice and in body, a proud man with a spear and a great singer at feast and fire. But a diminished man now, his flesh shrunk back, his eyes corpse blank, his great voice fallen soft. Bahadur, her husband.

Yet when he caught her gaze he smiled for a moment. For he was there sometimes – the ghost of the man she had loved. And though for the most part she felt nothing for the dour stranger he had become, then there would a moment of a song, a smile dancing across his lips as he forgot his sadness, and for a single beat of the heart it was as it once had been.

From behind her, she heard Laimei shift her weight. 'Was it him you were hoping to see,' Laimei said, 'or my brother?'

Arite answered the challenge, turning and staring right back at her companion. Just for a moment, she thought she saw a trace of alarm in Laimei's grey eyes, a half-step taken back to give herself room to fight. For Arite too had been a warrior, long before. No great champion, but she had made her kills bravely and well, and Laimei must have seen for a moment the woman Arite had once been.

Then the champion's arrogance settled upon Laimei once

more, and she gave a nod to Arite – the kind she gave to a worthy opponent on the battlefield, before she honoured them with death.

5

The sun rising, the horns calling to the sky, and the doors of the gate swinging open. Not the western gate, where the supply caravans came in; not the south gate, where men went to spend their coin in the *vicus*, to drink and whore their loneliness away. It was the way to the north, to the wild country, and Lucius rode out of it, his armour shining brightly, with fifty Sarmatian cavalry at his back.

No bandit look to them now, for along with their tall spears they had the other half of their honour restored to them, the great scale armour that they had worn for centuries, horses and men alike. Iron was in short supply east of the Danubius, and so they chipped horses' hooves into scales, sewed them onto a cuirass that fitted like a second skin. With the armour oiled and waxed they looked like creatures from another world, and above them once more flew the tall banners, the hollow dragons that filled with wind when the Sarmatians charged and screamed war cries of their own. For the first time, the people of that country were to see Sarmatian cavalry in their full glory.

Two others rode with the company of cavalry. One was

their guide, a sour-faced man of the Brigantes on one of their shaggy little ponies, who chewed at his long moustache and looked nervously to the horizon as they rode. The other a mute witness in rotted flesh – one of the raiders, the corpse least disfigured by spear and rot, slung across the back of a horse and carried with them.

It was a hard country they travelled in – gloomy hills that were veiled in rain, rough heaths marked by tussocks of grass and heather. No sign of villages or towns, only scattered farms and steadings, and at these places they received a welcome as cold and empty as the landscape. Some were abandoned, and the others seemed to be peopled only by old men who stared at the ground and answered no questions.

After the third farm where only greyhaired men were to be found, Lucius turned to the guide who rode with them. 'I take it this is no cursed land,' he said, 'and there are those other than the old who live here?'

'There are, my lord,' the Brigante answered. 'When they hear the Romans are heading north of the Wall, they hide the women and children.'

'And the men?'

'They go to find their spears.'

'How did they know we are coming?'

The Brigante laughed, as though Lucius had told a particularly fine joke. 'Better to assume that they always know, my lord. If you were forced to share your home with a wolf, you would mark its mood and habits very well, I think.'

'It will do little good to question these old men,' said Lucius. 'We shall have to speak to their chieftain.'

'He shall come soon enough, my lord. He merely means to make you wait a little.'

And he spoke true, for soon there were figures on the horizon, Votadini men riding the ponies of the northlands and keeping a careful, watchful distance. Lucius could see spears and bows – little thin hunting spears, and bows better suited to picking birds from the sky than for piercing heavy armour. He supposed those men of the Votadini could say they were hunting if they were caught and questioned. No doubt they had weapons of war hidden away, the same kind of great war spears that the raiders had carried, but Lucius chose to take it as a good omen that they did not wear them openly here.

Among his Sarmatians, there was no sign of alarm. They sat calmly upon their horses, seeming unconcerned by the figures that gathered on the hills and from the woods. Occasionally he heard them speaking, offering insults (and some compliments) to the shaggy little ponies the tribesmen rode, as they tested the balance of their spears and watched the Votadini on the horizon with an idle interest. If they were frightened to be surrounded in strange country, they did not show it. Yet still, there was something about the Sarmatians that troubled him.

He called Kai over. 'The men, they are well?'

'Steady enough,' Kai answered.

'I do not like the look of some of them.'

Kai cast his eyes across the others, as though seeing them for the first time. Then he said: 'It is bad luck to ride to war without women. They are not used to it.'

Lucius shook his head – another superstition that he would have to undo, or find a way to bargain with. 'Keep them watchful,' he said. 'And remind them of the good fortune I bring. They think me lucky, do they not?'

Kai grinned. 'For now. See you don't lead us into an ambush, or their faith might start to waver.'

They kept at first to the river that flowed past the fort, holding it at their right side as a hero in a labyrinth might unspool a line behind him, a path in water that would lead them back to the fort if they needed to flee. And when it was time to strike away from the river and out into the rolling hillsides, Lucius felt a little shiver of fear when the Wall fell out of sight behind a fold in the land. But their guide seemed sure of the way, leading them confidently but in a wandering path, shying away from markers and signs that only he seemed to see – border grounds and sacred sites that it would not do to cross uninvited, he explained.

At last, they came to a place where a yew tree grew beside a tall boulder. A cairn of stones gathered in the shadow of tree and rock, marked with soot and paint, and the remnants of old offerings scattered about it.

'This is the place,' the guide said. 'We make our gift here, and their chieftain will come to us. Or not, as is his whim and will.' He smiled, and knocked his knuckles against the wood of the tree. 'A good omen to see it empty.'

'What would a bad omen be?' said Lucius.

'It would be filled with the corpses of their enemies. This is where they make their trophies after battle.'

They waited. A hard wind rolled across the open country, as Lucius listened to the calling of the birds. Then another sound drifted through the air – the improbable sound of cart and horse, out there in the wilderness.

'Stand ready,' he said to the Sarmatians. 'And remember, we are not here to fight.'

A voice behind him said: 'But are they?'

Lucius smiled. 'For their sake, let's hope not.'

Then there was a new shape on the horizon, and for a moment Lucius could not quite believe what he saw. Not a cart, but a chariot – he had heard the stories told by other centurions, of the Britons who rode to war in such things like warriors from the dawntime. This one creaked and rattled as it moved across the hills, and he did not think it could have been ridden to war for half a hundred years. Yet still he could hear the Sarmatians sounding out their appreciation, both for the chariot and for the man who rode in it – a short, red-haired warrior who rode bare chested despite the cutting wind, his body crisscrossed in blue ink, lithe-muscled as one of the great cats that hunted in the distant corners of the Empire.

When the chariot pulled to a stop close by, Lucius saw that this man alone among his people openly carried a war spear, the broadheaded blade marked with feathers and charms. But it was dressed too in sprigs of holly, the sign of the truce, and Lucius came forward with his spear dressed in the same fashion.

Lucius had expected a slow and tedious conservation through their guide, but at once the chieftain greeted him in good Latin. 'I am Mor,' he said, 'chieftain of the Votadini. We greet the lord of the Wall, the chieftain of the Fort of River and Pool, and offer you our gift.'

The chieftain waved, and from behind him a warrior brought forward a bleating lamb that Lucius caught up deftly in one hand, a farmer's grip that held it still and calm. He answered in turn: 'I greet you, lord of the north, chieftain of these lands and much beyond, and offer a gift of return.' And the guide rode up, and offered, with trembling hands, an amphora of fine Samian wine – half of a month's wages had Lucius spent upon that gift.

'Very well then,' said Mor. A flash of the spear, as the chieftain thrust it into the ground at his side. 'Will you greet me as a brother? In peace?'

Lucius buried his own spear in the earth and clasped the arm that was offered to him. Despite himself, he smiled as he looked at the man, his eyes taking in the long red hair falling about the other man's shoulders, the smile of a rogue on his face and looping blue tattoos twisting across his chest. After a life spent guarding one border or another, Lucius knew that there were many kinds of men who had won a chieftain's torc – frightful killers, puppets of ambitious priests, weak sons of great men. But, rarely, there were those who won their place with cunning and kept it with honour, and Lucius could only hope that this was one such man.

'I greet you as a brother, and in peace,' said Lucius.

'You are a newcomer to this land?'

'I am. The new Prefect of Cilurnum.'

'Oh, you should call it by our name. The Fort of River and Pool is rather more beautiful, is it not?' The chieftain looked among the Sarmatians, whistled as though he looked upon a herd of fine cattle. 'And your brave men, where do they come from?'

'A long way from here. A country called Sarmatia.'

'They have a strong look about them,' said Mor. 'But sad, too. Like trees in November.'

Lucius tried to keep the surprise from his face, but it must have shown, for Mor laughed, and said: 'Do not look so surprised to hear me speak so. We expect our chieftains to be poets, too, in this country. You will learn this, in time.'

'I see that I was well advised to come to you,' said Lucius. 'Glaucus Montanus said that you were a man we could trust.'

The chieftain grinned merrily. 'I think that you lie, but kindly. Glaucus Montanus said I might be of use to you, but he has never trusted any of us. Not in ten years of peace.' The smile fell from his lips. 'I am glad to see you replace him. I like the look of you more than him.'

'Oh,' Lucius said, 'I am sure that you flatter every new Prefect this way.'

'I do. But it is the truth, this time. I hope the peace between our peoples may last another hundred years at least. Yet I think there is trouble that brings you north of the Wall.'

'Why?'

'You would not have brought such good wine otherwise.' Mor shrugged. 'Not the worst trouble, though. Or our spears would not be in the ground, and we would not be talking now.'

'This is so. Raiders went south of the Wall three days ago.'

Mor hissed through his teeth. 'I have heard this spoken,' he said. 'Yet I did not want to believe it. There are many dead?'

'Yes. Farmers. The raiders.'

'Your people?'

'Some.'

'I am sorry for it.'

'Is that true?'

'It is.' The chieftain looked about the hill and heather, the forests in the distance. 'There are deer and wolf enough for men to hunt, out here. There is no need for us to hunt one another. Yet it always seems to end the same way. With men hunting men.'

'Then you may help me. I have the body of one of them here. Name him or his tribe, and I can stop this from happening again.'

The chieftain went still. 'I have no need to look upon him to know that it is not one of my people.'

'Look anyway, then. A courtesy to me.'

The chieftain made no answer. Lucius clicked his fingers, heard the heavy tread of the horse, smelled the sharp scent of rot.

Mor glanced down briefly. 'I swear it upon my gods and forefathers,' he said, 'it is no man of my clan and tribe who went killing south of the Wall.'

'I believe you.' *Yet I think you know who it is*, Lucius thought to himself.

The chieftain lifted his arm, bracelets of bronze and silver sliding down to his wrist as he pointed to the north. 'You shall have to look further to find those who might have done this, and I would not travel that way in such small numbers.' He eyed the Sarmatian horse that Lucius rode with a lover's longing. 'Not even with such beautiful horses, and fine weapons.'

'Such horses may be yours, one day, if our friendship stands. But why further north?'

'It will be one of those tribes who makes war upon you. The Selgovae, perhaps, or the Damnonii. They are killers and thieves – worse, they are fools. No man who lives in the shadow of the Wall wishes for war.'

'Why is that?'

'When there is trouble, it is Votadini farms that are burned, our women raped, our men killed. No matter the tribe that did it.'

'That is not why I am here,' said Lucius. 'It is not my way.'

'But it is the way of your people. Romans come north of the Wall in search of blood, not answers.'

Lucius said nothing for a time. He listened to the calling of the wind, hoping he might find inspiration on it. The whisper of a god, as the Sarmatians called it.

'There is an answer I want,' Lucius said at last. 'The answer to a riddle. Perhaps you might help me find it?'

'What is that?'

'A man rides south of the Wall on a tall Roman horse, leading his men to rape and pillage. He rides back north of the Wall, a lone survivor. A man taller than any of your kind. Who is he, and where does he go to?'

'A trick of the light,' Mor answered at once. 'Or the dark.'

'Ah, but that is what Glaucus Montanus says. And we both know that he can never be right. It is not his way.'

The chieftain laughed softly, ruefully. 'Aye,' he said, 'perhaps that is so.'

'You have no such horses here?'

'None but the kind you see. They are good for what we need, to move across rough ground. But we do long for things of beauty.' The chieftain shook his head. 'The Romans will not trade them to us, and they guard us more jealously than they guard their women.'

'Where would a tribe from the north get such a horse? And what kind of man would ride it?'

An aching silence grew between them, the chieftain almost seeming to age before his eyes. 'That is the riddle,' said Mor. 'And that, I cannot solve for you.'

'I like you very much,' Lucius answered. 'But I think you do not speak the truth.'

The chieftain seemed to bristle, and there was a rattle of spears close by. 'You call me a liar?'

'No. But you do not speak the truth. At least, not all of it.'

The chieftain's gaze dropped, his fingers picking at the rail of his chariot. He made no answer.

'There is something you want to speak to me of,' Lucius said. 'Words that might give me answers to these riddles.'

'There is. But a great *geas* was laid upon me not to speak of it.'

'*Geas?* I do not know this word.'

'I do not know how to speak it in your tongue. Command. Destiny. Fate. It is all of these things.'

'Then I shall not ask you to break it,' Lucius said. 'But I know sometimes an oath must be broken, and there is no shame in it.'

'I grow fond of you, Roman,' Mor answered, 'and so I tell you this. Do not go to the north. There is only death waiting for you there.'

'I like you too, chieftain of the Votadini. And so I tell you this. You must stop those from the north from passing your lands. Or we shall have no choice but to return, with spear and fire.'

The chieftain snatched his spear from the ground, so sudden and quick that Lucius could have been struck from his horse in an instant. But Mor turned his back on the Roman, raised his weapon high and called back to his people. A shiver passed through the men on the horizon, and they sang back to him – no song of war, Lucius thought, but a sound of mourning, one of the sweet old songs for a time that is lost and never to be recaptured. And the song faded softly, as the chieftain rode away, one wheel of the chariot jumping and twisting against the uneven ground so that it seemed it would surely break apart. Yet it held, held long enough at least to see the chieftain back over the horizon.

Beside Lucius, the guide shivered, and said: 'The song, it was—'

'—I know what was said,' Lucius said irritably.

'But you do not speak our language.'

'I do not have to, to know what that song meant.' He tapped his spear against his shield and Kai trotted forward, answering the signal.

'I suppose he gets out and walks,' Kai said, looking towards the departing chieftain, 'when he is out of view of strangers. I don't suppose he can get far in that thing, fancy as it is.' He shifted his weight in the saddle, and said: 'What did he tell you?'

'Nothing but riddles and mysteries.'

'Do we darken our spears with blood today, or keep them bright?' Kai's eyes were upon the horizon as he spoke – perhaps a hundred men or more were gathered there and who knew how many more beyond it, but he asked the question as calmly as a man making an idle wager on the cast of the dice.

'Keep them bright, I hope,' Lucius answered. 'Though we go no further north without more men.'

Kai grinned. 'I shall tell the others the good news then.'

'Good news? I would have thought they would want to fight.'

'They did, until they saw the chieftain.'

'They fear him?'

'They like him,' said Kai. 'More than most of the Roman chieftains we have seen. A proper warrior, that one.'

'He is.' Lucius was still for a moment, irresolute. Some hope had slipped away into the woods and the trees, some question remained unasked and unanswered. A mad urge to stir his horse and follow the chieftain, the sense that if only they could speak for a little longer, some good might come of it. But instead, he turned his horse towards the south. 'Let us go, then,' he said.

Back towards the Wall, with more questions than answers. Sometimes Lucius thought he heard that song, the song of a dying people, still echoing in his ears as they rode. But there was no sound except that of the birds and the wind as they followed the river, their path out of the labyrinth of hill and heather, until the Wall rose before them once more.

A joy in the heart, to see the strength of Rome written there in stone. For Lucius knew, as all Romans did, that the strength of men often failed, but with their walls of stone they had conquered the world. A smile upon his lips, which faded as he looked back to the men who followed him. On the ride back through the open country, he had thought to see some of their sadness slip away, a little of their old spirit return – that restless hunger for life and careless joy that had taught him so much, far out to the east. For the rain had lifted and the shifting light crept through the clouds, the watchers on the horizon had drifted away, the ground become open enough to ward them against ambush. There seemed nothing to fear, and so perhaps they had been able to imagine themselves back upon the steppe – riding a patrol of their own lands, returning from a raid across the border, simply enjoying the feel of the sun on their faces and the movement of the horses beneath them.

All that was gone now. Looking upon the Wall, they did not see what he did. They saw their prison, the chain of stone that bound them, the symbol of a shameful defeat.

He heard one of them whisper, close by, those words that had become as prayer to them, here on the other side of the world: 'Twenty-five years.' And they rode quickly to the fort – eager, it seemed, to dull their minds with wine, distract themselves with dice or with women. To escape, at last, to the refuge of sleep, and dreams.

6

Kai woke to darkness.

It should not have been such a fearful thing. For though his people liked to sleep out beneath the stars when they could, in the hard winters on the steppe they would take to their tented wagons or the huts in the winter valleys. But there, the darkness was never so complete – always a gentle touch of starlight through the felt of the tents or the gaps in the walls, and often a fire burning close by. Here, enclosed in the stones of the barracks, the slats of the windows sealed shut against the wind, he woke from dreams of smothering into a world without light, gasping for air and clutching about himself like a drowning man.

Nearby, a voice spoke from the shadows. 'I do not blame you for being frightened. This place, it is like a tomb.'

'I wish it were, Gaevani,' Kai said. 'You would be silent then.'

A shifting on the cot next to him – Kai could not see it, but he could well imagine the other man's crooked smile. 'Oh I think you know that is not true. I would be a troublesome ghost, for you at least.'

Somewhere close, a cookfire kindled, a little light spilling into the room. Kai breathed deep, inhaled the rich, familiar smell of the horses that were stabled nearby, felt the fear diminish a little. He could see Gaevani now, on the next row of cots – facing the ceiling, one hand by absent habit running across his forehead. In the half-light, Kai could not see the old, knotted scar that was there, but he knew it well. He had helped to put it there, when they had fought against each other in a feud upon the steppe. And yet here, in this place, Gaevani was one of the few who still valued Kai's company.

'It is a land of ghosts, it seems,' said Kai.

'Ah yes. Your phantom on a tall horse. I would think it a tall tale from any other man, but you never had the wit to lie well.' Gaevani rolled over, and rubbed at his eyes. 'Forget your ghost. We have the night watch in three turnings of the hourglass. That is all. Rest more, if you can.'

'Living our lives by grains of sand and walls of stone.' Kai shook his head. 'I do not know that I shall ever grow used to it.'

'Oh, even a tomb such as this is not so bad,' Gaevani answered, 'so long as one has the right company.'

'My thanks, I think.'

'Not you, idiot.' Gaevani said. 'I meant the women in the *vicus*.'

'Laimei and Arite?'

'No! *Other* women. At a building with a straw goat hanging outside it. Saratos told me so. Sad-eyed women, but pretty enough.' He held up his hand, and Kai heard the clink of silver. 'A few of these is all that you need.'

'You mean to go there before tonight?'

Gaevani snorted. 'That's not to my taste. I have no need of

women outside the walls while there are men within it. And with men one does not have to pay, if you are handsome as I am. But I thought the women might be for your taste. Keep you out of trouble.'

'What trouble is that?'

The smile wavered then, as Gaevani hesitated. 'Was it bad fortune to have Bahadur posted here?' he said at last. 'Or was that your choice?'

'What makes you think that I had anything to do with that?'

'Come now. Lucius would do near anything that you asked. You could have sent Bahadur to the farthest side of the Wall from here, and his woman with him. I suppose I should be flattered that you chose to post me here, too.'

Kai remembered then, the arguments with Lucius. The look of gentle dismay his friend had given him when, over and over again, Kai had insisted that wherever he went on the Wall, Bahadur went with him. 'Perhaps I did have some hand in the choices,' he said.

'You think to make him forgive you? Or is it to keep his wife close to you?'

Kai made no answer at first. Then he said: 'I seem to have a way of turning friends to enemies, and my enemies to friends. Perhaps I may do it again.'

Shouting then, from close by – insults flying in the air, shadows intertwining, and Kai scrambled to his feet, looking for the shape of a knife, or the quick and jagged motions of a hand that carried one. But the brawl ended as quick as it had begun, with an embrace and rough laughter, one man pressing the heel of his hand against a cut on his face, a wound made by a fist and not a blade.

'Restless already,' said Gaevani. 'They'll cut each other to pieces, cooped up this way.' He shook his head. 'Do this for me – go to the *vicus* now. Take your coin, and go to one of the women that men pay for.'

'And why would I do such a thing?' said Kai.

'You are lonely. And it is better to pay in silver than in shame for a woman. Or blood.'

Kai let his eyes trace through the darkness, looking for a familiar shape. For somewhere in the shadows, he knew he would find Bahadur. 'I am lonely, it is true. So let me tell you—'

'—No, no, no,' Gaevani said, rolling away to face the stone walls. 'I do not wish to hear it. Not again.'

Kai said nothing. He merely stared at Gaevani's back, waiting. Until, as he knew would happen, Gaevani rolled over once more. For it was an almost sacred thing that Kai was asking of him. Another ritual, new born on their journey from the steppe, that no man would refuse to another.

'Tell me of it then,' said Gaevani, his voice weary, like a mother humouring a tiresome child. 'Tell me of the day you will go home.'

Kai looked towards the light of the cooking fire, let his gaze go soft as he stared at the dancing of the flames. 'It will be autumn,' he said. 'Late, late in the traveller's season. The winter wind blowing already. I will be afraid – afraid I will not make it in time. There will be much grey in my hair. My knees will ache when it rains. But on the journey, I will feel like a young man again.'

Kai smiled to himself. 'I will ride along the roads of the Romans. I shall be one of their citizens, and none shall dare to stop me. I shall cross their whole Empire, a free man, until

I ride through the last of their gates on the banks of the Danu. And at last, I shall be free of them.'

He stopped, for he heard a rustle close by. Others were gathering, eager like children to hear what he had to say, for they all loved to hear it, no matter how many times it was spoken. Each of them telling the same story in a different way.

'My horse will be frightened,' he continued, 'on the journey over the water. But she shall look at me, and be afraid no longer. She shall look at me, and know she is returning to the home of her kind, a place she has never seen.'

Kai hesitated, trying to remember. For less than a year had they been on the road, yet already he was beginning to forget that home himself. 'The tall grasses,' he said, 'will be dancing in the wind. The wildflowers dried to the colour of rusted iron. Those mountains in the distance – you remember them? Like a cradle about the land, the cupped hands of a god, always dusted with white snow. And I shall ride free across that open plain, following the hunting trails that will not have changed in twenty-five years, tracing the passage of the herds towards the winter campgrounds. And there, at last, I will find her. My daughter, Tomyris.'

Silence, for a time. Each man there imagining that self-same scene. Each one seeing someone different there, their own children that they had left behind upon the steppe. And Kai was lost, for a time, in his own mind, his eyes moving as he saw things that were not there. The tall grass of the steppe bowing in the wind like a man before his king, the herds of horses dancing across the open steppe. A figure standing beside by a river, children tottering about her feet, a woman with his black hair and a restless, impatient energy to every step that she took. Words mouthed and half formed – the words that he would speak to his daughter. Then the vision faded, and he returned once more to that dark room at the edge of the Empire, half a world away.

'She will be a mother, by then,' he said. 'Think of that – many little Kais roaming around the steppe causing trouble.'

'Terrifying,' Gaevani said dryly.

'She shall not recognise me at first,' Kai said, 'old as I will be. But I shall know her at once. And we shall sit together by the fire, and tell our stories.'

A little sigh, from those in the darkness around him – a sharing, for a moment, of the dream.

'You are finished?' said Gaevani.

'I am,' Kai answered. 'One day, you shall tell me of your return. I will listen.'

Gaevani laughed. 'That is the difference,' he said, 'between you and me.'

'What is that?'

'I *know* that I shall never go back. You have yet to learn it.'

Somewhere close, the calling of the horns and drum. And though it was not yet his turn to stand guard, Kai rose to answer it.

'And where do you go now?' Gaevani asked, watching Kai with a doubtful eye.

'To take your advice,' Kai answered. 'To go and find a woman.'

It seemed such a simple thing, to deceive Laimei. Not upon the battlefield or the sparring ground, where she seemed to see every feint, every trick of hand and horse – waiting and watching, stony-faced, for you to make a mistake, to offer a gap in the guard for her spear to find. But when Arite told her, with a careless indifference, that she was going to buy some wine, Laimei merely shrugged and returned to polishing the scaled cuirass laid across her knee.

Neither the child's curiosity nor the adult's insight did she seem to have. Or perhaps that was not true, for on matters of war she was exacting and precise – every link of her armour checked, the spear tested and weighted over and over again, the men of her warband endlessly drilled in the movements of man and horse. Perhaps it was that Laimei did know she was being lied to. Perhaps she simply did not care.

Still, Arite kept the pretence as she set off towards the wine sellers' quarter. A glance behind, fearful of being followed, before she took a turning that she should not have taken, and then another. Until at last she reached a darkened corner of the *vicus*, where one half-collapsed building leaned over and cast shade upon the rest, the burned beams open to the sky, reaching up like blackened fingers. A coin forger's house, she had heard it said, until the fire had flared high and torn through wood and thatch in a matter of moments.

As she waited, she cast her eye up and down the alley. For the most part only children came to that place, to dig at the broken building in search of some piece of silver or copper or tin. But still, it would do to be careful. There were whisperings of women who disappeared in the *vicus* – men too, sometimes, to be quietly entombed in the basement of one house or another, or thrown into the river to wash up in the reeds downstream, bloated and purpled with rot.

And so when the footsteps came, she dropped by instinct into a swordfighter's crouch, a hand to the knife at her belt. The figure who approached threw up his hands, came forward like a prisoner with slow, shuffling steps. But it was Kai, smiling as he did so.

'What did you tell the others?' she said.

'What I always tell them. That I come to give my silver to a woman.' He shrugged, and lowered his hands. 'It has the benefit of being true, though not how they think it.' The clink and rattle of metal against metal, as he passed the small pouch to her. 'Half of my pay,' he said. 'For Laimei. And for you.'

'I am grateful for it. We must care for the boy you brought back, too.'

'He does not speak?'

'No words. Perhaps he shall heal.'

'And what of Laimei?'

'She speaks rather too much.'

Kai threw back his head and laughed, and in spite of herself, Arite felt a half-smile creep across her face.

'Your sister is like a prize stallion,' she said. 'Expensive to keep.' She weighed the coin pouch in her hand, and shook her head. 'You must leave yourself enough. This is too much.'

'Oh,' he said lightly, 'I may borrow and gamble from the others for what I need. My luck holds, so far at least. But they make us pay for everything. Weapons, armour. Even our own horses, they sell back to us.' His mouth twisted. 'The Romans know nothing of gifts.'

'Except for Lucius.'

'Except for Lucius,' he said, suddenly solemn, the words repeated like a prayer. Then, smiling once more. 'My sister, she *is* a hard taskmaster. She spends all the silver?'

'Oh it is beneath her to deal with such things,' Arite replied, 'and so it falls to me. And always there is something new she needs for her horse or her armour, and nothing but the best workmanship shall do for her.'

'Is she well?'

'Who can tell? She spends her days training the warband, and it seems to please her as much as it ever does. But I do not see how it may last. She wants for impossible things.'

'So do we all,' Kai answered.

A silence, for a time. Arite reached out to the burned building at her side, picking a burned and crumbled piece of wood away, crushing it to ash between her hands. For still she could see it in Kai, the foolish, beautiful hope that the young have, the belief that the world shall bend to their desires, warp the way that they want it to. With the touch of grey in her hair, she had thought to leave such beliefs behind her. Yet still, sometimes, they were there for her, too.

'What is it like, north of the Wall?' she asked.

'It is good country up there,' he answered. 'Reminds me a little of our home. I hope they send us back there soon. Perhaps they will, after the Dance of the Horses.'

Arite thought of the endless drills she had seen upon the parade ground. 'That is what the warband trains for?' she said. 'A display of some kind?'

Kai nodded. 'Just so. Some Roman chieftain comes to visit soon – a Legate, they call him. Lucius says we must impress him with some fine horsemanship.'

'I hope you will.'

'If you wish it, it shall be so.' He hesitated. 'And Bahadur? Is he well?'

Arite shrugged. 'Sometimes he is. And sometimes...'

A pained smile, and the silence returned.

A winter before, when they had both thought Bahadur

dead, it had seemed such a simple, natural thing, to find comfort together. Especially among the Sarmatians – once, it was said, it was the custom to simply hang one's quiver outside the tent of the man one wished to call a lover. Yet some traitorous desire had grown there unbidden, remained even after Bahadur had returned. And with that desire, together they had broken Bahadur's heart.

There in the alley, she found herself suddenly afraid of the silence and what might grow within it. There was a dangerous light in his eyes, as he looked on her, and she imagined that he must see the same in the way she looked at him.

'Stay safe, Kai,' she said. 'And be careful.'

A hand reaching towards her – hesitant, almost frightened, like a child waking in the dark, reaching for comfort. And she took a step back. 'That is what I mean,' she said.

She turned from him then without any further word, strode out of the alley, out into the light and air.

7

The torches were lit, the circle carved upon the ground. Looming above them, the shadow of the Wall.

Six men waited at the southern edge of that circle – a lonely gathering in such a wide-open space. At the front was Lucius, the firelight gleaming on every curve of his cuirass, the crest of his helm standing high and proud. He kept his eyes forward for the most part, occasionally letting them drift to his left, where a man sat on his horse with the comfortable ease of a nobleman. The Roman ruler of these lands, Caerellius Priscus, Legate of the North.

They spoken little since that man had arrived in the late afternoon, a day earlier than expected. Lucius had begun to give his report when the Legate arrived, but the other man had thrown up his hand at once, smiled, and said: 'Let me see them, first, in the Dance of the Horses. Then I shall know what we will need to speak about.' And so it had been done. To the parade ground they went, the final orders given. Lucius, the Legate, and four bodyguards with them in close company, men who were well fed, heavy muscled, proud and arrogant like all elite soldiers were. Lucius allowed himself a tight little smile. Those bodyguards were about to see how useless, how helpless, they would be, if the Sarmatians decided to mutiny. There might have been two hundred of them, and it would do them no good.

They waited there, the Wall high before them, the fort of Cilurnum looming heavy in the darkness. A clouded sky, the occasional volley of rain brought in by a squall, and the torches dulling his night vision. And so it was that Lucius heard them before he saw them – the rattle and clink of armour, the heavy tread of the horses. Shadows in the dark, and a shiver of excitement to know that they were coming.

They bore no fire to guide them, riding surefooted in the night. A great column that seemed numberless in the darkness, though Lucius knew them to be a hundred of his best men. They were drawing closer now, close enough to see them, the torchlight dancing across faces carved from iron – the eerie cavalry helmets that mimicked the faces of men, left no flesh exposed, only eyes hidden in hollow shadows. Always in the Dance of the Horses, the Roman cavalry wore those masks. The men from a dozen different nations, captured or surrendered or made a tribute by their chieftains, becoming faceless men of iron as they fought for those who had conquered them. Automatons they seemed in movement, too, nothing wasted in the motion of man and horse as they came to a halt at the edge of the circle.

A moment's stillness – the terrible waiting, as before a battle, when all gathered know that the killing is to come. Soon and inevitable, but not yet.

Then a screaming in the air, a war cry that was at once a song of lost heroes and the sounding of the order, the calling of the charge. The Legate started in his saddle as the voices broke the silence, for though he could never have heard that war song before, somehow in his heart he knew it well, the way a lamb will mewl and cry the first time it hears the howling of a wolf. These were the battle cries that had sounded for hundreds of years on the bank of the Danubius, where the Sarmatians had beaten ceaselessly against the walls of the Empire. This was a song that Romans died to.

And the Sarmatians were charging forward, lances dropping low, tilting towards the Romans. Lucius felt the others shifting beside him, heard the horses snorting in fear. He held utterly still, his gaze unblinking and fixed upon his captains.

At the last instant the Sarmatians turned, breaking on either side of Lucius and the Legate, the slap of the wind following the charge close enough to set the plumes dancing on their helms. The Sarmatians were turning then, wheeling back, moving like murmurations in the sky as they shifted formation through line and square and wedge.

Such pride there was to see them move so. Lucius had worried the Sarmatians might think this a trivial game, beneath their honour to dance and perform for a Roman Legate, yet it seemed they understood the contest better than he did, the wager of their lives for nothing more than honour and renown. Above all, they understood the power of the ritual – to gather in a circle by torchlight, enact the dance of horse and spear, and show how well they could kill.

The hundred Sarmatians broke apart into two bands of fifty. The spears were held towards the light of the torches so that all might see that these were no false weapons that boys might train with, but blades of iron, the light catching on the killing edges. And then they were charging once more, this time straight towards each other.

In a single beating of the heart, it was already too late for them to turn away – fully committed, it seemed that nothing could stop them, as though in some old feud of the steppe had suddenly broken open once more, and the Sarmatians could think of nothing but killing one another. Yet at the last moment the formations broke into columns, leaving channels just wide enough for horse and man to pass through. And then they were all as one, two rivers pouring into each other in a flood.

A moment's misjudgement, a single horse out of place, and there would have been blood upon the earth, men speared from their horses or tumbled beneath the hooves. But with a great thunder and a shaking of the earth as though a storm were rising from the ground itself, the horsemen were through each other, circling back once more in their formations. Again and again they made the passes, carving patterns through the air, each more intricate than the last, until they stood once more around the circle, the horses' flanks shining with sweat.

Then one of the riders came forward, grasped the great lance in the middle with both hands, held parallel with the ground. The Sarmatian barked out words in his own language – a question, spoken like a prayer.

'What does he say?' the Legate whispered.

'It is time for them to fight each other in earnest,' Lucius answered. 'They ask if you wish them to fight with the blunt or the sharp edge of their spears.'

It was a gamble Lucius made to ask that question, for there were countless sadists among the Prefects and Legates who would think nothing of throwing away the lives of barbarians for sport. It was needful for him to know what kind of man it was that he served, who held all their lives in their hand.

But the Legate smiled, and it was not a murderer's smile. 'The blunt,' he said.

Lucius repeated those words in the Sarmatian tongue, and as one they reversed their spears. Twenty of them came forward, each one bearing the mark of a champion. One carried a spear etched with dragons, scaled beasts twisting their way up the haft. Another's armour was dressed in the tusks of boars and the fur of a bear he had hunted alone. Yet another man's long, braided beard clattered with a dozen rings, trophies hammered out from the swords of defeated men. Lucius was glad not to see any saddles dressed with scalps – an innocent enough trophy among the Sarmatians, but they had obeyed his command to leave those particular totems behind.

Again, the stillness before a battle. To end it, no sign or signal given. But all at once, it seemed, the Sarmatians knew that it was time. Some whispered command from a god of war, a clarion horn sounded by the ghosts of their ancestors, some sound heard only by champions and heroes.

No war cries now, nor the songs to remind them of the heroes of old that bore witness. For these warriors needed no charms to bring courage to fearful men, no watchful heroes to guide their spears. The true champions fought in silence.

In a moment, five of them were down, struck from their horses. Lucius winced as he heard the splintering, echoing crack of a bone shattering, and saw a man clutching at his leg and biting at the ground in pain, one of the beautiful horses screaming and kicking at the sky with only two legs, its back broken. But there was a roar from the Sarmatians to hear the sounds of death upon the field, as though they witnessed something holy.

Those champions that remained twisted like sharks in the water, light shining on the scales of their armour as the blunted spears wove through the air. More brutal than artful, as killing always was, no matter what the stories said. A few split away from the mob and charged in once more, and men were sent flying through the air, graceful and beautiful until they struck the ground, rolling and tumbling and lying still.

Then, all at once, there were so few left. The ground strewn with the defeated, beaten and broken men who were dragged from the field by their companions. Three alone remained, and for a time they did not move against each other. Bowed over in their saddles with exhaustion, hunched up as though suddenly cursed with age. Still no war cries from them, only a ragged panting sounded across the open field, the desperate retching breathing of those who have been fighting for their lives. One could see them looking at each other, reading the hero's marks upon spear and armour, to know who they fought against. Lucius could see the man with dragons upon his spear was still there, another man whose head was framed by the jaws of a wolf. The last carried the tassels of red felt on his spear, like blood forever dripping and yet never falling to the ground.

Among those three, an unspoken accord. For two of the three came together, the dragon and the wolf – a silent alliance, some understanding that the third, the one who bore the red felt upon their spear, could not be faced alone.

To warriors almost spent, the little parade ground must have seemed an endless plain, like the great Sea of Grass they had left behind, far to the east. Their horses stumbled and walked towards each other exhausted – even at a distance, one could see the drool that fell from their mouths, their eyes rolling wild and white. A single charge left to them, if that.

The dragon and the wolf broke wide and encircled, and Lucius expected the lone champion to turn at once towards one of them. Instead, with a warrior's arrogance, he kept his course arrow straight, the lance held low, walking into the trap.

All was still, save for the slow pacing of the horses. Every detail was marked in the mind, and Lucius could have closed his eyes and etched it upon wax. Each scale upon the armour, and where it was chipped and marked. The gloved hands that flexed away cramp and clutched at the spears. The nervous tapping of a boot against the flank of the horse. Everything so clear, and Lucius watching so closely, eyes fixed upon that warrior with the red felted spear. Yet even so, he did not see it when it happened.

Like a shadow moving across the ground when a torch is lit – that was how fast the red spear moved, as though his horse stepped out of their world for a single moment and stepped back once more in a different place. The horse springing to the charge, one last great effort, the kind given only by a horse that loves its master more than life itself, towards the warrior with dragons on his spear. And a blunted spear was into that man's side, rider and horse twisting and falling and breaking upon the ground.

The warrior with the mark of the wolf was close behind, closing the jaws of the trap. But his horse was stumbling, exhausted legs giving way, the war cry twisting to panic. The horse did not go to ground, but the red spear was twisting back, turning in the saddle, that great long spear stretching back as well, held at the last moment in but one trembling hand, the rider almost flat against the horse's back, face turned towards the sky.

The wet sound of a body falling to sodden earth, the crying gasp of a horse that could no longer stand. And then, the warrior with the red spear was alone upon the field.

He folded over the horse, so still that for a moment he might have been dead, pierced by an unseen wound from man or god. For the gods, in their jealousy, sometimes struck down heroes at their moment of triumph, stealing them away to the next life. But Lucius could see a hand moving, running along the horse's neck with a lover's touch. And when the wind blew, it brought some soft fragment of speech with it, a wordless whisper of gratitude.

The Sarmatians who watched did not scream or cheer, for it was a sacred thing they had witnessed. Only the rattle of spears lifted up to the sky, a single word sounding out, and then the silence returning once more.

'What is it they say?' the Legate asked.

'Death,' said Lucius. 'They call out to their god of death.'

'Magnificent,' Caerellius whispered. 'They are all that the stories make them out to be. More, perhaps.'

'Thank you, sir,' Lucius said, with a weary sense of pride. For in truth, he had not known if they would last a year. Lucius had wondered if the shame of defeat would break the Sarmatians, if to leave their homes would drive them mad, and that then the Romans would destroy them. For it had happened before – companies of auxiliaries who could not stand to serve Rome, who disappeared from the annals, disbanded a few months after they formed, cut down in rebellion or butchered by the executioners and then quietly forgotten.

And instead the Legate was lifting a crown of oaken leaves, the prize granted for skill and valour. A treasure that every soldier dreamed of. 'Bring the champion forward,' said the Legate.

Lucius called out to the rider, in the language of their people. Slowly, almost insolently, that warrior turned his horse towards them, laid the spear across the neck of the horse, and set out to receive the prize.

It was only at the last moment, that Lucius realised who that rider was – some glimpse of the eyes behind the carved iron face of the helm, a particular turn of the wrist in the way that warrior held a spear that was so hauntingly familiar. In the moment before the helm was lifted, Lucius knew the face that he would see beneath it.

No long hair spilling down, for this was not one of the old stories of Amazons and warrior women. But in spite of her close-cropped hair, and for all the scars she bore, there was no mistaking her for a man. It was Laimei who bore the red felted spear, who was the champion of the field, and came forward to receive the prize.

Lucius waited for the Legate's fury, the speaking of a punishment. For there was no greater god in the Roman army than orders and discipline, for one to bear arms for Rome except for those that Rome chose itself. And Rome would never allow a woman to go to war.

It would be a decimation of the soldiers at least, every tenth man tied down and stoned to death by his comrades. For Lucius, something much worse – one of the rare punishments saved for the captains of traitorous men.

And then, from beside him, he heard laughter.

'What a splendid thing you have shown me,' Caerellius

said. 'I had heard of their warrior women, but I never thought to see such a thing for myself.' He leaned forward, placed the crown about the spearhead.

A twitch of hand and spear from Laimei – some old killing instinct, perhaps, to find a Roman commander so close. But it was so slight that only Lucius saw it, before the weapon tilted up and back, the oaken leaves sliding down to be taken from the haft of the spear, and she was laying the crown upon her head, and giving a brilliant, murderous smile.

'You have done well,' said Caerellius. 'They have done well. Choose from among your captains. Have them join us for the feast.'

The feel of danger passing, but it only lasted for a moment. For the Legate spoke again, and said: 'And make sure that *she* has a place with us. For it is only proper to honour the champion, don't you think?'

8

A feast, the Legate had called it – a flattering term for what they had to offer him, for it was a rough kind of hospitality out there upon the border. Cracked clay bowls piled up with fresh venison, good bread, a little olive oil, and oysters that had been gathered at the coast and sent down the Wall by a runner, losing a single oyster in 'tax' at every milecastle that he passed. There were none of the delicacies that a cultured man of Rome would be used to – fig and liver, fish drowned in wine, the tongues of rare birds. But Caerellius seemed comfortable enough with the simple food, the flaking plaster walls of Lucius's quarters, the cutting wind that wormed through the cracks and battled with the heat that rose from the braziers and the hypocaust beneath them. He lay upon a couch and sipped at the wine with the comfort of a man in his own home.

'A long road brought you here,' Caerellius said to Lucius. 'Not many have seen two edges of the Empire, east and north. The Danubius and the Wall.'

'I am a fortunate man, sir.'

'Oh, I would not say that. Neither of them are places

that Romans choose to go. Perhaps you are doubly unlucky, instead.' He picked up a roasted piece of venison, swirled it around in a bowl of fish sauce. 'What do you make of this country?'

'As good as any for a soldier. A hard place for its people.'

'Yes, and the cause of much trouble. The barbarians have little to lose, and it makes them dangerous. The tribes hate one another more than they hate us – the only way that we keep the peace. A hard country, as you say. But it may breed strong soldiers, don't you think?'

Lucius hesitated. The Legate had the elegant manner of Rome, the practised speech and rhetoric that Lucius was not used to unpicking. 'Were you a soldier, sir?'

'Only from afar,' Caerellius answered dryly. 'The senator's distance, I believe centurions call it.'

Lucius waited for the man to speak again. Or he tried to think if it was he who was supposed to lead the conversation – it had been so long since he had been around a nobleman. But Caerellius seemed content to watch the Sarmatians who were their guests.

Three had been chosen to join them. Laimei, a bruise purpling up her arm as she reached forward for a bowl of bread, her eyes sliding restlessly about the room. Gaevani – the second to last upon the field, the one who had borne the mark of the wolf on his armour – was speaking almost ceaselessly, slipping between Sarmatian and Latin as he ate and drank. The last of the three was Kai, who kept his eyes carefully averted from his sister, answered Gaevani's mocking questions with single word answers. Kai and Gaevani lay flat upon the couches, aping the Roman way. Only Laimei sat cross-legged and straight backed, as though waiting for a command.

'I never thought to see an Amazon myself,' the Legate said, offhand. At this Laimei, seemed to bristle, and Caerellius laughed. 'She speaks our language?'

'A little. But I believe she knows that word.'

'She has the warrior's pride. Do tell her it is a compliment I speak to her, Lucius. There are many like her, in the east?'

'All the women fight,' said Lucius. 'But few like her, sir.'

'Is it true what they say? That they must kill a man before they are allowed to marry?'

'Three actually, sir.'

Caerellius sipped his wine. 'And is it that she likes the killing, or does not like the husband?'

'You would have to ask her, sir.'

'I think I would be afraid to,' the Legate said with a smile. He fell silent then as another course of food was brought in, and watched the Sarmatians eat.

Perhaps he expected some savage display, but the Sarmatians ate carefully and delicately, passing the bowls around in a regular motion, careful to take no more than their share from each one, even though it must have been better fare than they had tasted for months.

Gaevani caught the Legate watching, and spoke in near flawless Latin: 'You hoped to see us tear into this food, I think? Mannerless barbarians that we are?'

'Of course,' the Legate said jovially. 'Like wolves at a kill.'

Gaevani shook his head. 'Oh, you have never seen wolves eat, I think. They take their turns as we do – very courteous creatures. And their leaders take the choicest cuts first.' He grandly offered an untouched plate to the Legate, who laughed as he took his share from it.

'But there are three great virtues the stories teach our

people,' Gaevani continued. 'Courage in battle, courtesy to women, and,' he paused, and slapped his belly, 'restraint in eating.'

'You may make for rather poor Romans in that case,' Caerellius said lightly. 'We manage only one of those on a good day.'

'Do not worry,' Gaevani answered, 'we shall do our best to teach you.'

Laughter about the room, a laughter that Caerellius led. Lucius smiled politely, but he did not share in their mirth. For he could see that the Sarmatians were careful with their food, but careless with the wine – they drank it down unwatered, the flush of it already on their cheeks. Lucius caught Kai's eye, nodded towards the cups.

Kai gave a mutter in his own language, and Gaevani pointedly put his cup of wine back upon the table. 'Forgive us. Restraint in eating we value, but restraint in drink robs the world of joy. We must take our cheer where we can, in this hard country, as I heard you call it. There is little enough comfort compared to the place that we call home.'

'The silver coin and service of Rome is not enough reward for you, I take it.'

'We were promised a war,' said Gaevani. 'By your Emperor.'

The Legate stretched out, placed his hands behind his head. 'The world is not a peaceful place. I am sure you will get one.'

'We are not good at waiting.'

'Gaevani,' said Lucius.

'Forgive me,' said Gaevani, laying a hand on his chest. 'I speak only from the heart. I submit to your punishment.'

'Oh, none is needed,' said Caerellius. 'I admire your courage. And I hope you shall not have to wait long for your war.' The Legate coughed and cleared his throat, drank down the last of his wine and raised the cup in a salute. 'I know that you are far from your homes,' he said. 'That it may be a shameful thing to serve your conquerors.'

No answer. Kai stared down at the ground, and Gaevani fell to picking restlessly at the couch, a strand of straw teased out from a gap in the fabric. Only Laimei met the Legate's gaze, unblinking and unyielding.

'We are a people of many nations,' Caerellius continued. 'You are brothers to us, if you will have us. And all we ask is bravery. All we expect is victory, and the keeping of oaths once given. And what we offer is the chance to reshape the world, to be masters of it.'

Silence answered him. For they were holy words the Legate was speaking, and perhaps he knew it. Even Gaevani no longer smiled, nodding along in acknowledgement as the Legate spoke.

The Legate clapped his hands, a breaking of the spell. 'Now you must forgive me. You came to celebrate, and I have spoilt the mood. I must have some words with your commander, if you shall wait outside?'

'I am sure they are tired from the Dance of the Horses,' said Lucius. 'We may send them home, and grant them the reward of a good night's rest.'

'Oh, they cannot go just yet.' The Legate said, and smiled wide. 'And they shall have more of a reward than that. I must grant a boon to the champion. Whatever she asks for, I shall give – tell her to think on that, while we speak.'

Kai spoke those words to her in the Sarmatian tongue – soft and hesitant, as though he feared she would be angered by them. But she rose like a sleeper waking, a light in her eyes that Lucius did not like to look upon. And worse than that, for the first time Lucius could remember, he saw her smile.

Out into the courtyard, fresh air upon the skin. A relief to be outside with the stars above, though still the ground tipped and swayed a little beneath his feet – Kai shook his head. Too much wine.

'Never thought I would be so glad to leave a feast,' he said.

'Why?' Gaevani asked. 'Good food and good wine. Enjoy it while you can.'

'Better to eat under open sky, around a fire. And I do not care for the company.'

'The Legate?' Gaevani leaned against the wall and picked at his teeth. 'He's not bad for one of their perfumed men. Perhaps we may do well out of his visit.'

'I do not know,' said Kai. 'He reminds me a little of you.'

'How do you mean?'

'One who always smiles, but who loves himself a little too much.'

Gaevani laughed – too loudly, the sound echoing from the walls. 'That must be why I like him so much.' Then he shrugged. 'A good thing too, since he is our master now.'

'I swore to follow Lucius. As did you.'

Gaevani nodded to the closed door, outlined by the light of the braziers that burned beside it. 'That does not matter. That is what he speaks of with Lucius now, and that is why he promises a boon to our champion. We are being bought.'

'And what do you think of that?' said Kai. 'I have no wish to be caught in some Roman's game.'

'I think we shall have little choice. We should at least get a good price for ourselves.' Gaevani turned his head towards Laimei. 'But I do not trust our merchant.'

For Laimei had not yet spoken – she paced about from wall to wall, circling about the columns, her feet pattering restlessly against the stone. On their travels Lucius had spoken to them of Rome, of the menageries of the Emperor where wild beasts were kept, great black cats from some place far to the south. Perhaps they looked a little like her, behind their bars of iron.

'You have something to say?' she said, ceasing her pacing. 'Something that matters, I mean, rather than your endless chatter.'

'The prize should have been mine,' Gaevani said to her. 'You were lucky. If my horse did not stumble—'

'But it did stumble.'

'And I suppose you shall try and say that you knew it would be so?'

She made no answer, save for a small, tight smile.

'What prize will you ask for?' Kai said.

'What matters that to you?'

'It matters a great deal.' He nodded back towards Lucius's quarters. 'Gaevani is right – this is a game we play. That man holds our lives in his hands.'

'He holds *your* lives in his hands, you mean. And games are for children.' She lifted her head proudly. 'I already know what I shall ask for.'

'Laimei, think—'

'What need is there to think?' she said. 'Men think, gods know, heroes choose. I choose a place in the warband, the place that is my right.'

Kai said nothing for a time. A part of him had known that was what she would ask for. All that she longed for in life, that place of honour at the head of the warband, a place that one had to fight to get and fight to keep, for always were there jealous men who sought the glory for themselves. Yet, for a moment, he found he had no answer for her. He turned to Gaevani, hopeful that the other man would speak, but Gaevani remained silent, his face unreadable in the darkness.

'That is a thing that he cannot give,' Kai said at last. 'Women do not fight for Rome. If you ask for that, Lucius will be—'

'What do I care for him?'

'He has sacrificed much for us. Almost everything.'

'Then let him give a little more,' she said, 'if he is so eager to be one of us.'

'And what of the Legate? We amuse him, for now. But ask that of him, and they shall raise you on a cross.'

'The Sarmatians will butcher him if he tries.' Again, the terrible smile upon her face. 'You do not understand, do you? It is not Lucius or that fool of a Legate who rules these men. I do. I am still their champion.'

She stood there, smiling and proud, standing in a warrior's stance and utterly fearless. And even then, as she spoke words that could only bring disaster to their people, Kai could not help admiring her. As he always had, even in the depths of the feud, even when they had faced one another with spear in hand. For she was the last of her kind, perhaps. No more would their women bear spears in the east – Rome would see to that. Nothing that he might say would dissuade her, and in that moment he did not want to. Let a hero speak, one last time. It was how all those in the old stories earned their place in the stars, with some attempt at the impossible.

A voice in the darkness, then. A single calm word that Gaevani spoke: 'No.'

'No to what?' Laimei answered.

'To all of it,' Gaevani said, his voice patient, and mocking. 'You do not rule them. The Sarmatians shall not fight for you. You will not ask this of the Legate.'

'You think to speak for the others?' she said.

'Better than you do. For this is not the steppe, and you are not a champion anymore.'

She reached up, and tapped the crown of leaves she wore.

'You earned that trinket,' he said, 'but no right to command. They shall not rebel for you.'

'You think them cowards, then.'

'Oh, they will die gladly for honour,' said Gaevani. 'But not for your pride. And they will not throw away the lives of their people for you, either.'

She hesitated, made no answer.

Gaevani shook his head. 'Of course you would not think of that. What a simple world you live in. What do you think they shall do to our people back upon the steppe, if we rebel here?'

'I do not know,' she said. 'Who can say?' But, for once, there was doubt in her voice.

'They are ruled by Rome, now,' said Gaevani. 'Kept safe by Rome. And Rome shall murder them, if we rebel. They have our children there, a knife to their throats. Your champion's luck can do nothing about that. You have no power here.'

Laimei closed her eyes, tilted her head towards the sky. The stars were above them, for it was a rare clear sky in that place. It was on that night sky that the Sarmatians wrote their legends, not on wax and paper. And some of the familiar stories could still be read there: Syrdon the trickster, Arash by his hero's grave of stars. Some of those stories they had lost, the stars swallowed beneath the horizon, perhaps never to be seen again. And in that moment Kai could see the light of the stars shining upon Laimei's eyes, wet with tears.

'Is it true, what he says?' she said to Kai.

Kai could not think of how long it had been since she had spoken to him that way – since she had needed something from him. 'It is true,' he said. And he saw those simple words drive home like a spear into flesh.

An old, false instinct, then, to reach out and comfort her. He had not done that since they were children. With no mother left to them, and their father always raiding with the warband, it was they who had to hold each other close and take it in turns to whisper a mother's words to one another. And so he found his hand drifting towards her, a half-step taken inside her swordsman's guard, the killing circle that surrounded her. But she started from his touch and snarled at him, her hand drifting to her side towards a knife that was not there.

'You must ask for something else,' said Kai. 'This is what you must do. What a hero must do.'

Silence, for a moment, and in Laimei's eyes Kai thought he saw a madness building and growing like a fire that burned out of control. The great warriors all went mad in the end – the old stories agreed on that, for it was the price the gods demanded for that brilliance in battle. That at the last the mind would crack, the champion would turn upon their companions, or wage some impossible battle against a mountain or the sea. And their sworn warband, their friends and companions, would have to gather together one last time, and murder their ruined champion.

But, it seemed, that time was not yet. 'Very well,' she said, her voice hollow, 'I shall do as you ask. This once, I shall do it. But never again.' And then her hand lifted up high towards the stars, and Kai saw her pointing towards the sword of Arash that hung in the sky above them. For she had no blade of her own there to swear on, and so she made her oath on that sword of stars. 'But I shall be revenged upon you both,' she said, her voice rising high and haunting, a priest at a ritual. 'I swear it to the gods.'

'So,' the Legate said, pouring himself another cup of wine, now that they were alone. 'Tell me of the raid.'

Lucius made no answer at first. He made a show of collecting his thoughts, though he had practised these words ever since he had heard that the Legate was coming. In that silence, he sought to gain the measure of the man.

He saw black hair touched with silver at the temples, a face lined with laughter, not marked with the remnants of pain and care. Caerellius did not carry the signs of disgrace on him – no hunch of the shoulder or roving eye, no catch in the speech from one who fears to speak. Yet here he was, in the forgotten north of the Empire. Perhaps a little too much ambition had brought him here, sent out to quietly do his service and be forgotten.

'Three of ours dead,' Lucius said at last, 'and twenty of the raiders. Some farms burned – about thirty farmers slain.'

'Survivors?'

'A boy of the local tribe, the Brigantes. Though he cannot speak of what happened.'

'And did any of the raiders escape?'

A moment's hesitation, where Lucius considered the lie. But the Legate's smile seemed to broaden in that silence, to show teeth. *I'll know*, it seemed to say.

'A rider on a tall horse, sir,' Lucius said. 'A Roman cavalry horse, I think, though I cannot prove it.'

'I see.' Caerellius swirled the wine around in his cup. 'Strange, no?'

'Yes, sir. I made a show of force north of the Wall, spoke with a chieftain of the Votadini who has been loyal to us in the past.'

'Any answers there?'

'No,' said Lucius. 'But I do not believe it was his people on the raid. He was frightened, I think.'

'And are you?'

'No, sir. Only cautious.'

'Very good.'

The speech was plainer now from the Legate, and it gave Lucius an uneasy feeling, that the man chose to play the politician before his soldiers and not their commander. *I can be replaced*, Lucius reminded himself. *They cannot.*

'Did you fear my coming?' said Caerellius.

'Always wise to fear a Legate's visit, sir.'

'Of course. But there is the right kind of fear. I would have you fear me as your commander, not as some murderous tyrant.'

'I shall try to fear you in the right way then, sir.'

Caerellius laughed and lifted his cup, offering the toast. 'To Rome,' said the Legate.

'To the Emperor,' Lucius answered.

The taste of the wine, sweet and spiced against his lips. A silence, while the Legate watched him.

'The Emperor is not well,' Caerellius said at last. 'Few know this. But I share it with you, now.'

A stillness, then, in the room. They were innocent-seeming words that the Legate spoke, yet still had the taste of treason to them – to speak of the death of a god.

'I wish good health for the Emperor,' Lucius said. 'May he rule for countless years more.'

'Of course. But if he does not, much might change.' Caerellius cocked his head to the side. 'I have heard stories of you,' he said.

'And what do the stories say?'

'That you are fearless. And foolish.'

'They are wrong on both counts, sir.'

Caerellius laughed. 'So I can see.'

'And what do they say of my Sarmatians?'

'*Your* Sarmatians, are they?' The Legate wagged a finger at him. 'Careful. That's the first mistake you have made yet. They belong to the Emperor. And to me.'

'Yes, sir.' *They belong to themselves*, he thought.

The Legate lay down on the couch once more, toying with a wisp of straw that had crept from a cushion. 'They are better than any cavalry I have seen,' he said matter-of-factly. 'And it is a marvel that they are so disciplined so soon.'

'It was but a little work to teach them our cavalry tricks – they know most of them already.'

'A fierce people,' said Caerellius. 'Will they rebel, do you think?'

'They have sworn their oaths upon a sword and before a fire,' said Lucius. 'That means much to them.'

'Oaths have been broken before.'

'Not by these people. Sir.'

The Legate nodded. 'Perhaps it is so. Still, I see a weakness there.'

'What is that?'

Caerellius looked up at him and smiled wanly. 'You, of course.'

The feel of danger – that cold touch that danced across the skin. 'Sir?'

'You do not see the way they look upon you?' said Caerellius, seeming amused. 'Compared to how they look upon me? Oh, their loyalty is strong but it rests…' the Legate paused, and held up a finger and thumb a little space apart, 'on that much. Guard your life well, Lucius. For the sake of your men, if nothing more.'

They did not speak for a time. Somewhere close, the steady tread of a guard pacing outside his quarters, the creak of a gate swinging open. Some fragment of a song floating down from the walls, as a sentry sang to try and keep himself awake.

The Legate cocked his head to the side. 'What do you want, Lucius?'

Lucius hesitated. 'To serve Rome, sir.'

'Ah,' Caerellius said, 'that is your second mistake. Do not lie to me. For I know that you are not a true believer. Once, perhaps, but not now.'

Lucius's mouth was suddenly dry, the way it felt before a cavalry charge.

'Tell me what it is you want,' said the Legate. 'I may be able to provide it.'

For a price. Lucius kept his face impassive as best he could, but he could feel a bitter little smile picking at his lips. For it was always the way with Rome, this bartering of ambition and favours. Oh, they were fine merchants of ambition, and with it they had bought half the world. But he remembered the strange, traitorous feeling when he had been a captive of the Sarmatians – a people bound by honour and oath, or so it seemed to him. Men and women who could not be bought, in the way the Legate sought to buy him now.

'Why do you smile?' Caerellius said.

'I suppose I wonder why a Legate would ask a Prefect such a thing, rather than the other way around.'

Caerellius considered this. 'Very well,' he said. 'Tell me what it is you want, so that I may know whether I can trust you.'

'I want to keep them alive, sir. The Sarmatians.'

The Legate's smile wavered. 'A captain's love for his men. A beautiful thing, I suppose.'

'But not the answer you wanted. Sir.'

'No.' Caerellius glanced into the bottom of his cup, cast the lees of the wine into a brazier. 'Do you think the games of politics beneath you?'

'No sir. Only that I am unfit for them.'

'A simple soldier, eh? Only not so simple. If only you had more ambition…Well, there is nothing to be done.' Yet the Legate still picked at the fabric of the couch, seeming to wait for something more. And Lucius was like a man fumbling in the dark, trying to find the shape of the words, the thing he would need to speak to keep his people safe.

'If you come to ask me to risk my life,' said Lucius, 'or the lives of my people, for some great reward of power and fame, I will say no. But I will guard this wall upon the border, and I will not stray from here. You have nothing to fear from me or from this place while I am here. I am no enemy of yours.' He drained his wine carefully. 'Is that enough for you, sir?'

The Legate smiled tightly, and poured once more. 'Perhaps it is. You are certainly not foolish, as they have said. There may come a time when you must choose, though. Even a guard dog must have its loyalties, when it is pressed to a choice.' He raised the cup to toast again. 'To *your* Sarmatians. I like them, even that Amazon.'

'Thank you, sir.'

Caerellius nodded, wiped his hand across his mouth. 'I shall see that it is built well.'

'What is that, sir?'

'The veteran's colony, for your men, when they have served their twenty-five years. It shall be a little to the south, at Bremetennacum – it is better countryside there. They shall be glad to see the back of the Wall, I am sure.'

Lucius hesitated. 'A kind offer that you make them. But they long to return home. They shall go back across the Danubius, to Sarmatia.'

'It is not an offer, Lucius. Surely…' Caerellius fell silent, and looked at Lucius as though seeing him for the first time. As he might have looked upon a wilful, foolish child.

The firelight danced and flickered, casting shifting shadows upon the walls. Ash from the braziers curled through the air like snow, and there was the rich smell of wine upon the air, the scent of cooked meat. It was a still, quiet place they were in, and yet Lucius found himself listening for the calling of warhorns, arrows whispering through the sky. Still, he had not learned – he always expected to be defeated upon the battlefield, not in small, quiet rooms such as this one.

'They are never going to go home, are they?' said Lucius.

'Of course not,' the Legate answered patiently. 'Why would the Emperor send five thousand unruly cavalry back to an uncertain border? You said it yourself, they are people of honour, and people of honour have long memories.'

Anger was there, hot and sharp within his throat, and Lucius tried to breathe it away before he spoke. 'They were empty words, then, that you spoke to them.'

'Be careful, Prefect,' said Caerellius. 'I like you. I like your soldiers, too. You think that, perhaps, you have nothing to lose out here on the frontier. But you would be wrong.' The Legate stood, wiped his hand against some imaginary stain on his cloak. 'And they were not empty words. But Rome has not lasted as long as we have by being foolish. Or sentimental.'

Lucius stared down at his hands. 'And what do you think they will do,' he said, 'when they are told they cannot go home?'

'They will do what soldiers always do. They shall find wives among these local women, raise their children. And eventually, long memories though they may have, they will forget.'

'You do not know them as I do.'

'Perhaps,' said Caerellius. 'We shall see. But come now – let us see what your Amazon asks for her boon.'

Lucius lifted his head. 'A wager, then,' he said. 'For I already know what she shall ask for.'

The Legate seemed amused. 'What does each of us win?' he said.

'A favour, from the other.'

Caerellius shook his head. 'The favour of a Legate counts for something more than the favour of a Prefect. A favour from me, but a promise from you. From a man of honour, which I can see that you are, a promise makes for a rich prize indeed.'

Lucius nodded. 'Very well then. What will she ask for?'

'I think she shall ask for something beautiful,' the Legate said. 'A weapon or a horse. Champions are vain, women even more so. Some pretty prize is what she shall wish for.' He smiled. 'And what do *you* think she shall ask for?'

'To be given a place in the warband, as befits a champion.'

Caerellius laughed. 'She is brave but not that brave. Foolish, but not that foolish. I think I know a little more of women than you do. But very well, call them in.'

At that, Lucius found he could not resist. He lifted his head, sounded out that same war cry that had echoed on the parade ground, and at once, the Sarmatians answered the call, quick as hounds – so quick, with the bodyguards running behind them, that they might have swarmed upon the Legate and cut him down in a moment.

Pride there was to see them, fearless and brave. A bitter satisfaction, to see the Legate fearful. And yet Lucius found himself afraid, too, as he looked upon the Sarmatians, and he could not say why. He found himself afraid to speak, seeking some unspoken message written upon their bodies. For their eyes were guarded, their heads hung low. Somehow, already, they seemed defeated.

'Ask for your boon, Laimei,' he said at last.

She lifted her head, and looked towards Caerellius. 'Give me a good spear,' she said, the words slow and dull. 'The kind your great warriors would bear.' She turned her face away, and for a moment Lucius thought he saw shame there. 'A memory,' she said, more to herself now, 'of when I used to fight, to hang upon my wall.'

The Legate was gracious, at least, in victory. A serious look, as he asked his questions of her – the length, the weight, decoration and engraving, and she answered courteously, something of the champion's pride returning to her as she spoke. Lucius could almost believe her to be speaking the truth.

The Sarmatians saluted – here they were still unpractised and hesitant, like children aping their father. Then they were gone out into the night.

As he watched the Sarmatians walk away, Lucius felt the Legate step beside him, heard the whisper in his ear.

'Your third mistake, it seems.'

'So it seems,' Lucius answered. 'And what promise do you ask of me?'

Lucius had thought the other man might wait a moment – savour his victory, or think again upon the prize that he might have. But it seemed he already knew what he would ask for. 'Only this,' he said. 'You promise never to tell them of what we have spoken. They must not know that they shall never see their homes again.'

Lucius closed his eyes – the way, as a child, he had learned to close his eyes in an evil dream, and open them again to wake himself. 'Sir, I—'

'Too much depends upon this,' said the Legate. 'I cannot have a rebellion here. And so I need your word of honour. Upon the Eagles, and your oath to the Emperor.' His mouth twisted. 'Upon the gods of the Sarmatians, if they have come to mean anything to you. An oath of sword and fire. Do you swear it?'

And at last, Lucius said: 'I do.'

9

Outside the Prefect's quarters, Kai waited.

He was alone there, for as soon as they had been dismissed from the feast Laimei had stalked into the night towards the *vicus*, while Gaevani had given another ironic salute before he staggered off to the barracks. Kai had smiled to see him go – it would have been a good time to make a wager, to bet a handful of silver that Gaevani would empty the rich food into the gutters before he made it to his bed.

But he had no one to make such a wager with. Lucius was still inside, no doubt striking some bargain with the Legate. The thought held no fear for Kai as he waited there, for he had that strange, invincible feeling that only came when one followed a great captain. A leader that could be loved, who inspired the kind of loyalty that made all choices seem so simple. Fight at the captain's command, die if you had to, and it would all come easily, for that man had earned the right to your life, would always know the right thing to do.

At last the footsteps did come – the heavy, even tread of the soldier trained upon the parade ground. And Kai smiled to hear it, glad to have been proven right. For he had been certain that Lucius, tired as he was, would want to feel the air and see the sky once more before he slept, like a Sarmatian.

Together, they shared a silence. For Kai and Lucius were near enough alone then. Kai could hear the steady tread of the soldiers on the Wall, the rattle of nailed boots upon the stone. Some woman's shriek of pleasure or pain sounding out from the *vicus*. But it was a quiet time in the fort, and Kai could close his eyes and imagine those free, wild days before the war, riding and hunting free upon the steppe. The days that had been lost, but would come again.

He opened his eyes again, and knew what he had to say. 'I am sorry. I did not know she rode among us in the Dance of the Horses.'

'You are supposed to be my second in command,' Lucius said. 'My word must be your word, and your word must be law. Men will die if it is not.'

'The men did not wish to tell me. I suppose that they thought her lucky.' Kai looked to the ground. 'If you wish to give my place to another, I accept it. And any punishment you have, I accept that too.'

A hand settled upon his shoulder. 'There is no punishment I will give you for this,' said Lucius. 'And I will not give your place away. There are no others who are worthy of it.'

The hot touch of tears in his eyes that he brushed away quickly – the Sarmatians held no shame in weeping, but he knew that the Romans thought it unmanly. 'It is settled with Laimei,' said Kai. 'Gaevani spoke to her.'

'What did he say?'

'Difficult to explain if you were not there. But he taught her a lesson of sorts.'

'Good. Good.' And Lucius grinned then, weary and merry,

with that strange kind of exhausted joy that comes after a hard battle.

'Are you well, Lucius?' Kai asked.

'I am well,' the Roman answered. 'I shall be glad when *he* is gone.'

'Aye. You shall be with your own kind, then.'

'My own kind, is it?' said Lucius. 'I do thank you for that.'

'It is the truth,' Kai answered. 'Some cruel trick the gods played on you, birthing your Sarmatian soul to a Roman body. But you have found your people now.'

'Perhaps.' Lucius looked towards the gate, the parade ground that lay beyond it. 'And perhaps your sister brought her luck after all. The men did well today.'

'We have such rituals ourselves,' said Kai. 'It did them much good. It reminded them of their home.'

Lucius hesitated. 'You still miss the steppe?' he said.

'More and more every day,' Kai answered. He tried to smile. 'But twenty-five years, it is not such a long time to wait. I shall see my daughter again.'

Innocent-seeming words, but Lucius flinched at them, as though struck. And before Kai could question him, Lucius spoke again. 'Tell them that I am proud of them,' the Roman said, a catch in his voice, 'if such a thing means anything to them.'

'It will mean everything to them.' Kai grinned at his captain – even after all they had been through together, he still marvelled at how little Lucius understood of the Sarmatians. 'You still do not see it, do you?'

'See what?'

'They think you god-touched, Lucius. The Great Captain, they call you. A hero from the old times.'

'I killed your king, and you think me a hero?' Lucius shook his head. 'A strange people.'

'*Your* people.'

'If you say so.' And Lucius looked tired then, old beyond his years. In the half-light, Kai could imagine the grey in the Roman's hair spreading even as he watched, like a rot or a sickness. 'I must sleep,' the Roman said. 'And so must you. Drill first thing in the morning. A few of them are still carrying their spears too high in the charge.'

Kai nodded. 'They are used to facing taller horses.' He hesitated. 'You worry too much, Lucius. That Legate has filled your mind with Roman foolishness, I think. We will keep our promises to each other, and so all shall be well. There is no more to it than that.'

There were tears then from Lucius, shameful as they might have been to him, and the Roman's mouth was working as though he meant to speak again. But instead, the Roman pulled Kai close, into a brother's embrace.

Then they parted, for no more needed to be said. Lucius went back into his quarters, and Kai should have returned to the barracks. But something made him hesitate – that pleasant sense of warmth and fortune that is brought by wine and the company of a good friend, the safety offered when a promise is kept. And so Kai did not go west, but south. Towards the gate of the fort, and towards the *vicus* beyond.

Each step a fool's step. But he was bargaining with himself as he went, the way drunk and lonely men always have. Just to see Arite's house, but no more than that. Just a knock at the door, and then flee into the night like a child playing a trick. Just a few words spoken, and nothing more than that.

The *vicus* was quiet that night. Kai had thought that more

of the men would be out there celebrating their triumph at the Dance of the Horses, but perhaps it was that they had already drunk themselves into a stupor. Or that they had gathered solemnly at the barracks with no appetite for wine and song, simply wanting to revel in the feeling that sometimes came after battle, the sense of touching something holy. For it was only there at the border between life and death that one could truly catch a glimpse of the gods.

He made his way through the streets, to the house that Arite and Laimei shared with the boy who did not speak. In his dreams, he often wandered there, and always they were dreams of warmth and pleasure, of homecoming and peace. But now, beneath the light of a half-full moon, he felt a cold touch against his skin.

For the door was swinging open. Rattling back and forth when the wind blew, in a way that might have had half a hundred causes. A warped plank of wood, a rotten latch, a forgetful mind. Yet when he looked upon it, he felt the familiar sensation he had known many times before. In forest and field, upon ice and snow, with a horse beneath him and a spear in his hand. The way that the gods always sought to give a warrior his fair chance, to let him know the presence of death was close by.

A moment, then, where his courage failed him. For just as a horse hates to fight upon the bank of a river or the shingle of a beach, knowing its death lies waiting beneath every uncertain piece of ground, so he too feared to go towards one of these houses in darkness. Give him a battle upon the open plain with spear in hand, and the courage of his people would come easy, handed down in a thousand stories. But he knew no story of courage for the dark, closed places, only tales of heroes entombed beneath the earth, children dragged into caves by monsters.

Yet he remembered who was in that house. Laimei, to whom he was bound by blood. Arite, to whom he was bound by much more. The child whom he had saved, a gift from the gods whom it would be blasphemy to scorn. He had no weapon at his side, and so he picked a stone from street, curled it into the palm of his hand – the first and oldest weapon that men had found upon the earth. And with it, he stepped carefully into the house.

He held his left hand forward as he moved into the darkness, with the strange, calm knowledge that he could lose that hand if he had to, if it would buy him the time to fight back. He could almost hear a blade swinging from the darkness, feel it parting flesh and scattering his fingers upon the floor.

But there was nothing. He could see the shapes now, as his eyes adjusted – empty blankets, a simple table, little bags of grain. The few trinkets they had brought from the steppe – a piece of patterned cloth that held a golden coin, an arrow broken and bound back together, a shard from an old iron spear. But no one there.

Still clumsy in the darkness, he reached for the table to find his way. At once, there was pain – a line of cool fire across his palm, the edge of a blade cutting into his skin, his fingers plucking it from where it was embedded in the wood of the table. He could not see clearly what it was he had found – a knife perhaps, though he had not felt a handle, or some broken edge of a blade. But the blood made his fingers slippery, and the blade fell and clattered on the ground, ringing like a bell.

Something stirred behind him, as though it were summoned by the spilling of blood, the way dark bargains were made with spirits from the Otherlands. For there was someone with him in the room – a figure in the corner, lying so still that he had not seen her in the dark.

She lay curled on the ground, unable to rise. The only movement a hand plucking weakly at the air, the only sound a soft whisper that he could not hear over the blood beating in his ears. But he knew at once that it was Arite, staring up at him with the glassy, dull eyes of the dying.

A moment where he could not move, where he was struck still as one is in a nightmare. And all that he could think, strangely calm and quite clearly, was a single thought, over and over again: *It is Laimei who has done this. This is the revenge she spoke of.*

Then he was at Arite's side – a parody of intimacy, as he put his hands to her skin and hunted for her wounds. Perhaps she thought it too, for there was a little mocking smile on her lips, before she gasped with pain once more. For it was there, in the curve of her back, the cut in his hand now pressing against a deep wound that she bore. Hot and quick beneath his fingers, he could feel her life pouring away.

Her lips against his, the taste of life and death upon them. Then her head resting against his shoulder, trembling and shaking. And he held her close then, whispered to her things that he could never remember afterwards, like words spoken in a dream that are lost with waking.

Perhaps she would have spoken too, then – words that would have been as precious treasures to him, that could carry him through the hard years ahead. But there was no time for her to speak, no time left to them.

For there was another presence behind them in the room. Kai heard no sound, felt no breath of air upon his skin, but yet he still knew, in the way a deer always turns towards a hunter just before the arrow is loosed. He turned then, thinking to see Laimei with a blade in her hand, come to finish what she had begun. Yet it was something worse than that.

It was Bahadur who stood there in the doorway. Arite's husband, looking down upon them, death written upon his face.

Part 2

THE PROMISE

10

There was a story told by the Romans – that Sarmatian men did not grow old. No greyhaired man was ever seen in tribe or village, no matter how far the Romans had taken their war into the steppe. But this was no blessing or bargain struck with the gods by some ancient hero, for if a man grew old enough that he could no longer ride a horse or steady a spear, it was his son's duty to gift him a warrior's death. To gather their kin into a circle on the plain, kiss his forehead, and open his throat with a sword. Long ago, that duty had fallen to Kai, yet when the time had come, Kai could not bless his father with an honourable death. The sword had fallen from his nerveless fingers, and Laimei had stepped forward from that circle and taken it up – their father had been the first man that she had ever killed.

The feud with his sister, an endless circling dance of hate and love, and the shame he bore from the rest of his clan – all had sprung from that moment. But something beautiful had begun then, too. For when all others had turned from him, it had been Bahadur who had taken Kai in, had given him a place in the warband when all others whispered that he was unlucky and unworthy. And together they had shared that mad and reckless joy that comes so rarely between men, each believing completely in the other, forming a bond that each had believed could not be broken.

Yet, in the end it had been broken, by Kai and Arite. And now Bahadur stood in the doorway, looking down upon them both.

An instinct to reach for the broken blade upon the floor, for Kai's first thought was that it was Bahadur who had done this to his wife. That he had become one of the men who sought to wash away his shame and hate with the blood of a woman, and had come back now to finish what he had begun.

Bahadur came forward then, his hands reaching through the darkness, clutching at the empty air. But they did not close about Kai's throat, or take up the blade upon the ground. Kai felt a hand settle upon his, guarding the wound twice over, and, as Bahadur knelt beside them and pressed his face close against the cut, Kai knew what he intended. Even with all that had passed between them, they still shared their own wordless language, each knowing the other man's mind.

'It smells like a clean wound,' Bahadur said. He licked the blood from his hand. 'No taste of bile. We must move her, now.'

'Bahadur...' Kai said, but at once he fell silent. For there was a frightful blankness when Bahadur looked at him. As though Kai were not truly there, as though Bahadur spoke to a ghost. He had needed that hand against the wound. That was all.

'Go now,' said Bahadur, 'and wake the *medicus*. Hold a knife to his throat if you must. I will follow with her.'

'You are certain?'

A little anger, then, before the blankness closed over Bahadur's face once more. 'I am stronger, you are quicker – go, now!'

A pulse of blood against his hand as Bahadur took his place, and Kai was hurrying then, stumbling on the wet floor as he ran out into the street. No time to waste, no time at all, yet still he found himself looking back one more time. And he saw Bahadur cradling Arite close, holding her like a mother holding her stillborn child – staring down at her grey face, her head hanging limp in his hands, and wishing, against all hope, to hear her speak.

Afterwards, only fragments, like a dream upon waking. The buildings of the *vicus* tumbling past his vision as though they fell from the sky. The guards at the gate laughing at him as he passed, for they must not have seen quite how much blood was on him, and they called filthy jokes, telling him to wait a few days before he visited that particular whore again. The face of the *medicus* swimming before him and gone just as quickly. A throat raw from screaming.

And when the world was still once more he was out in the open air, in the alley beside the infirmary. Alone, save for Bahadur, who stood before him dressed in blood, like a flayed sacrifice offered to the gods.

Kai waited for the old hatred, the self-mocking smile to wash across the other man's face. But there was still only that careful blankness.

At last, Bahadur spoke. 'She saved your life with that kiss,' he said.

'Is that so?'

'I would have killed you otherwise.' Hesitation then – a crack in the mask. 'I wanted to believe it was you who had done it.'

'I wanted to believe it was *you*,' Kai answered.

And Bahadur did smile then, a bitter little thing, a shadow of what it had been in the past. 'It would make things simpler, no?' said Bahadur. 'The gods do have a sense of humour, it seems.' He looked down, at the drying blood. 'But I thank you, for what you tried to do. Even if I know why you were there.'

'She did not know I was coming. I…' But Kai saw Bahadur's bloodied hands close into fists, and he did not finish his thought. Instead, he said: 'Will she live?'

'I do not know,' Bahadur answered, but without hope in his voice. For they both knew that the gods were jealous of that gift of life, and would snatch it back at the slightest chance. Even a little cut across the skin often spoke of death, festering black and green or sending red lines across the skin and followed by a fever that burned the life away. And it had been a deep wound given to Arite, the kind that few survived.

'She is strong,' said Kai, for want of anything else to say.

'Not as strong as your sister, it seems,' said Bahadur. 'For it is she who has done this, is it not?'

Slowly, Kai nodded. 'I think it must be.'

'Why?'

'She was angry tonight, after the feast. But I did not think…'

'When do you?' Bahadur shook his head, and spat upon the ground. 'I have given your family nothing but love, and it has taken everything from me.' Then, it seemed, he could speak no more. One hand to his face, catching the tears in his eyes before they could fall, the other held out like a shield, the palm facing Kai. And they stood there together, marked in the blood of the woman they both loved, until Bahadur's shoulders no longer trembled, and he lowered his hand to reveal eyes that were blank and dry.

'I must stay with her,' said Bahadur, 'and wait for her to die. And you must go to find your sister. That much, you owe to me.'

Kai nodded slowly. 'And what happens then, between us?'

'Nothing.' And with that, Bahadur turned back towards the infirmary, back to that place of death. But he paused once more at the doorway, and he spoke again.

'I used to wonder,' said Bahadur, 'why Arite loves you so.' And he glanced back, over his shoulder, and said: 'But why should I? I did too, a long time ago.'

He could not wake Gaevani at first. Stealing through the barracks, light-footed as a thief, Kai had found Gaevani snoring in his cot without any man crying out the alarm. But a hand on Gaevani's shoulder did not wake him, nor did a little shake. It was only the dull edge of a cold blade laid against Gaevani's throat that at last brought one eye rolling open.

'Go away,' he said, the scent of wine and bile upon his breath.

'You must come with me now,' Kai whispered.

'Why?'

'You cannot ask me why. Or who it is we follow. Only you must come now.'

'A woman, is it? A little late for...' Gaevani began, but his grin vanished as he saw the blood on Kai's hands.

'You see? We must go now. Already the trail goes cold.'

'Beyond the fort?'

'Yes.'

'At Lucius's command?'

Kai hesitated. 'No. I cannot tell him yet.'

'What is the punishment for deserting without orders?' Gaevani whispered. 'Is it stoning, or crucifixion? I cannot remember. Tell me how it is you are asking me to die.'

'Please, Gaevani.'

And in the end, it needed no more than that. Among the Sarmatians, one had only to ask and it would be given – a life gifted away for that single word, *please*. Gaevani slipped from his blankets and beckoned him to the other side of the barracks.

The horses woke reluctantly, a begrudging whinny from one of them. They were weary from the Dance of the Horses, more so than the men, for they had not known that battle to be a sham. When they had lined up against each other and seen the light upon the spears, they must have thought it a fight to the death.

There was no way to take their mounts from that place without being seen. Some men were awake already, lovers in each other's arms. Others woke as Kai passed, but though he heard muttered curses, saw eyes flick open and track him across the chamber, no man questioned where they went – that would come tomorrow, for they were a people without secrets. They shared their thoughts as they shared wine and silver, openly and carelessly. But that was for tomorrow. In the night, their trust held strong.

Out in the streets and towards the gates – more danger here, for not all in the fort were of their people. He imagined what manner of trick or bribe would be needed to make their way past the Sarmatian guards at the gate. He waited for a voice to call a challenge, to demand a password that he did not have. But when one made as if to question them, Gaevani said simply: 'It is a matter of honour.'

Back to the house at the edge of the *vicus*, and the last show of irritation fell from Gaevani's face. He looked as solemn as a priest at a sacrifice as he attended to the augury of the ground outside, the marks of foot and hoof that might whisper a message from the gods.

'I have the trail,' Gaevani said.

'You are certain?'

The other man spat upon the ground. 'As certain as I may be, picking a trail from a street that half a hundred have walked across. But look here,' he said, and pointed to a stone on the ground, marked with the rusted colour of blood.

Soon, they were out – beyond the *vicus* and into the darkness, the heather sighing beneath their horses' hooves. Lighting torches, leaning low in the saddles until they felt a knife-sharp pain at the base of the spine, searching the ground for a sign of passage. Many times they were mistaken, led astray by the footfall of a deer, retracing their steps until they were certain of the trail once more. Slow, achingly, frighteningly slow, as they travelled but half a mile from the fort. But it was there upon the ground, the fresh marks of a horse.

Soon, they were moving faster. A long way from their quarry, but still, there was a chance. For the tracks had led them to an old game trail and not veered from it – briefly, even, Kai and Gaevani stirred their horses to the trot. For a moment, there was a hope that he might catch his sister.

And it was then that Kai felt something against his skin – a dozen little cold touches upon his arms and his hair, a hissing past his ears, the reins suddenly slick under his hands. A familiar sensation that he did not recognise at first, for he did not want to believe it. Then a crack and roar from the sky above, and it could not be denied.

For rain was pouring down upon them, that gift of the gods to the farmer and the thief alike, that blessed the fields and washed tracks away. Yet still they pressed on, mad and hopeless, pushed their horses to one desperate gallop as their torches hissed and went out. Kai searched for a shadow on the horizon, the light from a campfire, a sign from a god that might guide them. But there was nothing. The gods had made their choices clear.

Gaevani cast away his burned-out torch in disgust. 'That's it. We go no farther tonight. We shall lame the horses if we try.' He hesitated. 'I cannot be certain. But I think the trail was turning north. She seeks to cross the Wall.'

'She?' Kai said. But even he could hear the lie in his voice.

Gaevani shook his head. 'It is Laimei we hunt, is it not? She has gone mad, at last?'

Kai nodded. 'It was her time.'

The rain fell about them. The horses tossed their heads, sounded their disapproval. But the men sat slumped in their saddles – neither of them, it seemed, had the heart to return.

'I angered her today,' said Gaevani. 'But I did not think...'

'This is not your doing,' said Kai.

'What shall you tell Lucius?'

Kai looked back towards the fort, the fires upon the Wall. For a moment, a useless prayer upon his lips for the sun to stay beneath the horizon. Let them be trapped forever in that evil night, if it meant the new day would never come. But the prayer would have been in vain. Even the gods could only hold time still for a moment – that instant before a spear found its mark, or at the sight of a lover after a long parting, or before the charge in battle. One more beating of the heart was all they could gift, before the river of time flowed on.

'I shall tell Lucius the truth,' Kai said at last. 'As I have always done. As he has always spoken to me.'

11

Perhaps it was how all walls fell, in the end – this was all that Lucius could think, as Kai gave his report. Not with some terrible horde from the north that swept away every Legion before it, that butchered and burned a path all the way to the gates of Rome. But with little betrayals, the breaking of a mind, the flash of a knife in the darkness. Impossible promises that could not be kept, oaths that sent men needlessly towards their deaths. And perhaps when that horde of barbarians did come at last, they would find the watchtowers empty, the torches guttered out. None but ghosts would watch the border, for the Romans would have defeated themselves already. A slow rot, and no final, glorious battle for the songs of poets.

When Kai had finished speaking, Lucius did not answer for a time. Then he said: 'Arite – will she live?'

'I do not know,' Kai answered – a crack in the voice, before he blinked his eyes and raised his head, standing tall. 'She sleeps, and does not wake.'

'And Laimei?'

'She is gone. And she took the boy with her. The Brigante child, from the raids.'

Lucius found he could not look at Kai any longer. Here they were in a Prefect's chambers, and still the smell of the wine hung in the air, sharp and rank from the night before. The centre of power for leagues around them; in a land where his word was law, his speech could bring death. And it seemed, he could not even command his own men.

'Why would she take the boy?' he said.

Kai did not speak for a time – swaying on his feet with exhaustion, he did not seem to understand the question. 'She was always frightened to be alone,' he said at last.

'You will tell me she is afraid of the dark, now.'

'Many champions are. It is said they see the dead there, in the shadows. The faces of those they have killed.' Kai hesitated. 'What will you do, Lucius?'

Death, to ask such a question of most Prefects. Lucius had seen men of the Legion flogged and beaten to death because their voices lilted upwards at the end of a sentence – the slightest hint of a question enough to condemn them. And he was certain that Kai knew it too, yet still he would risk his life for that question.

'How many saw you?' Lucius said.

'Two at the gate. Others in the *vicus*, perhaps, as we passed though the street. I do not know. It seemed quiet.'

There was hope, then. The passage of a bloodied figure through the streets was little cause for attention, for often were feuds settled on the edge of a blade. And had anyone seen it was a woman carried towards the infirmary, the people of the *vicus* would have thought even less of it. A woman killed by a man was nothing strange here.

He picked one of the wax tablets beside him – the wooden back stamped with the mark of his office, the closest thing there was to the Emperor's word and law in this place. And he began to scratch the stylus into the wax, and said: 'Here I write that you reported this to me. That I ordered you to make a quick pursuit. You went, sought a fugitive, found a trail, returned.' And Lucius began his work then, carving the letters that might save his friend's life.

'Do not write it.'

The stylus went still. 'Why?'

'For all will know it then,' said Kai. 'That she did it, and that she is gone.'

'Why should they not know it?'

Kai looked to the ground. 'Arite may yet live,' he said. 'Laimei may come back.'

'If any who saw you last night decide to speak of it,' Lucius said slowly, 'I will have to put you to death. There will be no clemency. You did right to try to find her, but still, it is desertion.'

'I know.'

Lucius cast the stylus down in disgust. 'Very well. It shall not be written. Let yourself be stoned to death on behalf of a murderer.'

'If it is to be so, it will be so.'

Neither of them spoke for a time. Lucius could feel the other man's eyes upon him, but he picked at the parchments and tablets and pieces of birch bark, the orders and inventories – all of the endless, useless business of the fort.

'What will she do?' said Lucius.

'There is no telling.'

'And why would she take the child?'

'Why would she try to kill Arite?' Kai shook his head. 'Among our people, they say that all the great heroes go mad in the end. Is it the way with the Romans?'

'Our heroes seem to die before they have that chance. And she has never seemed mad to me.'

For want of anything else to do, Lucius cast his eyes to a map nearby – so precise on the layout of the Wall, the numbering and distance of each milecastle. Great swathes of land marked with the names of the tribes who lived there – the Votadini, the Brigantes, the Selgovae. So little they knew of what was there. 'You think she went towards the Wall?' said Lucius.

'That is where the trail seemed to lead, before we lost it in the rain.'

'I shall send an alert across the milecastles. Not to look for her,' Lucius added quickly, seeing the alarm upon Kai's face. 'But so that we may know if any try to cross.'

'And then what?'

'I shall take a patrol out to try and find her,' said Lucius.

A heavy breath – half a sob – from Kai. 'It must be me,' he said. 'I must come with you.'

Lucius shook his head. 'I will not put you to that work. I do not care what shame you feel, I shall not make you do it.'

'You do not understand. She is my kin, and I must answer for her.'

Lucius hesitated. 'Your honour will get us all killed, I think.'

'I gave my word. You know that I must keep it. Wouldn't you?'

A longing, then, to speak the truth. To give up his honour and break his oath, the way that Lucius might have broken a rotten stick across his knee. To tell Kai that he was never going home. All that he had been taught of discipline and law forgotten at once. Instead Lucius said only this: 'We shall both go.'

And at that, there was a touch of brightness to Kai, a ghost of a smile on his face. 'Together,' he said, 'as it should be.'

'As it should be.' But the lie hung thick in the air between them, and only Lucius knew it.

It should have been such a simple thing, to find a Sarmatian woman with a stolen child at her side, riding a monstrous horse of the steppe. Kai had more of a fear that they would find her too late, that they would find a body raised upon a tree by a river, the way the Brigantes and the Votadini were said to make their trophies of war.

Yet there was no trace of her. None of the milecastles reported a sighting, and when they sought the tribes south of the Wall, it was the same as when they had ventured to the north. The same vanished people – old men alone answering the summons in the farms, no man or woman without silver in the hair at the steadings, no children tending the roaming herds of sheep and goats that wandered across the grass and heather. Like a land where some curse had stilled every womb long before, the way that the gods sometimes murdered a nation in the old stories, leaving one last generation to grow old and die with no children to follow them. Those Brigantes that remained were a hard-faced people – tall and proud, with the tough look of those who lived in border country. And though they shared draughts of heather beer, they remained close-lipped about any more than that.

In desperation, Kai and Lucius ventured further north once more, thinking that perhaps Laimei might have found some way to cross the Wall unseen. And there, they found even less. A day spent waiting by the tree and the stones with gifts in hand, but that smiling chieftain, Mor of the Votadini, did not come to them this time.

On that third day, as they rested the horses in the shade, another silent steading of the Votadini behind them, Lucius said to Kai: 'I expect you shall ask me to believe that she may work magic, and make herself unseen?'

'No,' Kai answered. 'She is no ghost of the trees and water. But whether she is south or north of the Wall, I cannot say.'

Lucius hesitated. 'She may be dead, Kai. By her own hand, or…'

'No.' Kai shook his head firmly. 'She would never take her own life, and deny herself a death in battle. And I think if she had fought and died, we would have some sign of it by now.'

'I tell you this,' said Lucius. 'These people are hiding something. They send their greyhairs out to treat with us. They knew that we were coming. And their silences speak of secrets.'

'What will you do?'

'I should do what Romans have always done,' said Lucius, his mouth twisting as he spoke. 'Raise them upon crosses beside the roads, put them to knife and fire. Make them speak.'

'But you shall not.'

'No.'

'Because you do not have the heart for it, or because you believe it would do no good?

'Let us call it a little of both, shall we?' Lucius placed his helm back upon his head, his eyes shadowed into dark hollows. 'Now, let us finish our day of finding nothing, and being lied to.'

And yet, in the end, they did find something. Not a

mutilated corpse slung from a tree, not a trail leading them to a fastness in the forest or a clearing where Laimei stood in a duellist's circle, waiting for them to come and give her a warrior's death. They found only a word spoken too quickly, a lie poorly made.

For at the last steading they came to on that third day, a merry old man of the Votadini greeted them. Toothless and ancient, skin deep-furrowed and bronzed by the sun, like some centuries-old tree of oak, he waved and called out to them in his own language. Giving no sign of alarm to have fifty mounted cavalry arrive at his house, grim-faced and dressed for war, he chattered away at once, not waiting for their interpreter to catch up with him. And Kai had learned a few snatches of the Votadini speech, enough to hear the man speak of the heavy rains (there had been none), tell of his many sons who were gone to war against the Romans and were soon to return (a war that had finished twenty years before), hear him call out greetings to the Sarmatians as though they were his long-lost brothers. And the Sarmatians laughed at him, but kindly, as they might have done at the trickery of a playful dog. None of them had ever seen a man so old as this – he would have been put to the sword more than twenty years before, back upon the steppe, and to them he was a marvel, a sculpture carved from ageing flesh.

And when at last the river of his speech dried up, their interpreter put to him the same question they had asked everyone else they had spoken to – if he had seen a woman and a boy on a tall Sarmatian horse. But he had got no further than a single word when at once the old man spoke. And it was the same thing that they had been told by all others that they had spoken to. 'No, I have not seen a woman of your people.'

Kai looked about himself, to see if any other had noted the quickness of the speech. But Lucius seemed weary in the saddle – it was the end of the day, a day of rare heat in this country that had them drenched in sweat beneath the heavy armour. And his companions, still fascinated by the sight of the old man, paid no mind to his speech.

A secret for Kai alone, to do with as he pleased. And he turned it over and over in his mind, like some rare forbidden treasure, as the sun fell from the sky and the fort, the Wall, their home, loomed once more before them. He turned it over, and tried to think of what it might mean, and what he would do.

12

The Romans called the building the infirmary, but the Sarmatians had another name for it – the House of the Dead. A place they would walk halfway around the fort to avoid and made the sign against evil if they had to pass it, for the Sarmatians knew that spirits of the dead clustered thick about such a place, always jealous of those who still lived and eager to beckon them to the next world. Better to die in the open air and staring up at the sky than to go willingly into a tomb such as that.

Already, that place had claimed some of their own. A man called Garas who had trodden upon a dirty nail in his first hour in the fort – his blood had burned with fever for three days and three nights before the gods took him away. Another man had taken the wasting sickness of the lungs, hacking red phlegm into his lap with every breath, and had drunk and gambled and whored with relentless intensity until they brought him to that place to die, drowning in his blood upon dry land. Halan, a man Kai had known well, had fallen from his horse in the Dance of the Horses, and a purple bruise bloomed against his skull and sent him to a sleep he could not wake from. The Romans had taken Halan into the House of the Dead, while outside his companions listened. They heard a sawing of bone, a high-pitched screaming, and then silence had followed.

Now Kai lingered there upon the threshold of the infirmary, and not for the superstitious reasons that kept many from that place. It was the living and not the dead whom he feared.

When Bahadur emerged at last, with slow footsteps that dragged upon the ground, he might well have been mistaken for a corpse that had risen and walked. Grey skinned, the smell of blood and rot upon his clothes, his eyes dulled by days spent without sleep. And when those dead eyes fell upon Kai, no life returned to them.

'What is that you want?' said Bahadur.

'To speak with you.'

'And what else?'

'To know if she shall live or die. If she has spoken anything to you.'

'It should make no difference,' said Bahadur. 'You shall not see her again, either way. And her words are not for you.' But Bahadur's voice cracked and broke as he spoke those words – a singer's voice he had, and it did not suit cruel speech.

'Bahadur—'

'Say what you must, and then go. Please.'

Kai nodded slowly. 'I may have found a trail to follow.'

'Something the others missed?'

'Aye.'

'Good fortune to your spear, then,' Bahadur said, the words hollow, spoken with empty ritual. He hesitated. 'Will you ride alone?'

'I will.'

'Laimei is the better hand with a spear than you. I do not believe you can defeat her.'

'I still hope it shall not come to that.'

'You think Laimei may come willingly?'

'Perhaps she will know it is her time to die. The champions always do, in the end.'

The crackling of fire from the braziers, the howl of the wind about them. And the rain was falling softly, a thin veil of water drawn between them. It was better that way – growing dim and indistinct, Kai could imagine his friend as he once had been.

'If I do not return…' Kai let his voice trail away to nothing, not daring to speak the words that he wanted to.

Yet still, it seemed, there was something between them. That particular joining of the mind is not so easily broken as friendship, for Bahadur answered the question that had not been spoken: 'I will know that you did what you could,' he said, the trace of a smile on his lips. 'But do not ask me to make a song for you.'

'I wish that you would sing again. It was always such a beautiful thing.' Kai hesitated. 'Arite always said so, back upon the steppe.'

The smile was gone at the sounding of that name. The dead eyes looked on him once more. 'Home,' Bahadur said absently.

The rain fell harder about them, but Kai did not feel it on his skin, and Bahadur did not move. For perhaps in that moment they both dreamed the same thing, that they were back upon the steppe. No stone buildings squatting around them, no gutters running with mud and filth. Only the long grass dancing with the wind, the wildflowers shining under the sun, the world open beneath an endless sky.

Then from somewhere close, a horn that called the changing of the guard. The creak and roll of a wagon, the heavy step of booted feet. The steppe of their minds vanished like smoke, and they were once more on the far side of the world.

Bahadur lifted his hands, wiped the rain from his eyes. 'Go now. And do not worry. I will be with her when she dies.'

'I know,' said Kai.

There was no swimming up from dark waters. No visions of her lost children, or a wandering through a shadowy version of the world Arite knew from her waking life. There was nothing, and then there was light, sharp and sudden and painful.

A sense of the wound in her back, and with it an animal fear of being surrounded by enemies and unable to fight. And so she lay quite still until she could be certain of where she was. Smells came first – a sharp tang of herbs that she did not know, the smell of urine and faeces, the odour of rot. Opening her eyes but a little, and stone walls swam before her vision, shadows dancing from crackling braziers. And a shape close by, wonderful and familiar.

For Bahadur sat on the ground beside her, his head forward and buried in his arms. Unsleeping, for she could hear his breathing was ragged, saw one hand rise and slap irritably at a mosquito as it landed on his arm. She knew that rigid, sleepless posture, for it was how she had sat beside fever-struck children, beside her own mother as the old woman rotted from within, coughing blood as the sickness took her away. The way that one sat beside the loved, the dying.

A hideous thirst came to her then, her throat raw as if it had somehow been flogged from within. It seemed impossible that such a thirst could ever be quenched, and for a moment there was the mad longing for death, the way that those put to torture will beg for their lives to be ended. If close to hand there had been only a dagger and a bowl of water, she did not know which she would have reached for. But there was only the bowl, with a rag dipped in it, and she reached for both with trembling fingers.

Then a hand closed over hers, held it tight, while another was dipping the rag in the water and lifting it towards her mouth.

'Be still,' Bahadur said. 'Do not move.'

She tried to answer, but could not. Drop by drop, she took the water, until her throat loosened enough for her to speak, her voice a rasping whisper.

'I can smell rot,' she said. 'Is it the wound?'

'No,' he answered. 'This whole place stinks of it, but the wound does not fester.'

She felt the damp air against her skin, listened to the patter of the rain. She could see the cast of her skin now – corpse grey, seeming so thin that she could see the blue webbing of her veins, the pulse of the blood beneath her skin.

'Then a fever shall take me, I think,' she said. 'I am weak enough for it.'

'Do not speak that way.' He lifted her hand to his lips, and she felt his kiss against her palm. 'You shall live. You must live.'

A memory beckoned at her mind, then, but she would not let it come. For this was akin to that moment after waking from a dream where half the world is forgotten. All that remained was that moment, and the man beside her. They were alone, and there was nothing to come between them. Not the children they had buried, nor how cruelly they had hurt each other, nor the slow destruction of all that they had built together. Just the simple pleasure of touch, the oaths of love that they had sworn over and over again. The gratitude of living.

At first, when she had woken, there had been a strange, almost frightened look upon Bahadur's face. But now it seemed that he felt as she did. For the fear was gone from his face, a shy smile upon his lips. He was the man once more that she had loved, long ago.

'You shall not die in this place,' he said. 'The gods have spared you for a reason.'

Perhaps it was true what he said, for she felt their message then. And as they always did, the gods spoke through pain. Sharp and sudden, behind her eyes and beneath her skull, a white flash that stole her sight.

'Laimei,' she said – the only word she could seem to speak, for her throat was closing once again.

'She runs,' Bahadur said. 'Kai goes to hunt her soon. Do not think of her now.'

The fear returning – strong, stronger than she had ever felt it. Even facing the long spears in battle, even when she had watched her husband and her lover riding towards death, there had not been a terror such as this, the fear that she would die before she spoke. For the blood beat thickly in her ears, her heart skipping like a drum beneath the hand of a careless player. The gods were often jealous of those who crawled free from death, would pluck them back to the Otherlands with no warning given – an invisible spear that stopped the heart, an unseen cord that choked away the breath. And let it be so, she thought to herself, offering her own dark bargain. Let them take me back, so long as I may speak this before I die. For there could be nothing worse than this, to see those she loved hurtling towards death for the wrong reasons.

'You must stop Kai,' Arite said. 'Laimei tried to save me. It was the others…'

There was so much more to tell. The men who had come in the night – the water-warped door catching and sticking for a moment as they tried to force it, enough time for her to take up Arite's sword. The shadows in the darkness, the dancing of blades. The screaming of that child, Chodona – silent for so long, and returning to voice once more, calling out in wordless terror as those men lifted him away. The wound in her back, strangely painless at the moment the blade struck, even as all the strength fell away from her at once, even as she tumbled to the ground, looked up at those who had killed her.

And those men – their faces, and their speech. It had all been wrong, like the workings of an evil dream. More frightening than the wound in her back, the knowledge that they were killing her and she did not know why.

But there was no time left to speak. The dark reached up, and the gods, hungry and jealous, took her back once more.

13

'Well then,' said Gaevani, sitting low and sullen in his saddle, 'what is it we are here to do?'

Kai made no answer at first. He leaned forward, stroked the neck of his horse as she drank from the river, and tried to think of how to answer.

Two days he had been forced to wait for his chance to go beyond the Wall, until the call was made for scouts to venture into the north country and learn its mysteries. For there were certain places that always spoke of death to the horsemen – the banks of rivers, the boggy soil amid the low heather, the rocky ground beneath tall cliffs – and so men were needed to learn the land, the stories that waited to be written there. The places where it was good to fight, and where it was good to die.

A handful of silver had earned Kai his place among the scouts, and a little more had ensured that it was Gaevani he would be paired with. And though Kai had spoken nothing of it, Gaevani seemed to know at once that something was amiss. For once they were clear of the sight of the fort, alone amid the rolling hills, Gaevani pulled at the reins of his horse and brought it to a halt.

'I know it is not by chance that you have brought me here,' said Gaevani. 'You want me to try and follow a three-day-old trail after a storm? Or is it the sun you would like me to pluck from the sky, while I am doing impossible things for you?'

'No. I did not bring you here as a tracker. For I have the trail myself. Here,' Kai said, tapping a finger to his forehead, 'and here,' as he placed his hand upon his heart.

'And what must I do?'

'Simply keep the silence.'

'To that,' said Gaevani, 'I was never well suited.'

'Go back to the fort,' said Kai. 'Give me enough time that I shall not be followed. Wait until the end of the day, and I might even come back with you. This trail is for me to follow alone.'

'And what am I to tell them?'

'Whatever lie you wish. Or the truth.'

Gaevani muttered to himself and turned his face towards the sun, perhaps seeking some signal from the gods there. As the light fell across his face, shining white upon the thick scar that cut across his forehead, Kai thought how little he knew of that man. There were those such as Bahadur whose thoughts he could feel as if they were his own. Even with his sister, he could feel the shifts of her mind like the breaking of waves, for all that the depths of her heart were mysteries to him now. But he never knew what Gaevani would do, or why he would do it.

'I wish that you had chosen someone else to come with you,' Gaevani said at last, his voice heavy with regret.

'Why? You shall go back now.'

'No. I shall not.' Gaevani's hands dropped to his horse's mane, pushing the hair one way and another with his fingertips. 'Less danger for both of us if I come with you. I know what the Romans do to those who do not obey.'

'A flogging at worst for you if you go back alone. I do not know what waits for us on the road ahead.'

Gaevani shrugged. 'There are worse things than flogging.'

'Death?'

'Worse things than that, too.' He smiled, suddenly merry. 'But you know that, or you would not be here. So let us not waste time, or give me a chance to change my mind. Where is it that we go?'

The falling sun reddened the sky by the time that they came to the steading that Kai sought – the place where the old man had spoken his lie too quickly. And when they entered the steading, the crude wicker door catching and dragging on the bare earth, the man sat by the embers of his cooking fire, the merriness gone from his face. He did not seem afraid to see two men dressed for war – no doubt, living on the border, he had seen such things many times before, in the endless conflicts between clan and clan, between clan and Rome. Men bearing sword and spear, their faces cruelly set, demanding answers that he could not give.

Indeed, they might have been long awaited guests from the way he greeted them – some words in the native tongue, a gesture towards a skin of heather beer, offering up the single cracked clay bowl beside the cooking fire. Yet if there was no fear on the old man's face, Kai thought he could see regret for what was to come.

'Where is she?' said Kai, in the language of the Votadini, words he had practised over and over again. Even so, there was a muttering from behind him – Gaevani had an ear for the music of language in the way that Kai did not.

But clumsy pronunciation did not seem to matter to the old man before them. Perhaps it was, so close to death, that his vision pierced through the veil of things, that he saw the question written upon Kai's heart, and knew that the Sarmatian would not leave without an answer. For there was no need for threat or torture, it seemed, as a trembling hand lifted, and pointed to a wall of the steading.

'That way?' Kai said. 'Close?'

The old man nodded. And he was weeping then, as he repeated words that Kai did not know, over and over again.

'Do you know what he says?' Kai said to Gaevani.

'Forgive me, forgive me.' Gaevani's eyes narrowed. 'At least, I think that is what he says. Who can tell what it means? His mind is broken.'

Perhaps it was true, and the next day the old man would not remember. Kai hoped it was so, that whatever code of honour or oath of silence the old man had broken, he would forget, and be joyful and chattering free as birdsong once more, a child living each day as a lifetime. But perhaps those tears would never cease – a lifetime of sorrow, building and now overflowing. What had the coming of Sarmatians reminded him of? Sons he had sent to war and never seen again, or a life that he wished he had lived, but had not. Some secret shame that the old man had read upon strange faces from another land. And so it was a relief, to be back under open air, to smell the horses and hear the turn of the wind. Only the low sun worried Kai, a sky streaked with blood.

Gaevani, it seemed, thought it too. 'An ill omen,' he said, 'to be abroad in such a land after darkness.'

'You may always return.'

'*You* may always return. Come back tomorrow, with a full day ahead of us. Speak with Lucius of what you have heard.'

'No. Tomorrow, she may be gone. We go there now.' And he nodded south, towards where the old man had pointed. A little forest lay there, a river winding through it. A piece of land like many others they had seen, yet looking upon it, Kai had the still feel of omen. He had the knowledge of his sister's mind and knew that it was a place that she might choose – more for a river to fight beside than for trees to hide in. For while it was true that horsemen feared to fight on the uncertain footing of riverbank, in the old stories it was the place where the heroes always chose to make their stand. The place where champions were tested at the last.

They stirred their horses forward, into the woods and towards the water, as the sun disappeared from the sky.

There is a particular delight known only to a few. The wounded man, hacked and bloodied, pulled from the battlefield and laid by a river to die, who listens to the beautifully sweet sound of flowing water and suddenly knows he will live against all odds. Or those consumed by illness, the flesh falling from their bodies and the fever like a rolling fire in their veins, who crawl their way back to life once more. That joy of having sipped from the cup of death, but not drained it fully.

And Arite knew it too – lying in the house in the *vicus*, waking in the place where she had almost died and knowing that she would live. Her world nothing but those four walls for now, as weak as she could ever remember being, the pain constant and gnawing at her back. Yet still, to live was a joy to her, though she had nothing but her memories to keep her company.

Perhaps it was that she now understood the old people of the steppe, those greyhaired Sarmatians who clung so stubbornly to lives wracked with pain and loss. All women, for a man was granted a warrior's death by his sons as soon as he could not hold the reins or steady a spear. But not the women. Most were carried away by starvation or fever or were murdered by childbirth long before their hair turned grey, but there were still some who lived long. She remembered one who was said to have seen a hundred winters, who kept close to the hemp fires to dull the pain, who had to be carried everywhere she went, her bones as fragile as Roman glassware. Back then, Arite had pitied that woman, but now having wandered so close to death, she thought she understood the pleasure of such a life. To lean close to her memories, as one may draw close to a fire on a winter's night.

And indeed, some of those memories were hot enough to burn her. The children she had lost – their laughter as they tottered around, their screams as they clung to her in the midst of a raging fever, or the still, shrunken, grey-faced bodies that were brought back from feud and cattle raid, speared through and sent to the next world. And there was fire, too, in other memories. Of the nights spent with Kai, when they had clung to one another for comfort but had not guarded well enough against the love that had crept in like a thief in the night.

The scrape of the door catching upon the ground. A quickening of fear to hear that sound again, a sound that spoke to her now of knives in the dark, of fighting for her life, of pain and darkness. But it was only Bahadur returning.

'You are awake, at last,' he said.

'I am,' she said. She tried a smile. 'I decided that I would like to grow old, and so it seems the gods have heard me.'

He knelt beside her, and took her hand in his. 'Grow old?' he said. 'Not such a grand thing to wish for. Time will take care of that, you need no help from the gods.'

'To live long, I mean. Don't you?'

The smile faded. 'I do not know.'

'We would have more time together.'

'We would,' he said. 'And I would be glad of it. But...' The words drifted away.

After a moment, she took her hand from his. 'I have suffered as much as you. More, perhaps. But I think of summers past. That midsummer festival, after the raids, when the wine ran free. Do you remember—'

'I do not wish to speak of that,' he said, his voice sharp. 'I do not wish to speak of the past. Why spend time thinking of such things?'

She said nothing at first. Then: 'Why not? We have spent half our lives making memories together. What was it for, if not to share them now?'

'And for most of them, he was there. Kai. So unlike you, I do not have a past to live in. He taints all of my memories.'

'Then forgive him.'

'I cannot.'

Silence, for a time. Her mind was not what it had been, her thoughts dull as after a night spent steeped in wine. Something spoke of danger to her, something she could not hear or see or touch. She lay safe, beside a man that she knew loved her – she knew that more truly than anything else. Yet the pulse beat hot beneath her skin, the breath came short.

'Where is Kai?' she said, and Bahadur started, as though struck.

'Why do you ask such a thing of me?' he said.

'You told him what I said, did you not?'

He did not answer at first. Then: 'I thought you spoke in fever. In madness.'

She tried to rise, then, clawing at the table, trying to stand up upon shaking legs. And he was upon her – a moment, just a moment when his hands were at her wrists, trying to keep her to the ground with a terrible blankness written across his face – before he released her just as quickly, crawling back across the floor as though trying to flee from himself, while the world swam and tipped and pitched around her as she tried not to fall, fought to stay conscious.

'It was not Laimei who tried to kill me,' said Arite, her voice slow and even, for she would not be mistaken again. She would not give him that excuse. 'Men were here. Men I did not know. They cut me, and they took the child. And Laimei came after, and went to find them. Do you believe me now?'

He nodded, white faced, and did not answer.

'Where is he?' she said.

'He has gone beyond the Wall,' he said, his voice small, like a child's. 'He goes in search of her. I did not think—'

'Quiet.' She tried to stand once more, and made it to her feet, both palms pressed against the table. 'We must go to Lucius.'

'It is desertion,' said Bahadur. 'That is what Kai has done. You know what they do to deserters?'

'Lucius would not—'

'Can we take that risk?'

Arite closed her eyes, and tried to think.

'He shall come back,' she heard Bahadur say. 'With Laimei, or not, he will come back.'

'And if he does not?' she said, looking at Bahadur again, trying to remember, above all, what it was to love him.

He made no answer. She pushed away from the table, and stood unassisted. 'If he does not,' said Arite. 'You will go searching for him. Or I shall.'

'My love—'

'Do not call me that!' The words rang in the air, the way a sword sings against a shield.

He stood before her, trembling and silent, and waited for her to speak again. His face that of a condemned man, waiting to hear the sentence pronounced. And she found that she did have words for him – words that came from some deep part of herself, words that seemed to almost speak themselves.

'I saw something upon your face,' she said, 'when I first woke. I did not want to believe it. But you were afraid to see me live, weren't you?'

Whatever he had thought she would say, it seemed, it had not been that. Perhaps he had not known it himself, until she spoke it. And he fled from her then – the door scraping and catching, as he ran in terror out into the night. And she sank down once more to the ground, all her strength spent. And at last, she let herself weep for all that she had lost.

14

They were deep among the trees when Kai first sensed it – a feeling like oil across the skin. For the deer in the forest always know when the wolf walks soft behind them, the hare before the falcon falls from the sky. And men knew it too, sometimes, when they were hunted.

There was a longing to think it was nothing more than a trick of the mind. For there were many Sarmatians who had died because their minds would not let them see the ambush they rode into. Bowstrings would be drawn and sound like the bending of trees in the wind. Lances were seen dressed in truce leaves that were not there. Riders emerging from the trees would wear the faces of friends for a single, fatal instant.

And so it was that Kai had to force himself to truly see the men who were gathering in the shadows to kill them.

Whoever they were, they knew the art of the forest well. Only once did he see one clearly, and at a distance. Just a pair of eyes glinting in the twilight, bright and yellow like the gaze of a wolf, before they sank once more into the undergrowth. But he saw the shadows move out of the corner of his eye, trees bend against the wind. Circling around the way that Kai and Gaevani had come from, driving them deeper within the forest.

Beside him, Gaevani rode steadily, whistling some old travelling song of the Sarmatians. But when he turned in the saddle to face Kai, his eyes were flat and cold.

'Shall we try to run?' said Gaevani.

'Too late, I think.' And there was grief then, tight about the heart. Not for what was to come, but what must have happened already. To know his sister must have ridden into this self-same trap. 'And if they have killed Laimei,' said Kai, 'then I do not care to run from them.'

Gaevani shook his head. 'After all she has done to you, you would still fight for her?'

'I wish you had gone back. I am sorry.'

'I wish I had, too.' Gaevani leaned over, stroked the neck of his horse. 'But this is as good a place as any to die.'

No fear, not yet, only the strange calm that sometimes settled before a battle, the gift from the gods that gave a man the chance to die well. The mind filling with the particular details of the fight ahead – the choice of one grip or another on the spear, the character of the horse that he rode, memories of pain and how it might be overcome. And Kai looked about him for some way out of the trap, or at least some place they might sell their lives more dearly. He saw only thick forest behind them, proud oak and ash trees standing tall, thistles and brambles coiled thickly upon the ground like snares. The only way through were the narrow game trails left by hunters and woodcutters. There was no way back.

'The river,' Gaevani whispered then, his voice strangely flat. No more than that, two words that could have meant anything. Yet somehow, they both knew what they had to do. To not go back, but to go forward – deeper into the forest, further into the trap.

The forest was a thing of shadows that late in the day, and they followed the game trails as best they could in the half-light. Once a stumble from Gaevani's horse, snared in the undergrowth, and it seemed certain to fall. But a great howling hunting cry went up behind them, the pursuers breaking their silence upon seeing their quarry almost taken to the ground. The horse heard it too, and understood that to fall was to die – its feet danced against the earth, too fast to be seen, and once more it stood tall.

No pretence any more, no concealment of the chase. Only the weary, impossibly slow struggle of horses and men forcing their way through the undergrowth. As exhausting to battle against the forest as it was to fight against men, and Kai was close to calling for Gaevani to turn and make their stand where they were while they still had strength left. But he heard it then – the calling of the water, the chatter and rush of the river that ran through the forest.

Once more the cry behind them, but of alarm not victory, for the tribesmen must have known then what Kai and Gaevani intended. The whisper of arrows falling about them – most fell wide, striking tree and earth, and Gaevani plucked one irritably from the scales of his armour, looking at it as though it had insulted him.

It would all have been for nothing if the river ran too deep to be crossed. But they had wagered that a forest stream might run slow and shallow enough to be forded, and so it was, and they plunged into the water, ice cold against their skin, the weary horses lapping up a draught of it before they mounted the far bank. Kai did too, scooping a cupped hand through it and lifting the clear cool water to his lips – never had he tasted anything so good, it seemed, as that water. The last thing he might taste, save for blood.

For here they knew they could go no further – the horses weary, and the forest growing thicker around them. But Kai and Gaevani were laughing, the mad, merry laughter of men with nothing more to lose. For they would have the battle on their terms now, not be surrounded on all sides, dragged down, hacked to death without a chance to fight back. They would wear their wounds upon their front and see the men who killed them, a little victory that mattered for much. And at last, Kai understood why it was always so in the old stories, that heroes always made their last stand at a ford.

'I am glad of your company,' said Kai. 'I would hate to be alone.'

Gaevani smiled at him. 'Now we shall see,' he said, 'how brave these people are.'

The tribesmen came slowly through the trees, some two dozen men. The Romans had said that all the war spears had been taken, this close to the Wall. Yet here they were, broadheaded blades dressed with charms of feather and pelt. Unearthed from caches in the woodlands, dug up from beneath hearths in the villages, ready to be marked with blood once again.

Gaevani was shouting at them, insults in every language he spoke, obscene gestures across the water. They stared silently, until one man, young and hot headed, began to wade forward into the river. Gaevani was ready for him – a flicker of the reins and a flash of the long spear, and the tribesman was scrabbling up the bank as the blade bit into the water behind him.

A hesitance, then, from those men who had gathered to kill them. In the half-light, Kai glanced from one face to the next – the strange, intimate way that men look upon each other before battle. He noted the shuffling half-step back one took, marking him a coward who could be discounted from the fight. He saw the hot-headed man who had rushed into the water, who now impatiently tossed his spear from one hand to the other. An older warrior, bald headed, fingers missing from a hand and a dragging pace to his steps – he would be experienced, but slow. And he saw something else, too, a certain cast of the face that several of them held in common, the thick shock of dark hair that fell over their faces.

'They are kin to one another,' Kai said. 'That is why they do not rush towards us. They all wish to live.'

Gaevani grinned, his teeth bright in the twilight. 'Well, we do not always get what we want.'

'Translate what I say,' Kai said. But he hesitated before he spoke again. He thought at first to tell them that he was a soldier of Rome. That they would be hunted down, their homes burned, their women raped, if any harm came to Kai and Gaevani. For an insult to any part of Rome was taken as an insult to the Emperor himself, and was answered in kind.

Instead he said: 'A shame it is, for men to die for no reason. I seek a criminal of my people, and have no quarrel with you. Go, and let us all live.' And he looked at the oldest man there, and said to him: 'So that you may see your sons grow old.'

A moment after, and Gaevani was speaking his words again in the soft, musical language of the northern tribes. And a hesitance then, from those men who had gathered to kill them. Kai and Gaevani must have seemed fearsome, standing tall on the bank, their horses proud, wearing shining armour and carrying tall spears. Perhaps those tribesmen longed then for the comfort of the fire and heather beer, the company of their women. There was that other magic working, too – the kinship between men, the old weakness that captains always fought against as they taught their warriors how to hate and kill. For Kai felt it then, as they stood and looked at one another, scarcely a spear-throw away. They might have been travellers come from a distant land, old kin returning from a long journey. They might have gathered together about a fire, traded wine and stories, and by the time the morning came about they would have been as brothers. For they were not tribes who had learned to hate one another, spent long and patient centuries nursing a feud – the Sarmatians were strangers to this place. In that moment, Kai found that he did not much wish to kill those men, to leave sons fatherless and fathers to bury their sons. Perhaps those men across the water thought the same, for the spears dipped low, and one of them took half a step away. How easy it would be to slip away in the dark, forget the warrior code and the law of the hunt for one night alone. For them all to live.

But there was another figure coming through the forest then – tall, taller than the rest by nearly half a foot, wiry and thin. Fair hair that marked him out among these tribesmen, a shape to his face that seemed alien to these lands. And as he looked on him, Kai felt that haunting sense of destiny. For he had seen that man before, beneath the light of the moon. He had ridden a Roman horse on the raid past the Wall, and fled back north before they could stop him. And here he was again, as though brought here by magic, come to be the death of them. For that captain barked an order, and the spears stood tall once more.

'It was worth a try, speaking with them,' Gaevani said softly, as he rolled his shoulders, reached down to calm his nervous horse. 'No hero's deed, but still, it was bravely done. I do not know another who would have spoken so well.'

Kai levelled his lance at the captain across the river. 'There is something here for us to do it seems.'

'So there is,' Gaevani answered. 'I wager a month's silver that I shall kill him and not you.'

'Why not a year's, since we shall not live to spend it?'

'Bargained well and done.'

Kai took a deep breath in, inhaling the scent of rain rising from the bracken, the odour of wet earth, the sharp sweet smell of horse sweat. 'Though our lives be short...' he began.

'Let our fame be great,' Gaevani answered, finishing the proverb. Hollow words, for there was no fame to be earned in that place, no songs made for them. They would be killed and forgotten, hung from an oak tree as a trophy until the flesh fell from their bones. There would be no fame, except what they earned from each other. To be witnesses, each to see that the other died well. But in that place, at that time, that seemed to be enough to fight for.

He heard the whisper of a bow, saw the flicker of the arrow through the air, yet the battle fever made it seem to move so slowly – Kai dropped his head, heard and felt the ring of the arrowhead glancing from his helm, even as he moved his horse to the bank, even as he thrust forward with the great two-handed spear, thrusting blind, but with the hunter's knowledge of where his quarry would be. A catch and a tear and a scream, and he looked up to see a warrior stumbling back upon the bank, the river running dark beneath him.

And then there was not one man there, but many. The water alive and teeming with them, the spears flashing forward, as Kai stirred his horse back and forth, wheeling and turning, chasing and stabbing in the dark at the men who strode into the river and were driven back just as quickly. A great cry of victory from Gaevani, and Kai saw a still figure bobbing and floating down the water, speared through by his friend. The first blood claimed by the Sarmatians.

But an answering shout beyond, the prize the dead man had bought with his life, as two of the warriors gained the riverbank beyond Gaevani. And a low splash from behind Kai, as three men pulled themselves from the water like drowned men come to life once more.

It was already time, then, and Kai knew what must be done. For a moment, one last glorious moment, Kai put his horse to flight, felt the echoing shock of the horse's hooves striking the ground, the moment of weightlessness as he was lifted in the saddle. And he and Gaevani were together, their horses nose to tail, as the tribesmen gathered around them, moonlight bright upon the spears.

They were on Kai then, blows glancing and striking from his cuirass as he twisted in the saddle. He feared less for the blades than the hands that were reaching to pull him down, and he held his spear in the middle like a quarterstaff, striking and shoving at those who reached for him. He counted upon his horse to kill – hooves striking out, and a bubbling scream as the horse bit forward and lifted part of a man's face from his skull.

A moment where those warriors drew back, perhaps

frightened by the horses more than those who rode them, horses that must have seemed like monsters to them in the dark. Beside him, Gaevani was still mounted but hunched low in the saddle, curled up around some hurt, the shaft of his spear slick and black with blood. And the light of the moon fell upon the tall captain of the tribe, a mark of destiny falling from the sky, a call from the gods, a challenge.

Kai knew that there was no chance that he might live. But he might kill that man before he died. For it was ever thus in the stories of gods and men, that they held the greatest task back until the end. It was not a man before him, but a knot of fate that Kai might cut, a bloody path for his people that might be averted. And Kai rose up in the saddle to answer, lifting the spear one last time.

It was then that beneath him, his horse began to scream.

Someone was below them, working with a knife on the belly, the ripping sound of cut flesh echoing up. The world twisting and tumbling under Kai as the horse sagged to its knees, something hot spilling and pooling on the ground around them. The spear snatched from his hands, and no time to draw his knife and hack at the hands that reached towards him, pulled, and sent the whole earth up to strike him.

Gasping, winded, he tried to rise again, the heavy horseman's armour dragging him back towards the ground. And there was more weight upon him then, the weight of men bearing down upon him, fixing him to the ground the way one is frozen in a nightmare. And he was screaming then, the shameful fear coming upon him all at once as he waited to feel the probing knives at the joints of his cuirass, for them to begin the butcher's work of killing a man in heavy armour.

But a voice was calling high above it all – their tall captain speaking. And for a mad moment Kai had the instinct to respond, for they were words that he knew. Commands of the Roman army, spoken in Latin.

Fear came then, the fear of not knowing his enemies. To be caught in a trap that he knew nothing of, to die without knowing why. He tried to speak and call out, before something was bound about his face, worming into his mouth and down his throat like a living thing, and he was plunged, once more, into darkness.

15

Before the gates of the fort, Lucius waited.

Runners and messengers came one after another, trying to drag him away from that place, to get him to attend to the hundred endless tasks of a commander – punishments to be given, arguments to settle, orders to decide upon. Yet none of them seemed to matter so much as remaining in that place and watching the land beyond. Hoping to see his friend come back.

A feeling like madness, to be waiting for men he knew would not return. For the patrols and scouts had all been marked one by one upon the tablets of wax, their reports given. Only two were missing, hours after they should have returned – Gaevani, and Kai.

A changing of the watch, and braziers lit high upon the walls. A muttered exchange of passwords with those new guards who came to man the gate, and then once more, the waiting.

His rare gift, Kai had once called it. For Lucius remembered a night about the fire, on the journey that had taken them to the Wall. A night when they had drunk too much *posca*, for reasons that Lucius could not now remember. A festival day, perhaps, or merely a reckless need had taken them over, the need to forget the long journey ahead and all that they had left behind. And so, drunk, they had spoken to each other as heroes, picked out the blessings that the gods had given to them both. Lucius had named Kai as a prince of kindness, a man unafraid to stand alone, and Kai had pulled a sour face at those words.

'Those are not thought great virtues among my people,' he had said. 'But I suppose we are not grateful enough for our blessings.'

'What of me, then?' Lucius had asked, suddenly and shamefully needful for praise.

Kai had grinned at him. 'You wait. Better than any I know.'

'That is all?' Lucius shook his head. 'You might praise a stone for such a quality.'

'Wait long enough, and the world shall turn to your advantage. Watch long enough, and you shall see the thing that no one else does.' Kai had looked around the campground, suddenly wistful. 'Anything may pass, if one only has the patience for it. It is an art my people have never learned. We would not be your slaves if we had.'

Now, the sun had almost gone, the sky marked blood red above the Wall. The gate guard looked at Lucius – a nervous man, for the gate was open when it should be closed, and already it seemed that the Sarmatian had learned to think of the world in the Roman way, to fear the danger that came when things were out of order, out of time.

A count to a hundred breaths – that was the bargain that Lucius struck with himself, the prayer he offered up. Let the gods know that was all the time they had left to conjure up their miracle. For once he closed the gates, it would be done. There could be no trickery with the roll call, no wax tablet deliberately lost or left unmarked. Two men marked down as dead or as deserters, which was merely a different, slower kind of death. And for all the powers that the gods were said to have, even they could not alter the flow of time.

A hundred breaths came and went. One last time, he looked at the land beyond the gate, the ground lit by the low, blood red sun. Hoping against hope to see one at least riding back. To see Kai return alone, if that was how it must be.

There was nothing but the heather dancing in the wind, as though some unseen riders passed through it. The ghosts of Kai and Gaevani, perhaps, riding home to keep in death the orders they had been given in life.

At last he could wait no longer. Whatever gift of waiting he had, it was defeated there and then. He gave the signal, and the gate swung closed.

He turned on his heel at once – the temptation already there to countermand the order, to throw the gates open once more, to take to his horse and search in the darkness for his murdered friend. But instead he stumbled back through the streets of the fort, waving aside the men who stood and saluted before him. Such a longing he had to be alone then, as he made his way back to his quarters.

But he found even that wish, simple as it was, could not be granted. For there, standing to attention outside his chambers, flanked by guards on either side, was Bahadur.

The Sarmatian's skin was grey, and the sweet stink of wine rolled off him – he looked and smelled like a corpse preserved, in the way Lucius had heard the Egyptians favoured, gutted and stuffed with herbs to stave away the rot. Yet the man's eyes were alive, almost feverish. They burned with the fire that prophets and traitors both shared, his lips moving, silent and restless, animated by the urge to speak, or confess.

A flicker of his hand, a word of command, and his guards were gone. A beckoning finger to Bahadur, and the man followed Lucius into the privacy of the Prefect's quarters.

Bahadur made the salute well enough as he entered, stood straight and tall as a Legionnaire after ten years' service in spite of the wine he had drunk. Yet there was still a restlessness to him, if one looked close enough. A slight shift of his weight from foot to foot, a momentary glance towards the door. Eager, no doubt, to return to his wife's side.

Good, Lucius thought to himself. *Let him wait a little longer*.

He took his time to study the Sarmatian. Silver streaking the black hair, the winding tattoos inked across a solemn face. Thin – too thin, with that empty look of a man who has never quite recovered from a long illness. They had known each other a little, in the war to the east. Kai had spoken of him as a joyous, lighthearted man, quick with jest and song, but Lucius had never seen that side of Bahadur. He had only seen that man broken by Roman captivity, half starved, an emissary of defeat and conquest. Disciplined enough as a Roman soldier, yet there was something hollow in that discipline. Lucius had seen it before, among those who walked with the Legion, those men who kept to their orders because they had nothing else left to follow.

At last, Lucius said: 'You are well spoken of.'

The older man blinked. 'Sir?'

'A man that others look up to. A leader, or once you were. You could be again.'

A careful smile. 'I did not think to be promoted today, sir.'

'Do not mistake me. I do not think to promote you. I merely say what others say, not what I believe. For I do not know that I can trust you.' Lucius picked restlessly at the wax tablet on his desk. The place where he would have to mark his absent soldiers. 'Tell me,' he said, 'where is Kai?'

The smile fell away then. 'He has not come back?'

'Strange for you to worry about the comings and goings of a man that you hate.'

Bahadur lifted his head proudly. 'After what has passed between my wife and him, you think it strange that I should keep watch over him? You would set your dog to guard your herd, I think.'

'Perhaps I would. Do you wish to see him dead?'

Bahadur's mouth worked for a moment, but no words came at first. And when, at last, he did speak it was as though Bahadur were discovering the answer himself, in that moment. 'No.' And he shook his head, as though the word itself were not enough. 'He was to me, once, what he is to you now,' said Bahadur. 'So you shall understand.'

Neither man spoke for a time. Lucius let his eyes wander over the cracked plaster, the scored frescos on the walls. How many other commanders had sat in that place before him, how many would come after? Scratching at the borders of the Empire, sent in disgrace, trying to hold together their ragged band of soldiers against madness and defeat. And a traitor's whisper sounded in his mind, that perhaps it would be better if Kai were lost. For he could close his heart then, treat the Sarmatians the way the Roman army had taught him to. With ruthless discipline, bribing them with raids upon the natives for what little gold, wine, and women they could find.

Yet fear followed that thought close behind, fear of the long, lonely years ahead, spent upon the border without a friend at his side. For all the war that Lucius had seen, it seemed as though he had never been so frightened of anything as that.

'Tell me what you know,' said Lucius. 'I will not punish you for speaking the truth to me now. But if you lie to me, I shall—'

'I do not fear the lash.' A curl of the lip. 'Your Emperor did worse things to me than you ever can, and he needed no whip to do it.' Bahadur looked to the ground. 'I do not know where he has gone. That is the truth. Only that he said he had a trail to follow. Laimei's trail.'

'No more than that?'

'No more than that.' A shadow of a smile on Bahadur's face. 'Perhaps he knew that you would ask, if it came to this.'

'Perhaps he did,' said Lucius.

'What will you do?'

'Wait. What else is there to do, when men keep such secrets from each other? Wait to find Kai hanging from a tree, or dig him from a shallow grave. Or wait to put him to death for desertion, if he does return.'

'Let me go after him. Please.'

'That I cannot do. I cannot risk more lives on a mad chase such as that.'

Something changed upon Bahadur's face – for a moment, another man seemed to stand in his place. 'If he does come back,' said Bahadur. 'I shall stand for his punishment. Whatever must be said, I will say it.'

'Even if you were to take his place before the executioner?'

'Even then.'

Lucius hesitated. 'A strange kind of hate you have for him.'

'Do not mistake this for what it is not.' And then the light was gone from Bahadur's eyes, the hollow man was there once more. 'I must prove myself better than him, braver than him. That is all. And I am.'

It had been a long time since Lucius had allowed himself to be angry. To hate. But he did hate then – the stubborn man who stood before him, the wretched Sarmatians choking themselves with their honour, the miserable scrap of countryside of which he was an unwanted master. And he hated himself, too.

'You will nurse your wounds forever, it seems,' Lucius said. 'The only man in this fort lucky enough to bring his wife with him, and still you think yourself wronged by the world. It is too late to take his place. Kai has gone to die for you, and you are a worthless, broken man. I am certain Arite knows it too.'

And Lucius waited, then, the tyrant's smile upon his lips. He waited for Bahadur to speak the words that would doom him. For it was death to speak against the commander – a single hot word would be enough to have the Sarmatian raised upon the cross, or his guts unspooled while he still lived, or his bones broken by stones and thrown into the river to drown. What a pleasure it would be, to have someone before him that he might hate, and kill.

But there was no anger. No reaction at all, except a diminishment, something more lost by a man who perhaps thought he had nothing left to lose.

'You may be right,' said Bahadur. 'But perhaps I am better than you think I am.'

'Oh yes?' said Lucius. 'Why?'

'Because I shall tell you this, in spite of all that you have said to me here. I shall tell you what my wife said to me.' Bahadur drew himself tall. 'It was not Laimei who tried to kill her,' he said. 'Men came. Who they were, she could not say. But they came for the Brigante boy, from the raid across the Wall.'

Lucius said nothing for a time. Then: 'Why?'

'Why indeed? Something a better man than me can answer, no doubt.' And with that Bahadur offered a perfect salute, and strode from the room.

Lucius was alone, then. A rare moment where there were no commands to give, no soldiers or slaves before him. It would be thirty beats of the heart, perhaps, half a hundred breaths, before someone came to take that solitude from him. And Lucius took advantage of that time in the only way that he knew how – he put his head into his hands, and wept for the loss of his friend.

16

When they carried Kai away from the river, he did not expect to live long.

He knew that he was worthless as a captive to these men – he had no knowledge with which he might buy his life, no ransom that the Romans would pay for him. The tribesmen would know their mistake soon enough, and put him to a slow death for their own amusement. And even when he was laid to the ground with surprising gentleness, he thought it impossible that he would sleep. That he would lie awake all night, waiting for the sawing of a knife against his nose and ears, arrowheads sliding beneath his fingernails, a stone shattering his ribs. Yet, somehow, he fell asleep almost at once, deep and dreamless. A gift of sleep that was an omen from the gods – but an omen he would not know the true meaning of until it was too late.

He woke to the low, uneven light of the rising sun breaking through the trees. All about him the sounds and smells of a camp awakening – woodsmoke and the scent of dew upon the leaves, that still feel of morning. A relief, he realised, to sleep once more beneath the open sky, not sealed away in a Roman tomb of stone and mortar. He could almost pretend that he was back upon the steppe, a child once again, waking slowly and smelling the cooking fires in the middle of a long journey, soon to feel the comforting touch of his father's hands upon his shoulders, stirring him from the blankets to tend the herd.

And hands were upon him then – once more, strangely gentle, lifting him to his feet, a palm upon his back to guide the way, catching him when he stumbled upon dead branches and sods of earth. Soon he could smell the smoke of a fire, drawing ever closer.

They brought him close enough to feel its heat, and the hands grew heavier and rougher as they threw him to the ground. A wave of nausea then, to think of what that fire might mean for him. For every people had their own art of torture – Romans raised their prisoners upon the cross or broke them on a wheel, while the Sarmatians favoured the knife, the slow lifting of skin from the body, the uncoiling of the guts beside a screaming man staked to the ground. Perhaps these tribesmen chose fire, and there was the metal taste of fear upon Kai's tongue, shameful words threatening to bubble up from his throat.

But the sack lifted from his head – whatever fate was to be given to him, at least he would not go to it blind. And he found himself sitting beside a cooking fire, around him the solemn-faced men he had fought against a day before. And closest to Kai, the one who was not like the others.

The captain. Tall and lean, the knotted scars of a practised swordsman marking his hands and arms, and a blunt, hard face unlike any of those he commanded. Golden hair touched with silver, the kind that some of the Sarmatians had. It reminded him of Arite, and he was thankful for the memory, that he would die with her in his mind. It was easier to be brave, thinking of her.

They stared at each other for a time – each, it seemed, waiting for the other to speak first.

'I have seen you before, I think,' Kai said at last, in Latin. 'Upon a horse, at night. You were running from me, then, towards the Wall.'

'That was you?' A rumbling chuckle, deep in his throat, as the golden-haired man answered in the same language. 'The gods, it seems, have a sense of humour. What is your name?'

'Kai of the River Dragon. And yours?'

'I was called Ballomar, once. Among these people, my name is Corvus. And I am of all tribes, and none.'

'Corvus?'

'Yes.' And the other man ran a hand through his thinning fair hair. 'A jest of sorts. Then again, the people of these lands have always said that death follows me.'

Kai swallowed heavily, and asked the question that, in his heart, he already knew the answer to. 'Where is my companion?' he said. 'Where is Gaevani?'

'Him, we could not take alive. He fought bravely, to the end. He was a good friend?'

It was some time before Kai could answer. No grief yet, only the first touch of guilt wrapping about his heart. And that memory, clear in his mind, of Gaevani reluctantly choosing to come with him into the forest – a man trapped by honour, dying for his companion. 'Yes,' Kai said at last. 'He was my friend.'

Corvus shook his head. 'You should have stayed in your fort, Kai of the River Dragon. What brings you to the woods north of the Wall, where no Roman soldier should go?'

'A woman of my people came this way. I came to search for her. You have taken her captive?'

'We have,' said Corvus. But he spoke a little too quickly.

'Really?' Kai smiled. 'Tell me her name, then.'

Corvus hesitated, caught, and did not answer.

'I did not think so,' said Kai. 'She has escaped you, too, it seems.'

'Cleverly done,' the captain said. He leaned over, stirring the pot of the stew above the fire. 'Tell me, where do your people come from?'

'Sarmatia.' Kai expected the word to mean nothing to that man, but Corvus nodded at once.

'The steppes to the east of the great river,' he said. 'Good horse country, or so I am told.'

'You know of it?'

'Yes. I am a brother to you, of sorts. A brother of the river. The Donau, we call it. The Danu to you, I think. The Danubius to the Romans.'

Kai said nothing for a time. Then: 'You are of the Quadi?'

'No. The Marcomanni.' The captain cast more wood upon the fire. 'We are both a long way from our homes,' he said. 'Our people fought together once, not so long ago. The free people against Rome.'

Kai said nothing for a time. For it was another life that this man spoke of, when there had been a strange alliance of tribes who had never met one another. No emissaries exchanged, no kings striking bloodpacts, only rumours that travelled north and south along the river, travellers and traders bringing word of a war against Rome. That should not have been enough, and yet some beckoning hand of the gods had led them all to the great river and sent the tribes across the water, all at once.

And for a brief and glorious time the border was broken open, the rich lands of the Empire lay before them. Fields of golden wheat, sweet grapes crawling up the vines. No more famines, the killing winter forgotten for a single, beautiful year. And then Rome had taken its revenge, and put them all in chains.

'You have heard of my clan?' Corvus said.

'I have,' Kai answered. 'And I know that you surrendered to Rome before we did.'

'You are proud. That is good. Yet now even you wear the eagle of Rome.'

'I do what I must.'

'Ah, then you are clever, too. That is even better.' Corvus fell quiet then – oddly shy, it seemed to Kai. A man considering something shameful.

'Speak, or act,' said Kai. 'You are a warrior. How would you feel, bound before your enemy, only to find him too much of a coward to do what he must?'

Corvus lifted his head. 'I do not wish to kill you.'

'Then tell me what you want.'

'I want to graze my herds on the good lands south of the Wall. I want to live free, without a Roman yoke about my neck.' A hardness then, about the eyes. 'And I think that you must want the same thing. You are a man are you not? A warrior. Not a slave. You must wish to be free.'

Kai hesitated. 'What we wish for and what we may have are not the same.'

'But they could be.' The captain smiled at him. 'This is no idle dream, a phantom of the mind. You might reach out and touch it, hold it in your hand. If you have the courage for it, and I think that you do.'

'And what must I do, to have this dream of yours?'

'A simple thing,' said Corvus. 'I wish for you to bring me your commander. Lucius, he is called, yes? That is all you must do. Give me the words that will bring him north of the Wall.'

And Kai was grinning then, the smile breaking over his face faster than he could halt it.

'This amuses you?' said Corvus.

'Oh yes,' Kai answered. 'For you give me a gift I did not think to have, and I thank you for it. That I may die bravely for my friend.'

Corvus sat back heavily. 'It is so between you and the Roman?' he said.

'Yes. And even if I hated him, it would be so.' Kai lifted his head, proudly offered his throat. 'Kill me and be done with it. He is our Great Captain, and I swore my sword oath to him. There is nothing more to be said.'

'And what did he swear to you?' Corvus said, his voice dangerously calm. 'That you would go home someday, no doubt?'

Kai hesitated, and the courage that but a moment before had seemed to flow warm and strong through his veins began to cool a little. 'What would you know of that?' he said.

'You are a clever man,' said Corvus. 'But not clever enough to wonder that I speak Latin better than you. Or what a man of the Marcomanni is doing here, so far from home. For you see, I was promised the same thing.' And Corvus lifted up the sleeve of his tunic, and showed the mark of the eagles upon his shoulder.

Together, they stared at in silence. A whole story written there, in ink and scar, in the way the nail of Corvus's finger absently scratched over what remained there, picking at an old wound. The way his eye lingered on it, dull and empty, as Kai had seen crippled men look upon the sight of their maiming.

'They brought my people here, as they brought you here,' said Corvus at last. 'Gave us the same promises that they gave you.' He paused. 'Did you leave children in the east?'

'A daughter,' Kai whispered.

'What is her name?'

'Tomyris.'

Corvus nodded. 'A good name. I left two sons and three daughters behind. A more fortunate man than you it seems, to have so many children. Or perhaps not. Perhaps my pain is worse, for there are more who are lost to me.' He tossed a twist of dried peat upon the fire. 'We came to this place,' he said. 'Fought and bled for Rome, until there were few of my battle brothers left. Sickness took some.' He gestured to the tribesmen who shared the fire. 'The spears of these people took the rest.'

'And yet you stand at their side.'

'Yes. For we have an enemy in common. Your enemy, too.' And Corvus went still, lost in memory for a time. 'The rumours started. Little whispers at first, late at night. That the Emperor would never let us go home.'

'Soldier's talk. A worthless thing to break your oath over.'

'I thought so too, at first. But it is like the way a blade may splinter against bone and leave a piece of itself behind. The wound itching and festering.' Once more, Corvus's finger picked at the mark of Rome upon his skin. 'I had to know. If I was wrong, I alone would pay the price. And so I took our centurion beyond the Wall, to a quiet place much like this one. I put him to the torture that I have spared you. And he did tell me the truth, at the very last.'

'A man may say anything, if you work on him long enough.'

'He may.' The ghost of a smile on Corvus's face. 'But I do not think you have done that yourself. Or you would know, as I do, the strange honesty of a man who knows he is about to die. For he was a good man, like your Lucius. He was ashamed of what he had done to us.'

Silence for a time, as they listened to the fire. A silence broken only by a single voice, a song of mourning. For on the other side of the campfire lay a tribesman who was dying. A faceless man that Kai's horse had maimed, that ruined head in the lap of a man who must have been his father, who sang some winding prayer for the dying, chanted over and over and over again. The father looked at Kai, the hate carved deep upon his face. This was the beginning, then, of their people learning to hate one another. The start of a thousand feuds that would span generations.

'Lucius would not lie to me,' said Kai.

'An Emperor is he?' Corvus snorted. 'A senator? A Legate? One whose word is law? Or merely a disgraced centurion, saying what he must to make you do what he wishes? To not have his throat cut by his men?'

And Kai wanted to speak then, to defend his captain. But the words caught in his throat, as Kai remembered the feast with the Legate – the greyish colour of Lucius's skin that night, the haunting light in his eyes, the little sour twist to his mouth. The way that the Legate had looked on them – a man with knowledge of a secret, and a trick well played. And within Kai, the first stirrings of a particular kind of hate. The sense of betrayal.

'I think you know it is true,' said Corvus.

'Say that it was,' Kai answered. 'And if I found a way to bring him to you? You shall kill him?'

'Yes,' Corvus said simply. 'No torture. It will be a clean death. And without him, your Sarmatians will rebel.' And that captain of the Marcomanni spoke again, and as he did so Kai saw what it was that made men follow this man to hopeless war. An ache to see it, that same quality that Lucius had, to make men willing to die for him – that beautiful, terrible gift.

'We shall take the Wall,' said Corvus, 'take the land south of it, and make it a kingdom of free peoples. No more tributes sent to Rome. No slaves to our conquerors, soaking in wine to forget our shame, dying of the flux or on a Votadini spear for a cause that is not our own. Your Sarmatians will take this land as their own. You shall be the princes and the warriors that you once were. Not slaves with swords.'

Kai took a heavy breath. For it was a beautiful dream that this man shared with him, and it cost much for him to fight it. 'You forget,' he said, 'the lessons of the Danu. The Legions will return. They always do. Their Emperor does not forgive.'

'The Emperor is old, and dying. The Empire weak, and spread too thin. They will scratch a new line in their map, and try to forget us.' Corvus shook his head. 'But you are right. We waste time. Will you do this, or not?'

Kai said nothing.

'Lucius will die. You cannot prevent it. We have people in

the *vicus*. North and south of the Wall. Many eyes that watch, many hands that keep busy. An arrow, an ambush, poison in his wine. But you can give him a clean death. And you can have your answer.'

'And if I do not?'

'You shall die,' said Corvus. 'Cleanly, and well. But you shall die for a man who has broken his oath to you, and that would be a shameful thing.'

'You do not know that.'

'I know that they would be fools to send you home. The Romans are not fools.' And Corvus was looking on him then, with something a little like pity. 'Do you not wish to know, one way or the other?' he said.

A longing to be brave, then, and for the world to be simple. Perhaps those were the same thing. For always when Kai's courage had failed him in the past, it had been that itching, restless need to know that had unmanned him, that had made him think, and not act.

Corvus pointed to the horizon. 'The sun shall rise over the forest soon enough. When it is above the trees, you shall have to choose.'

Kai stared into the fire. He kept silent, and pretended to think. But, deep in the dark and secret places of the heart, he knew that he had already made his decision.

17

The sentries on the Wall saw the rider coming from afar. A single man bearing the tattoos and charms of some tribe far to the north – the Damnonii, perhaps, or the Venicones. Tribes that had not been seen this far south for half a hundred years, whose presence spoke of nothing but war and death.

And this man came alone, riding openly towards the Wall, a war spear resting across his thighs, something dark and wet bound to his saddle. There were truce leaves upon the blade of the spear, and as the man approached the gate of the Wall he held his hands high and smiled, called to those soldiers on the Wall as though they were long lost companions. Called to them and asked them to let him in, so he might speak with their chieftain.

Silence answered him at first. Then shuffling feet and the rattle of a ladder, a runner sent to the heart of the fortress. A time of waiting, while the stranger hummed and sang merrily to himself, and the bundle on his saddle began to seep upon the flank of his horse, slowly painting it red.

The Sarmatians on the walls began to jeer insults at him,

laughing at this strange emissary from the north who sought the impossible, who rode to the lands of the Empire and thought to make demands. A madman, or a fool, and one whom they would soon send on his way with their words or their spears. But the laughter fell silent as the runner returned – an order given, a password checked and double checked. And then the gates swung open.

When the stranger came into his quarters, Lucius tried to keep his eyes on him. For a thousand clues were there to be found, if only he had the wit to look for them – little scars upon the hands and face might tell Lucius that this was a practised warrior, the pallor of his skin might tell him if his tribe were hungry or well fed, desperate raiders in search of food or honour-bound warriors prepared for a long war. Yet it seemed Lucius could not make himself seek any such thing in the stranger before him. He could only look at the wrapped and bloody bundle in the man's hands.

'What is your name?' Lucius said at last.

'I am Drust,' the man answered. 'Once of the Venicones. Now of the Painted People.'

'The Painted People?'

'That is our name now, for the free people of the North. And you are Lucius.'

'You know my name?'

'I do,' said Drust. 'My people know many things.' He patted the bloody bundle, almost affectionately. 'And we know how to make people speak their secrets.'

'Very well,' said Lucius, trying to keep his voice steady. 'What is it that you bring me?'

The tribesman shook his head. 'Better that we are alone for that,' he said, haughty as a prince.

Behind him, Lucius saw the Sarmatian guards grin to each other, their hands tighten about the weapons in anticipation of the punishment they would soon be meting out. But the smiles fell from their faces as Lucius gave a wave of the hand, a barking order to dismiss them.

When they were alone together, Drust gave a half bow to Lucius, and then laid the bleeding bundle upon the table – his movements strangely gentle, as though he feared to wake what lay within it.

For Lucius, it was a fear of a different kind. He had faced death on the battlefield many times, had duelled with a Sarmatian king for the fate of his people; he had even dared to bargain with his Emperor, a god that walked upon the earth. Yet it still seemed that nothing cost him so much courage as to lift his hands to the fabric, to unwrap it and see what lay inside.

And his eyes played tricks at first – for a moment he did see Kai staring back at him, the warmth of the eyes gone cold forever, the gentle smile cut from his face by the edge of a blade. But then there were tears of guilty relief flowing down Lucius's face, for it was the hacked and mutilated head of Gaevani that lay upon the table.

'I shall have another present to give you soon,' Drust said, 'unless you do as we command.'

Lucius lifted his head to look upon the stranger. 'Speak, then. What ransom do you want?'

'Only the simplest of things,' said Drust, smiling as he spoke. 'That you come north of the Wall, to a place of our choosing. There, you shall find your Kai. There you may trade your life for his. That is the only ransom that my master will accept.'

Lucius said nothing for a time. Then: 'Your master? Better that he came himself, rather than send his dog to bear his messages.'

'He knows better than to trust a Roman with his life.'

Lucius leaned back in his chair, cast the blanket over the bloodied head once more. 'So that is what he thinks of you?' he said. 'He would risk your life and not his own.'

A wavering, then, across that man's face. 'Enough of this,' said Drust. 'What message am I to take back?'

'How may I know that Kai still lives?'

At this, the stranger laughed. '"Though our lives be short, let our fame be great" – that is what he said to tell you. And he said that you would know what it meant.'

'Yes,' said Lucius. 'I do.'

'Come tomorrow. Come alone. Or we shall send him back to you a piece at a time.'

Lucius felt himself go still – like a man carved from marble, he must have seemed to the stranger. And then the sword sprang into Lucius's hand as if of its own accord, and at last the stranger did look afraid. All arrogance gone, and he clutched at the truce leaves he still carried as though hoping they might protect him. But surely, he would know they would be of no use, for unlike the tribes of the north, the Romans thought nothing of breaking a truce, counted a promise to a barbarian as something less than a promise to a dog. For the Romans were the ones who brought desolation and called it peace – the only truce they recognised was that between the living and the dead.

But Lucius knew, here at the end of his life, that he was

a man unlike the rest of his people. That he would have a chance to prove it. And he held the sword flat before that stranger from the north, and laid his fingers on the tip of the blade.

'An oath upon a sword,' said Lucius. 'Ask Kai to tell you what *that* means, and you shall know that I will come to you tomorrow.'

In the shadows of the trees, they waited. Corvus, twenty men of his warband, and Kai. All of those others were mounted on the shaggy-haired ponies that the northmen favoured, and Kai alone bore the shame of being without a horse.

Yet still, there was something familiar to that waiting. How many times before had he taken his place amid trees, besides rivers, in the hills and upon the plains. In war, in bloodfeuds, in cattle raids – many times had he known that simple, terrible waiting, where the day seemed endless and the sun seemed to crawl across the sky. The warrior's soul hoping to see the enemy appear before you, the coward's heart praying that they would not. But never before had he laid an ambush for one he had called his friend.

He looked up to that slow sun, moving inch by inch from east to west. Like an executioner's axe as it travelled, for it would be his death if it touched the horizon and Lucius did not appear. But he found himself wishing it on its way, praying to see it suddenly tilt and swing and fall from the sky, even though it would bring his death. The gods could not still or turn back the flow of time for anything more than a moment, yet perhaps they might make it flow faster, and let the passage of a day come in a single beat of the heart.

Then, a rider was coming over the nearby hillside. Even at such a distance, Kai could see the red crest of the helm, the links of the chain cuirass polished to a high shine. And still then there was hope, to see twenty or fifty or a hundred riders follow him, to see the flowing dragon banners arching through the sky and the tall spears tilted high, to know that Lucius had come to fight and not to surrender.

But that rider came alone. A slow and wandering path he took, like a traveller across the steppe who is in no hurry to reach the new grazing grounds, who stops to contemplate the shape of the clouds in the sky and the dance of wildflowers in the wind, looking for omens and for beauty both.

A wrenching, about the heart. A longing to call to his friend, to tell him to ride and to flee. But a greater longing was there still – an aching need for the truth. And so Kai kept his silence.

Further and further the Roman rode into the trap. All about him, the northmen laid arrows to their bows, gripped their spears tighter, laid comforting hands upon their ponies. And Corvus was whispering to Kai then.

'Call to him,' he said. 'It is time.'

Kai hesitated a moment longer. For he could see that Lucius had stilled his horse, was looking out across the countryside, a little smile on his face as he savoured such a view for the very last time. It was the soul of a Sarmatian he had, a soul that longed for the free and open places, and it had been some cruel joke of the gods to lock him in a Roman body, sealed in narrow stinking buildings, marching in close order. For but a little span of time, in the steppe to the east, and here north of the Wall, that man had been allowed to become what he was meant to be.

Kai could see his lips pursing – perhaps Lucius would whistle or sing, some old marching song of the Legion or a poem of the Sarmatian steppe that he had learned. And Kai knew that he could wait no longer. That to hear such a song might rob him of what little courage he had left.

And he called out to Lucius, as if he greeted a friend. Lucius answered him in kind and stirred his horse forward, even as the tribesmen rode out of the forest and spread in a half circle around him.

'There are no others with you?' said Corvus.

'No,' Lucius answered.

'Difficult to believe they would let a Prefect ride north alone.'

'I had an escort for the first few miles, for the show of it. But I sent them away.' Lucius cocked his head to the side. 'It is true, then. You know our customs. You are a deserter.'

A shiver passed through Corvus, then. For no matter how much he must have cursed and renounced his oath to Legion and Empire, still that word must have carried the power to wound him.

Lucius nodded to himself. 'I thought as much. It was the only thing that made sense.'

'Much good may the knowledge do you now,' said Corvus.

'Indeed. We always know the truth of things too late.' Lucius turned to look at Kai, and said: 'You are hurt?'

'No,' Kai answered, trying to keep his voice steady. 'Not in any way that matters.'

'Good,' Lucius said, his voice still cold. And he looked back to Corvus. 'How shall it be done?'

'He shall come to you,' said Corvus. 'You shall give him

your horse. And we shall let him ride free.'

Kai saw Lucius's eyes flicker among those gathered there – the soldier's gaze, judging their weapons and their horses, making the judgements of weight and speed. His gaze lingered on the great cavalry horse that Corvus rode, the only one among them that might keep pace with a Sarmatian horse.

At last, it seemed, he was satisfied there was no better deal to be struck. 'Very well,' said Lucius. 'Send him forward.'

Kai stumbled forward, the awkward, bowlegged walk of a man who had learned to ride before he learned to walk. His people counted it a shameful thing, to go unmounted, and there he was doubly shamed – by having no horse beneath him, and by what he was about to do.

And he could see Lucius trying to smile then – a trembling, wavering shape to his lips, as he slid from the saddle and held out the reins to Kai. 'Do not think badly of yourself, Kai,' he said, speaking the Sarmatian tongue, speaking for Kai's ears alone. 'For wanting to live, I mean. You must know that I am glad to trade my life for yours.'

Kai closed his eyes for a moment, breathed deep and heavy. He had thought himself ready for many things – for all that might come to pass. But he had not thought that Lucius might try to comfort him, there at the end.

'Go, Kai,' he heard the Roman say, 'and live.'

And then there were words to be spoken – the comfort of anger to fuel them.

'So that I may see my daughter again?' said Kai, opening his eyes once more. 'And the steppes of my home?'

The smile wavered then. And Kai knew – he knew it all in that moment, yet still it would need to be spoken. There was a sudden reluctance, then, to ask the questions that he had traded oath and honour for, the way that great armies before a battle will while away half the day in watchful silence. Listening to the rolling wind, the smell of the summer bracken thick in his nose. Waiting, afraid to destroy the world that he had built.

Behind him, Kai heard a muttered order from Corvus, the sound of hooves against the earth as the northmen began to edge forward. And he felt the battle rage then, a roaring fury that he would be denied what he had fought for. 'Have I not done as you asked?' he cried out. 'I ask nothing but these few words with him. You shall have your blood soon enough.'

A hiss and a whistle, and the tribesmen fell back to their places.

'Will you swear to speak true to me?' Kai asked.

Lucius looked back at him proudly. 'What use are oaths now?' he said.

'True enough. I shall have to trust you one more time.' From the corner of his eye, he saw the tribesmen begin to circle around them once again – still at a distance, the noose not yet tightening. But he did not have much time.

'I ask you this,' said Kai. 'Will I truly go back to the steppe, after my twenty-five years? Will I see my daughter again?' He hesitated. 'Will you keep your promise to me?'

A little half breath taken by the Roman, a shiver across the skin. 'No,' he said. 'They will never let you go home.'

No anger yet, not even grief. Only a little hollowing around the heart. Perhaps it was what Bahadur had felt, when he had learned of what had passed between Kai and Arite. To discover that a promise could be worth so little. How easily one might be betrayed.

'I wish that you had told me,' said Kai. 'Perhaps I could have lived with the breaking of the oath. If only you had told me.'

'I wish that I had told you,' Lucius answered. 'I was sworn to silence, on an oath to the Emperor. I wish that I had broken that oath. But it is too late.' He looked towards the tribesmen, gathering like vultures around them. 'This was the deal you struck with them? My life for this answer?'

Kai nodded, not trusting himself to speak.

'I hope it is a good life you make here, with them.' Lucius looked around, drinking in the sights of land and sky for the very last time. Then he offered his scabbard to Kai, hilt first, and said: 'Come. I am ready. And if it is to be anyone, it should be you.'

The Roman sword was in Kai's hand, the hateful weapon of the conqueror. 'I am sorry, Lucius,' he said. 'I had to know it for certain. I knew you would not lie to me here, at the end.' And with that, he turned his back to the Roman, and called out to the tribesmen who gathered about them. 'Let us finish what we began beside the river. For you still have to answer for Gaevani's life.'

A warning call, from Corvus, the deserter: 'Kai. There is no need for this.'

Kai ignored him, and in the Sarmatian tongue, he said to Lucius. 'Take the horse. Run, if you can.'

Only a moment for Lucius's eyes to flit from one tribesman to the next, to judge the distance to the horse. To weigh the odds in his mind. He answered. 'No. I shall not leave you here.'

No time left to argue – no time left at all. And there was something like relief in Kai's heart, then, that helped to wash away the shame. 'Let us die together,' he said.

No sign of surprise from Corvus – nothing but a glance about at the men he had gathered there to be certain of the odds in his favour, a little shrug of the shoulders, a blankness to the eyes. Corvus waved them on, and the tribesmen began their careful advance, as wary as hunters tracking a dying boar. They would take their time, and there would be little chance, it seemed, for Kai and Lucius to die well.

But then, a sound in the air. A sound that did not belong, that struck them all to stillness, like a spell. The sound of laughter.

It came from Lucius – a berserker's laughter, high and mad and merry. And he was pointing to the horizon as his voice, hoarse and cracked, called out a song of the Sarmatians. Not one of the slow, winding songs of doomed men that a company of horsemen would sing when surrounded and soon to die. It was a call to victors and champions, to greet boon companions riding home at last.

And at first Kai thought the Roman sang to phantoms of his mind, to the spirits of his ancestors come to claim him for the ride to the Otherlands. But when Kai risked a look back, he saw them too – horsemen on the hill, the tall spears and banners of Sarmatians. Impossible, but there they were, a company of men and horses riding to rescue them. And he was frightened then, like a drowning man in sight of land who fears to die with safety so close.

Corvus was screaming at them to kill Lucius, for he could see his great victory slipping away with each passing moment. But already among the tribesmen he could see the eyes rolling wide, glancing towards the safety of the forest. For those monstrous horses of the Sarmatians were coming for them – to stay and fight was to stay and die.

And so it was that only six of those men answered their

captain's call. No time any more for the patient work of the hunter, to circle and wear down their prey, and so they rushed forward blindly, calling the old war songs of their people. One on a pony, ahead of the rest – Kai thrust at him, missed with the sword, the slap of the air rushing past as the tribesman's own spear passed wide. The man was past Kai then, but no time to turn and face him. For the others were almost upon them – the spears bright, the iron in the air. And Kai felt Lucius's hand upon his shoulder, that comfort of touch that was one fighter's gift to another. *Do not be afraid*, that touch seemed to say. *I am here.*

It was akin to fighting in a nightmare – all about him the iron spearheads danced, and Kai's own movements felt impossibly, frighteningly slow. Yet much like a nightmare, it seemed the blades of his enemies could not truly wound him. For the tribesmen fought hesitantly, frightened by the great horse that towered above them. They still had something left to lose.

The haft of a spear swinging in, striking low, taking Kai's breath from him. A cut and a counter, the feel of his sword catching and tearing against flesh, a scream that seemed both close and far away, all at once. The tribesmen falling back, as the blood fell upon the heather, and as Kai's vision swam with the pain, he saw the deserter come dancing forward, the hopping steps of one preparing a spear throw. His eyes fixed upon his mark, upon Lucius.

And through the pain, Kai found the strength to call one word. 'Lucius!'

The spear passing in flight – a beautiful throw, a hero's cast that in the still, frozen instant between one heartbeat and the next Kai could not help but admire. But the spear found nothing but air, as Lucius twisted aside in the saddle, watching it in that detached, calm way that comes upon a warrior close to death, as the spear passed a quarter inch from his throat.

And there was clear ground about them then, the earth torn and ripped and bloodied as though it too had fought against them, though no dead man lay upon it. The tribesmen falling back, turning and running, for Kai could hear it now, the hoofbeats of the Sarmatians, the roaring of the wind in their banners. And watching the northmen run, there was a mad urge to go after them, to chase them down, to throw himself upon their spears. For dying had seemed such a simple thing, a moment ago, and living frightened him more now.

For he could see who led the Sarmatians who had come to rescue them – unarmoured, the long spear glittering in her hand, it was Laimei who rode in the champion's place at the front. All glory fell to her, it seemed.

And for Kai? In the battle, perhaps for the last time, he and Lucius had been brothers once more. When he looked to Lucius, he knew what waited for him. For the other man's eyes were a mirror to him, a mirror to his shame. A gaze that grew colder even as Kai watched, as whatever brotherhood had once been there began to flicker, fade, and die.

18

For the great champions, the presence of the gods can be seen in all things. It is in the hesitance of the warrior who does not strike when you are unguarded. It is in the clouds that suddenly sweep across the moon as you wait in ambush. It is in the horse that will not charge, the spear that shatters when it should not, the arrow that the wind itself seems to turn aside. The world seems to bend itself to your will, so long as you follow the champion's code – to never hesitate, to be fearless of death, to be careless with your life and the lives of others. A champion does not grow old this way, for the gods are fickle and give their favour only fleetingly. But it is a life that is glorious, and mercifully free of doubt.

That was all Lucius could think of, when he saw Laimei ride up to them, a company of Sarmatians at her back. For she seemed unsurprised to see them there, regarded them almost with a kind of weary boredom, with no apparent regard to the chains of fate that had brought her there. All was as it should be – to her, at least.

'I am glad to see the Cruel Spear,' Lucius said. 'May I swallow your evil days.' It seemed wise to offer the ritual greeting of the Sarmatians. He was a Prefect of Rome, and at her back were men that he commanded by oath and by law. Yet in that moment, in that place, he felt certain they would follow her commands and not his.

She inclined her head to him, but did not answer. He saw his gaze flicker towards Kai, yet for once there was no hate in her eyes when she looked upon her brother. Only something a little like pity.

'How is it you come to be here?' said Lucius. 'And why—'

'No time for your questions.' She nodded towards the tree line. 'There may be more of the Painted People close by. Many more.'

'There are things I must know.'

A little hiss of irritation. 'Then I shall answer your questions as we ride,' she said. 'We have no spare horse for my brother. He shall ride with you?'

It was Lucius's turn to remain silent, as beside him Kai stared at the ground, trembling with shame. For all that Lucius wished to call that man onto his horse, he knew that he could not bear to be that close to Kai. And so without a word being spoken, one of the Sarmatians came forward, offered a place to Kai. And as they rode towards the south, towards the Wall, Laimei told her story.

'After the Dance of the Horses,' she said, 'I found Arite dying and the boy taken. I followed the trail, north of the Wall.'

'North of the Wall?' said Lucius. 'How did you cross?'

'A milecastle lay empty,' she said, 'and before you ask, I do not know how or why. Why do your people do or not do anything? It does not matter. I found those who took the boy. I killed them.' She shrugged, as if she spoke of some simple thing. Not the tracking and killing of armed men in the dark, done by her alone.

'Where is the boy now?' asked Lucius.

'With the Votadini. With their chieftain, Mor, who I think you know.' She raised her head proudly. 'I am of his tribe now. They have taken me in. For they are a little like our people, in one way at least. They are not ashamed to see a woman fight.' She glanced towards Kai, riding miserably at the back of the formation. 'There seemed little enough for me to return for.'

'I see. And how did you come upon us here?'

'The scouts of the Votadini spoke of men coming north of the Wall, and of one riding alone.' She nodded towards the other Sarmatians. 'I came to speak with them, and they told me you sent them away.' She curled her lip. 'I knew then that my brother must have done something foolish. For that was the only thing that might make *you* be so foolish as to ride in this country alone, great prize that you are.'

Lucius said nothing for a time. Then: 'He came searching for you, you know. That is where all this trouble began.'

She flinched, as though struck. 'I think the trouble began long before that. Long before you have known us.' She hesitated. Then: 'Why?'

Lucius took a deep breath, and said: 'We thought that it was you who tried to kill Arite. You that took the boy.'

And at that, she laughed – not the harsh roar he might have expected from one who lived for sword and spear, but a strangely gentle sound, soft and echoing, like distant birdsong. 'No doubt he told you stories,' she said, 'of the madness of champions? I hear those stories too – jealous tales, told by weak men. I am wiser than you both, it seems.' She paused. 'Arite lives?'

'She does.'

Laimei nodded appreciatively. 'I did not think to see anyone live from a wound such as the one she bore. She has a strong soul, that one – I do not know why she chooses the company she keeps. The company of weak men.' She glanced back once more towards her brother. 'What will you do with him?'

In his mind, Lucius saw Kai pleading with him to flee on the horse, to take a path to safety. He saw the Sarmatian standing between him and the tribesmen, willing to fight and die to protect his captain. And he thought too of Kai sending those words with that messenger who had come to the Wall. How he had summoned Lucius to die.

'In truth,' said Lucius. 'I do not know.'

Soon enough, there was the sight of the Wall upon the horizon. No sense of joy or pride to see it, only the weary relief that it might bring safety, the chance to think. For though his skin lay cold, Lucius's mind felt feverish – so much had come to pass, so much of his world turned up and over upon itself, that he felt the old Roman longing for stone and warmth and darkness. And so Lucius turned his horse towards the Wall, at the same moment that Laimei turned hers to the north, the wild country.

'I go to the Votadini,' she said. 'You should too. Mor shall wish to speak with you.'

He looked to the other Sarmatians, and to Kai. Would they follow her or him? Had they been Legionaries, he would have commanded and they would have obeyed, bound as much by their fear of torture and death as by their oaths. But for the Sarmatians, for all the time he had spent among them, still there was no telling what they would do, or why. And a traitorous voice told him that this was what the Romans had learned long ago, the lesson that had let them conquer the world, the lesson he was relearning once more – that it was best to lead with the whip, and perhaps the promise of gold. That codes of honour would fail when one needed them most.

In truth, he did not know if any of them would follow him south. And in truth, he did not wish to ride alone. So he turned his horse to the north, and he followed Laimei. As though she were the captain, and he a rider at her command.

The taste of heather beer upon his tongue, the smoke from the fire stinging his eyes, the scent of meat upon the air – the feelings of a feast, as unlikely as it seemed to Lucius on such a day as that. For they were in the heartlands of the Votadini now. Not at a truce meeting by tree and river, but sitting by an open fire in the shadow of the chieftain's home, as children danced and played about them, and the herds grazed upon the grass nearby.

'My palace,' Mor had said when they arrived, and the bright-eyed chieftain had laughed then, for he must have known how his home must have seemed to Lucius. A fine round roofed hut, mud daubed and well roofed with reeds, but a building that a well-bred Roman might think fit for a stable and nothing more.

'One may be a great chieftain without a palace,' Lucius had answered.

'True enough,' said Mor. 'It is in meat and milk that we measure our wealth north of the Wall, not in great buildings of stone. We are a little like your Sarmatians, I think. And so let us sit out here, amid my treasures – my people, and my herds.'

An easy silence had settled for a time. Horns of beer brought to them, venison smoking above the fire. The Sarmatians had busied themselves with the food and drink, seeming unconcerned to find themselves in the camp of a tribe they did not know, surrounded by half a hundred men with spear and shield. Perhaps it was that, for the first time in more than a year, they might let themselves believe themselves back upon the steppe. That they might believe themselves to be free.

Only Kai and Laimei did not join them at the fire. Kai sat, hunched and miserable, at the edge of the camp, while his sister busied herself with the horses, barking orders in her own language at the warband of the Votadini.

Mor watched her go, and smiled reproachfully at Lucius. 'You did not tell me you had such women with you,' he said.

'There are none quite like her.'

'So I see.' The chieftain lifted the horn of beer to his lips. 'You know, when she came to us and asked for a place among the tribe, I asked if she would be my wife.'

'How did she answer?'

'She asked how many wives I had already,' Mor answered ruefully.

In spite of himself, Lucius laughed. 'And?'

'I said three, which is not so many for a chieftain of my people. But too many for her, it seems.'

'In truth,' said Lucius, 'I think she has made her marriage to spear and shield.'

'Ah yes, it is so. And who could speak against that? More constant companions than most men. Especially chieftains such as us. We come and go. But there is always war.' Mor reached his hand towards the fire, testing the heat. 'And soon,' he said, 'there will such a war here as these lands have never seen.'

A silence, then, and Lucius let it linger for a time. 'There is much that I would speak of with you,' he said at last. 'And I hope that we may be truthful with one another.'

'Well,' said Mor, 'we know each other better, now. And we know our enemy, too.'

'You could have spoken to me before. Much might have been averted.'

'A shameful thing,' the chieftain said, 'to go barking to the Romans of what another tribe is doing. My own people might have hung me from a tree, had I done so. And we did not know if we could trust one another.' Mor glanced then towards Kai. 'It is always the way of men, no? Always, we trust those we should not, and do not believe in those who are our true friends.' He dipped a horn cup in the barrel of heather beer, and handed it to Lucius. 'And I might say the same to you. If you had told me of the boy...' The words trailed away, and there was a testing light, in Mor's eyes – that sharp patience of the instructor, the swordmaster, or the priest. For the chieftain was waiting, it seemed, to see what Lucius knew.

'The boy from the raids across the Wall,' said Lucius. 'He is of your people?'

'Ah, yes, you *are* clever.' Mor drank deeply from his own cup. 'Yes. They were our kin south of the Wall that the raiders went in search of.'

'Hostages?'

'Just so. And they only took one in the end, but that was

enough. They knew I had no taste for war. They feared that I might talk with you, fight beside you.'

'Will you?'

'Talk with you? Of course. Fight beside you…' Mor hissed through his teeth. 'That is another matter.'

'Let us talk, then. How many are there?'

'Many,' said Mor. 'Very many. They have gathered the northern clans together – the Venicones, the Damnonii, perhaps others, too. Together, they are many thousands, calling themselves by that new name, the Painted People. They hate each other, but they have sworn a blood oath that surpasses their hate. Corvus, that man who leads them…' Mor did not speak for a time. Then: 'His name is well earned. He truly is a carrion crow that walks as a man. Your people taught him the art of war a little too well. But to hate your people, that he learned all by himself. And to inspire that hate in others – that was a gift from the gods, I think.'

'Yes,' Lucius said, and it was his turn to look towards Kai. 'It seems he has that gift.'

'They are coming,' said Mor. 'They are gathering on the borders of this land. They mean to cross the Wall, take the land from you.'

'Poor farmland, bad pastures. A foolish thing to fight a war over.'

'Of course. But to them, it means much. To your people too, it seems. Why else would you build that Wall? Worthless land, you think it, but they shall fight and die for it. And so will you.'

'And you?' said Lucius. 'Will you let them march through your lands? Or will you remember your treaty with Rome?'

'They are too many for my people to stop,' Mor said. 'And

besides, it is your land that they want. And my people are not so foolish as to fight for land that is not our own.' Mor allowed himself a smile. 'That is the foolish Roman way.'

Lucius made no answer. He stared into the fire, following the twisting patterns of flame and smoke, and he tried to think.

After a time, Mor spoke again – gentle, and insistent. 'What shall you do now?'

'My Legate must know of this.' And as he spoke, Lucius said the words as a judge might give a sentence in the courts of Rome. A sentence of death.

'It is to be war, then?'

'It is. Bloody, and foolish.'

'You think that you shall win?'

'If there is one thing that I have learned, it is that Rome does not lose. And Caerellius, my Legate, he is ambitious. He *cannot* lose.'

Mor made no answer. He merely smiled again, and there was sadness in his smile.

'You do not think this is so?'

'Something is stirring here, north of the Wall. Something that your Empire cannot stop.'

And Lucius was laughing then, a hateful, mocking laughter rising in his throat and spilling from his lips. 'Do you know how many tribes and clans have told us that?' he said, with all of the pride that he so despised in his people, but that he could not seem to resist. 'All across the Empire, for hundreds of years. Carthage. Gaul. The Quadi. The Marcomanni. The Iceni. "We are different, we shall defeat Rome, for we are braver and nobler than they are." And one by one, Rome breaks them to its will.'

'Your Sarmatians too, yes?'

Lucius hesitated. 'Yes. Even them.'

Mor nodded. 'You speak true. Yet still, I tell you, it is so. What stirs here may not last long. No more than a season – perhaps not even that. But for a time, it has the power to destroy you.'

'And you think it cannot be stopped?'

'Of course it may be stopped. Anything may be stopped. But it will not be stopped by your Empire. By your Wall or your Legions.'

'Then by what?'

'It shall be stopped by magic,' said Mor, 'or by nothing at all. And I think that there is little magic left here in this land, except that which men may make for themselves.'

Lucius said nothing for a time. Then he drained the horn of heather beer, offered the last drops of it to the ground, to the gods. 'I shall keep your tribe from the battle, if I can.'

'*I* shall keep them from the battle, if I can,' Mor answered. 'But more than that, I cannot promise.'

'They killed your kin south of the Wall,' said Lucius. 'They tried to take a child of your people as their hostage.'

'True. But many a feud might be forgotten, if there is a war against Rome. It is the thing my people long for, more than anything else. A whispering at night, a vision they dream together. It will cost me much, to keep them from the dream. I do not know if it can be done.' The chieftain looked up towards the sky – judging the quality of the light, perhaps, or searching for an omen in the passage of the clouds. And Mor laughed, warm and merry. 'But that is then, this is now. Drink your beer and eat your meat. Do not look so gloomy. You live today when you could have died. That is worth celebrating, no?'

'Perhaps,' Lucius answered. 'But I lost a champion today.' And, once more, his eyes found Kai – apart from the other Sarmatians, arms wrapped around his legs like a child.

'He has betrayed you?' said Mor.

'He has,' Lucius answered. 'Though in a way, I betrayed him first.'

'And what shall you do? What would be the Roman way?'

'To raise him on a wooden cross by the walls of the fort, and let every man see him die.'

'And the Sarmatian way?'

'I do not know. A duel, I suppose.'

'And what is *your* way?'

In spite of himself, Lucius smiled. 'Oh, you are clever,' he said. 'I do not know that a chieftain should be so eager to know the hearts of men. It shall cause you trouble, I think.'

'It is true,' said Mor. 'And it has. I should have been a druid. Unravelling the mysteries of men and gods has always been my gift. But we have no druids left – your people killed them all, remember? Drove them to the sacred groves of Yns Mon, far to the west, butchered and burned them a hundred years ago. Killed our gods, too, I think. And so a man such as me must be a chieftain instead.'

And Mor leaned forward suddenly, clasped Lucius by the arm, an act of strange intimacy. And when the chieftain spoke again, it was with the beautiful, frightening quality of the priest or the prophet, of a man who believes utterly in what he says. 'We are alike in this – the gods put us both into the wrong bodies, sent us to the wrong part of the world. But perhaps there is something here for us to do. Something that no one else can. Do you believe it?'

Lucius said: 'I do not know.'

And the priest's fire was gone from Mor's eyes – he sat back once more, suddenly sad and weary. 'You must be south of the Wall by the time the sun falls,' he said. 'You are safe until then. But I can promise nothing after that.'

At the edge of the Votadini encampment, Kai ran his hands across the ground. Seeking, in the touch of grass and earth, some memory of a different time and place. It was a foreign landscape, the peated soil rolling in his palms, the grass quite unlike the tall dancing strands of the steppe. But still, he could touch the grass and the ground and pretend himself home, at his daughter's side.

A child's imagining. He would never see the steppe or his daughter again.

Distantly, he could hear the sound of Lucius and the chieftain speaking. Not the words themselves, but the rhythm of the speech. There was pain, sharp and insistent, when Lucius raised his voice. The music of Lucius's words had quieted Kai's mind, in times past. But no longer. Now, this sound of it brought shame circling around his heart, the way a wolf will stalk a helpless man, hamstrung and bleeding in the snow. Yet the wolf was more merciful. For it would open the throat quickly, and unlike shame, it would not eat you alive.

Close by, he heard the heavy tread of hooves, the soft footfalls that came with it. And when Kai looked up, it was Laimei who came towards him, walking upon the ground and leading her horse by the reins.

She stopped before him, and he saw her resting one hand on the flank of the horse at her side, the gentleness of that touch always a surprise to see. For she did not raise her voice in song or laughter, smile at anything save for a fine move with spear or sword. Men and women were there only to be commanded, broken to her will. Yet alone with a horse, there was something of the gentle sister she had once been to him, a long time before.

They watched each other silently for a time. Her face, as always, hard and unreadable – the warrior's gift, that empty, almost bored expression that gave nothing away.

Two times before, they had faced each other with spear in hand, back upon the steppe. And all warriors knew that the gods loved to speak in threes, and that if something had happened twice, it would surely happen once more.

At last, she spoke. 'He broke his word, then.'

'He told you this?'

She shook her head. 'No.'

'And yet you know. As you always have.' Kai shook his head. 'You should have been a dream reader of our people, a seer who may speak the future.'

A shrug of the shoulders. 'It is no piece of magic. You are a simple man, and you wear your wounds openly on your face. I know of only one thing that might hurt you so.'

'He broke his promise to me,' said Kai. 'To all of us. We shall never go home.'

She thought for a moment. 'My life is a simpler one than yours,' she said. 'I knew I would not live to see the return, and so it meant nothing to me. Who ever heard of a champion who lived to see thirty summers?'

'But you must have been afraid, when you saw they would not let you fight.'

'Yes,' she said quietly. 'I was afraid to grow old. I doubted. But I was wrong to do so. The gods sent me to this place.' Her eyes flickered about Mor's steading, and rested upon the signs of war – the old chariot, the war trophies gathered outside the hut, the horses in the fields. 'Women are queens here, sometimes. And warriors too, when they must be.'

'You have a place here,' said Kai, 'and a people to call your own.' He reached up and touched his cheeks, felt the whorls of the scars that marked him. 'But I have no people. And without Lucius…'

'And why do you speak of this to me?'

Kai shivered then, at the coldness of her words. For no matter what had passed between them, by some old instinct, he still found himself turning to her for comfort. Their mother had died in the birthing of him – a fortunate thing, the Sarmatians called it, for they thought it marked the birth of a fearsome kind of a man, who could kill before he had lived a single day. And so Kai and Laimei had raised one another, while their father fought in feud and raid and war. And now, there was nothing left of what had once been between them. He let his head sink low, felt the weary, defeated tears run across the scars on his cheeks.

But then, a touch upon his shoulder – the same shy, gentle touch his sister saved for her horse. The earthy scent of her hair, as she sat beside him, and leaned her head against his.

They waited there together for a long time, and watched the shifting motion of the horses in the pasture, the gentle way they took the grass from the ground.

'I sometimes wish,' she said, 'that I could put our feud aside. But I never did learn to surrender. And that is what it would be to me, a surrender. You understand?'

'I know. I hurt you. For what I did, and did not do, I am sorry for it.'

'Yes,' she said. 'But know this – I want no vengeance from you. Not anymore.'

'Laimei—'

She stood and turned her face away from him. 'That is what I offer you,' he heard her say. 'A truce. A wish of good fortune. Perhaps that is not enough.'

'It must be enough.'

And she should have walked away from him then – everything that he knew of her told him so. But she remained, hesitant and irresolute. 'Do you think me cruel?' she asked.

Kai tried a smile. 'It is the name you have earned – the Cruel Spear.'

'And is that what you think of me?' she said, and there was something strangely needful in her voice.

At first, he did not know how to answer, for he could not quite believe the question that she had asked. That she, who had carved a place for herself in the world through sheer force of will, who stood alone and proud and did not seem to need any man or woman to stand beside her, would still have that longing to be known and understood.

'No,' he said. 'That is not what I think of you. I remember you as you once were, for you spent a lifetime's worth of kindness on me, long ago.' He hesitated. 'Perhaps *that* is who you are – a creature of seasons. You had your season of love when we were children, and I have known nothing like it since. Now it is your season of war, and it is pure and true as your love once was. I wonder if we will both live long enough to see your next season. I think it shall be a remarkable thing.'

She smiled then, suddenly shy as a child. 'I know more of you now than I did before,' she said. 'I thought it was that you could not keep your promises, but you can. The promises of the heart, you keep better than any.'

And there was a knowing between them then, as the wind stirred the heather and the horses whickered close by – a closing of the circle. What a thing it would have been to remain forever in that moment. But the sun was beginning to fall from the sky, and the Sarmatians were whistling to their horses. The moment ended as soon as it had begun.

'The others will be going soon,' she said. 'And so you must decide if you will go back with them.'

'You will stay here?' Kai asked.

'There is nothing for me there, south of the Wall.' She hesitated. 'I do not think there is anything left there for you, either.'

And when Kai looked to Lucius, he wondered if she were right. The Roman sat there upon his horse, weary but still with the warrior's pride about him, the presence of a great captain in the way he moved and spoke. But there was a hollowness to his actions now – perhaps only Kai knew him well enough to see it, the performance Lucius gave that he might no longer believe in.

'Perhaps you are right,' said Kai. 'But I must find out.'

'Very well,' she said. 'But it shall not do for you to go unarmed.' She took two spears from a pile of weapons close by, and made to hand him one. But she hesitated a moment longer, before she gave it to him. 'He may kill you, if you go back.'

'Perhaps,' Kai said, feeling the weight of the spear in his hand. 'But that does not matter does it? Live one more day or live ten more years, and it matters not. Only to do what is right.'

'Yes,' she said, 'that is so.' And perhaps it was that Kai had been wrong – that she was not a creature of a single season. For a moment, there was the child she had once been, love written clear across her face.

Then the creak of leather, the sound of a spear falling into a palm, as Laimei leaned forward and rapped her spear against Kai's, metal against metal like the peal of a bell. The warrior's farewell.

19

The word passed across the walls and through the streets of Cilurnum – riders approaching from the north. The return of their commander, just as the sun was falling from the sky.

One could tell everything about a leader from the way their return was answered. When the tyrant returned, men became as statues in the hope they would be forgotten – there was the stink of vomit in the gutters, and the sentries shivering and trembling at their posts as their tormentor returned. Or when it was heard that a weak captain was coming back, everywhere were the empty smiles of thieves, lips moving as men practised the begging deception that would earn them fortune or favour.

Arite saw none of this when word came that Lucius was returning. No fearful snapping to attention, but men standing tall with pride. A light in the eyes, the soft music of words filling the air, the whispered sharing of stories. *Do you remember when... He told me that... I saw him...* For this was a captain that men loved to follow.

She was watching as the gates swung open. And she

saw, if only for a moment, a beaten, fearful man put on the mask he wore for his people, as Lucius rode back into the fort.

The smile was there. The little jokes, the warmth in his voice as he called to the sentries by name. Only a little trembling about the corner of the mouth, the restless tapping of his fingers on the pommel of his sword. And behind him, she saw Kai – her heart sang to see him, but only for a moment. For she saw how he sat upon his horse like a man before a hopeless battle, the beautiful, terrible sight that she had seen many times before, the way the men and women of her people faced death.

But just as quickly, the moment passed. Lucius was leaning forward to speak to Kai, and there was a whispering of orders, hands clasping hands. Then the Roman was gone – riding towards the heart of the fort, and Kai alone was left at the gate, as the other Sarmatians drifted away, back towards the barracks.

She called Kai's name, and at the sight of her she saw all the pain gone from his face. Just for a moment, a moment of brilliant joy.

Kai's horse was led away by one of his companions, and together they moved through the fort and towards the *vicus*. The unspoken words seemed to cluster thick in the air about them, secrets and confessions that would have to be spoken. Yet they wandered together, slow and silent, as though frightened of what lay at the end of the journey.

From time to time she would have to stop and sit upon the ground, for she was still weak from the wound, a cutting pain at her back with every step that was taken. Each time she stopped, she saw Kai give a twitch of the hands, a

half-step taken towards her, before he remembered himself
and stood away.

By the crooked house in the *vicus*, they sat together and
leaned against the wall. A heavy heat in the air, one of those
rare midsummer evening in the northlands where the air
shimmers even when the sun has almost fallen from the sky.

After a time, Kai said: 'I should not be here. Bahadur may
come back.'

'No,' she said. 'He will not.'

'Even so, I made a promise…' The words trailed away, and
he shook his head. 'But I have had enough of promises.'

She watched him then, but he gave nothing away. His face
had something of his sister about it, her careful, guarded
blankness.

'I thought I saw something at the gate,' she said. 'I thought
that Lucius was going to kill you.'

Kai nodded dully. 'I thought so too.'

'Why?' she said.

And the words came then – slow and relentless, spoken
with the quality of a confession, as he told her of what had
passed beyond the Wall. Of his capture, and what the deserter
had spoken. The question asked, and the answer given. The
peace made with Laimei, the wound given to Lucius that
might never heal.

When he had finished, and the silence grew thick between
them, she knew he had told her almost all. But something
remained unspoken – a raw wound that he would not touch,
that would fester and rot, if she left it alone.

'What did he say to you?' she said. 'At the gate, after the
others had gone.'

'That I must not mistake his mercy for love,' Kai answered.

'That he needed every rider that he had. Even the ones he could not trust.'

She waited, for she knew there were more words to come. She could see him piecing them together even as they sat there, slow and patient. Even as they heard the call of the guard changing, as the smoke from cooking fires grew thick and the wine shops began to clamour, she waited.

At last, he spoke again.

'I believed in my people,' he said. 'Then, when I could no longer believe in them, I believed in you.' A hard smile. 'But that was not to be my fate. And so I chose Lucius, and the promise. It meant everything to me. *He* meant everything to me.' He hesitated. 'Do you think me a fool, for thinking so much of that promise?'

'Perhaps. But he was happy enough for you to believe it, was he not?' And even as she spoke, she could hear the bitterness in her own voice.

'What has happened?' Kai asked, and there was such gentleness to his words that she shivered to hear it. How long had it been since Bahadur had spoken to her in that way?

'I woke in the infirmary,' she said. 'I crawled back from the land of death. And it was not for you, but for Bahadur, that I fought to live. And he was beside me – it was what I hoped for, to see him there. But the way he looked at me...'

'What did you see?'

She paused for a moment, not wanting to speak the words aloud. Then: 'That he wanted me to die.'

Kai shook his head. 'I do not know that can be true.'

'Of course, you will not believe,' she said bitterly. 'And of course, after all that has passed between the two of you, you shall still take his part. But I know what it was that I saw. For if I were dead, he would be free of his pain. He could nurse his wound proudly, and keep my memory like a treasure. A cold, dead, safe thing. A simpler life for him, then.' She looked to Kai, and knew that she was ready to cast him aside too, if she must. 'Do you believe me?' she said.

'It is a fearsome thing,' said Kai, 'to see that in another's eyes. I believe you, for I have seen it myself.'

'And after all that I fought for him. All that I have given to him, and given up for him.' She shook her head. 'But enough of this. Tell me, what will happen now?'

'A war,' Kai answered. 'And I do long for it to come.'

'Yes,' she said, 'it will be a simple thing for you. Like Bahadur, you think enough death may make your life whole again. I know a little now, of why Laimei chose the life that she chose. Why she clung to the horse and spear.' Arite embraced her knees and held them close against herself – some half memory, then, of being held in such a way by another. 'She wanted something that could not be taken away from her. She did not want to meet my fate.'

And she was afraid then. For the hard years stretched out before her – alone, burying men like Kai and Bahadur behind her, much as she had buried her children. Robbed of her spear and freedom both, waiting to die alone.

It seemed that Kai knew it too. For it was gone at once – the hesitance and the restraint, the doubt that had always marked him. Nothing more than a gentle touch, a taking of one of her hands in both of his, clasping them together with the quality of prayer. No more than that.

It had already been decided, of course. When she had called his name by the gate, or long before that. Perhaps from the moment she had met him long ago, back upon the steppe.

When her husband had brought him to their home – a young man, white-faced and weeping, shamed and alone. Bahadur had not known the doom that he had brought back with him, the beautiful, painful love that the three of them would share with each other, that none of them would escape.

But there was peace to know that it was so decided, and above all else, she wished she could share that feeling with Bahadur, that she could make him understand it. For it was true that a great champion knew it was the hand of the gods that guided their horse and spear, but lovers knew it, too. That beautiful, frightening sense of fate. And in his arms, she knew she would find, if nothing else, a forgetting of her pain.

Lucius was alone in the Prefect's quarters. His only company the occasional heavy tread of a sentry outside, the scratch and scuttle of a rat trying to find a path within. Before him, a table piled high with wax tablets – messages, requests, orders. Prefects and Legates spoke wryly of this particular enemy, the real killer of Romans on the fringes of the Empire. Out in the provinces, it was said more men fell on their own swords than died by a barbarian's hand.

A fine joke, Lucius had once thought it, but he knew the truth of it now. For this seemed an empty way to scratch out the years, without a friend at his side. Perhaps that was what had led Legions to their destruction – the Ninth lost beyond the Wall, the three Legions destroyed in the Teutoburg Forest. A commander's mind breaking with solitude, and then a mad, hungry march towards death. And he was frightened then, calling for more wood and stoking the braziers high, like a child who fears the darkness.

He sat there, and he tried to think. Tried to remember the gift of the Sarmatians – that beautiful courage, their hunger to live matched only by their disregard for death. This little flickering, fading light that he had thought to keep alive out here at the edge of the Empire, that he was fated to fight for, perhaps to die for. And he would have to stand his post until then, through the long cold nights, the loneliness and the fear. For them, he would have to live.

He called out to the sentries, was grateful to find his voice held strong, stronger than he felt. And when the man came in – an old, scarred veteran named Saratos – Lucius gave him six names to summon.

'And send me a woman,' Lucius said, 'from the *vicus*.'

The sentry shifted on his feet. 'They do not come to the fort.' *They are not allowed to* – that remained unspoken, for it was Lucius himself who had forbidden it.

'I am sure she will come for a few extra coins,' said Lucius. 'And at my command.'

'Yes sir. Anyone in particular?'

Lucius tried a smile. 'Anyone at all.'

After a time, a rapping at the door, and the six men entered. But one could hardly call them that – more boys than men, the youngest having seen perhaps thirteen summers. They were the youngest in the fort, those unlucky enough to be just old enough to be sent to the west. Birthed a year or even a month later, and they would not have had to leave their homes. But even so, they had the hard eyes of veterans – they fought young, out upon the steppe. They were light and quick, the fastest riders that he had. And if he was to send any of his fighting men from the Wall, away from what was to come, he would rather send them.

In his hand Lucius held the sealed wax tablets. Messages for the south – to Eboracum, Vindolanda and Coria. A moment's hesitation before he handed them over, for it would be war, then, once the report was made. The Sarmatians gathering together from across the Wall and the training grounds to the south, and perhaps even the Sixth Legion would come too. Bloody years lay ahead, once the wax seals were broken open. And he knew all too well that it was always an easier thing to begin a war than to end one.

At last, he handed them over, offered up his orders with a prayer to the god of war. To the god of travellers too, that he might speed the Sarmatians on their way.

For a moment, outside the door, he saw their hard eyes soften, as the boys grinned and laughed with one another. Children once more, out on an adventure in the dark, telling jokes to ward away the fear and daring each other to acts of courage.

Then they were gone, out into the night, and he was alone once more. Waiting for a long time, for a knock upon the door. Waiting for a woman.

Outside, a warm, fresh night, and a half clear sky. The messengers mounted, spare horses with them, the gates rolling upon to the open land beyond, the road a dark line cut into the earth like a path of iron. A clasp of the hands, a wishing of luck, their teeth white under the moonlight as they smiled at one another.

The bright young boys, light in the saddle. The youth of the Sarmatians, taking to the grey roads as the night fell.

None of them would be seen again.

Part 3

THE LOST

20

In the old stories, an evil omen was no subtle thing. A great black bird, as big as a horse, that settled in the high trees and cawed out its prophecy of doom to the people below. A hard west wind that turned the sheep in the fields to stone. A bard seen only under the light of the moon, plucking discordantly at a harp fashioned from the bones and sinews of lost children.

And yet, when the omen came to Cilurnum, it was such a simple thing. A wagon of grain that did not arrive, and a chest of silver that vanished somewhere upon the roads. A supply of food delayed, a late paychest – nothing more than that. Two scratched marks upon birch bark, noting the late arrival, should have been all that came of it. But a part of Lucius knew that sign for what it was. A knowledge that grew more terrible still as the days stretched on, and his messengers did not return.

He doubled strength to the patrols, and personally inspected the grain storage as thoroughly as he studied the walls of the fort, looking for the weak places where his enemies – rats, and damp weather – might pierce the defences. He thought of sending messengers further up and down the Wall, to the forts and milecastles beyond his territory. Yet he found himself too afraid to do it, for reasons he could not say.

Until one morning, the fort woke to find the *vicus* deserted.

The sun rose upon a place of emptiness and silence, save for where a Sarmatian could be seen wandering through the streets in search of his lover, calling out her name in vain. A wine shop that had served late the night before, its Brigante owner laughing and joking with his patrons, now lay empty, the jars of wine smashed open and spilling on the floor, no trace of the laughing man to be found. A cobbler, an old scarred man of the Votadini who had stitched and shod boots for near twenty years in that fort, had vanished and left everything behind, half-finished shoes left scattered across the workshop like ghostly footprints. Only a few of the native women remained behind, kept by some loyalty of the heart or simply with no other place to go. But no matter what their lovers said, pleaded, or threatened, they made no answer. They simply sat upon the ground, glassy eyed and mute. Too loyal to leave, but unable to speak of why they had stayed. The tongues bound by some oath to their tribe, sitting and waiting for death to come.

And when Lucius sent the patrols out into the surrounding countryside, an empty land waited for them. None remained, not even the old men and women they had found before. Crops cut down, pastures emptied of the herds. Even the water was fouled, as again and again they pulled animal carcasses from well and spring. Lucius found himself turning over the furrowed earth in his hands, half expecting to find it glisten with salt, the way the fields of Carthage were said to have been destroyed when the Romans had wiped that city from the earth.

It was as though a vengeful god had swept a curse through the land, gathering away every native in a single moment and sparing the Sarmatians. Yet Lucius knew differently, and looking at his pale-faced companions, he saw that the Sarmatians knew it too. That it was they, the ones who had been left behind, who were cursed to remain.

That night, Lucius did what he had promised himself he would not do. He sent for Kai.

He could not quite say why, or what he wanted. An empty hope, that what had been broken between them might be mended once again, or perhaps the strange compulsion to probe a wound that all warriors knew, to not trust the sight of open flesh and shattered bone unless it was felt again through touch. But if the Sarmatians had taught him anything, it was to trust the dreaming urge, the instinct, the unspoken message from the gods that was found in the longing of the heart. To trust that he would know why later, when it was past mattering.

When the Sarmatian entered the quarters and offered his salute, Lucius did not speak for a time. He studied the man who had once been his friend.

There were hollows under the eyes, the flesh creeping back from the skin. But there a life about Kai too, a lightness to his steps, and a steady gaze answered his own. A jealousy rose, hot and sharp in Lucius's throat, before he swallowed it down like bitter wine. A cruel thing, it seemed, for Lucius to be wounded by their parting more than Kai had been.

'What is your command, sir?' Kai said at last.

'I need you to tell me more,' Lucius answered. 'Of what you and the deserter, Corvus, spoke of beyond the Wall.'

A pleasure, then, to see a flush upon the cheeks. A reminder of Kai's shame.

'You cannot speak?' said Lucius. 'Did he swear you to silence?'

'No,' the Sarmatian answered, 'but I do not know what it is you seek, sir.' He hesitated, then said: 'Tell me what has happened.'

'The fields are empty. The *vicus* too. And the messengers I sent out have not come back.'

'We all know that.'

'And I must know how it has been done. For it seems to me more than the work of a bandit king north of the Wall.'

'You think the boys you sent are dead?'

'In my heart, I know it,' said Lucius. 'And I know that it is the messages they carried that killed them.'

Kai said nothing for a time. Then: 'The deserter, he spoke of friends, south of the Wall. Eyes in the fort, and around it. Perhaps they saw the messengers go.'

'An ambush? It would be quite a feat for this bandit king to take six Sarmatian horsemen on the road. And at night, when they rode to three separate places.'

Kai shook his head. 'You are right. There must be something that we do not see. How did it start?'

'What?'

'We must return to the beginning of things, if we are so lost. The night that we came here. The empty milecastle, and the raid on the south.'

Lucius nodded slowly. 'A deserter would know the forts. Enough, perhaps, to talk his way inside the gates, and butcher the guards.'

'So he takes the women and the children,' said Kai, 'so that

Mor of the Votadini will not act against him. And he gathers together the tribes north of the Wall, and makes his war upon Rome.'

Silence, for a time. Both of them seeking the same thing, to know the mind of Corvus. To imagine the world as the deserter saw it.

Lucius spoke first. 'But a deserter would know about the Sixth Legion,' he said. 'At Eboracum.'

'What of them?'

'Perhaps he may breach the Wall here. Perhaps he might scatter the Sarmatians, if I were dead.' Lucius's mouth twisted. 'Though it seems he thinks too highly of your loyalty to me. But they could not stand against the Sixth Legion. And he would know it.' The Roman hesitated. 'Is he mad, do you think?'

'No,' Kai answered. 'He is not mad. So he thinks that he can defeat them.'

Lucius closed his eyes, put his head into his hands. 'You must think. Something else that he said.'

Once more, the stillness. And then Kai said, offhand, 'He said that the Emperor was dying. It seemed strange to me, that he would know such a thing.'

Lucius lifted his head sharply. 'Are you certain of what you say?'

'Yes.'

And in that moment, perhaps for the last time, a vision shared between them. For they had spent many months making themselves of one mind – in battle, by the fire at night, journeying together upon the roads across the Empire. That fellowship between them was fading now, and yet Lucius was certain that Kai must have seen what he did – a tall horse silhouetted against a night sky. A man with a horse he should not have, who knew things that he could not have known.

'It is not that he thinks he can defeat the Sixth Legion,' Kai said. 'It is that he knows they will not come.'

Lucius knew then why he had brought Kai there. To think what Lucius could not allow himself to believe, to see the treason that a Roman could not see. The truth hung heavy in the air between them – both knew it, and still they did not dare to speak it.

'What will you do?' Kai whispered.

'The only thing that I can do,' Lucius said. 'I shall write another message.' He reached for birch bark and stylus, and was glad to find his hand steady. 'Only now, I know what it is I must ask for.'

21

A few miles south of the fort and the Wall, a circle of standing stones rose upon the top of a hill. Tall and forbidding and silent, mapped out in some pattern that had once been sacred and whose meaning was now forgotten. There must have been power here once, when the stones had rung out with the words of the gods. But the druids had been dead a hundred years, and in this place the gods were silent. Even the Brigantes seemed to shun the place – grieving, perhaps, for the holiness that had been taken from them.

It was there that Lucius waited, ten handpicked men at his side. The Sarmatians had marked this place when they had scouted the land, more as a curiosity than anything else, an ill-omened place best avoided. Yet as a parley ground it might do well enough. There must have been much blood spilled there if half of the stories were true, men gutted beneath the light of the moon and their hearts offered up to the gods. A fine place for another sacrifice to be made.

As the sun rose high above them, Lucius saw a group of riders coming from the south. No warband of the Brigantes or the Carvetii. No chariots or shaggy-haired ponies, no blue warpaint upon bare skin or hair stiffened with lime. Under the light of the sun he could see the gleam of iron, red cloaks trailing behind them, the mark of eagles and lightning bolts, the signature of the Empire. And those riders came towards the hill upon tall Roman horses.

Lucius stirred his own horse forward, went alone to the edge of the stone circle. One of the Romans mirrored his movements, and once more, Lucius saw the easy smile of Caerellius Priscus, Legate of the North, as he took his place a careful distance away. Once more, they spoke alone.

'You are superstitious, perhaps?' said Caerellius. 'To ask me to meet in this place, with the dead gods watching.'

Lucius shook his head. 'A simple place for you to find, and a good vantage point to see how many you brought with you.' He reached out to his side, and touched the old stone that lay aslant beside him, webbed with lichen and moss. 'But perhaps there is some magic still here. For I did not quite believe that you would come.'

'You gave a difficult invitation to refuse. Short, and persuasively written.' And Caerellius quoted Lucius's words back to him. '"Tell me how I may save my people." Like something out of an old story, it was. And besides, I am curious.'

'About how I knew?'

Silent, the Legate nodded.

'The horse,' said Lucius.

'The horse?'

'The Roman cavalry horse that Corvus rode. A strange prize for a bandit. But a fine gift, from a man who had such a thing to give. A Legate. And you do like to offer gifts.'

Caerellius said nothing for a time. Then: 'The horse alone?'

'No. Corvus spoke to one of my men. He knew many things that he should not. About me. About the Emperor. But it was the horse that made me certain.'

'One gives a gift,' the Legate said, 'and so often one is punished for it. It is an ungrateful world.' He shifted in the saddle. 'What is it you wish to know? Some questions, I must tell you, I will not answer.'

'My messengers. The boys that I sent. They are dead?'

Silence answered him. But there was a faint look of distaste on Caerellius face that served as answer enough.

'You might have bargained for their lives,' said Lucius.

'Perhaps,' Caerellius allowed. 'But you are a warrior. You understand that some chances cannot be taken.'

'And you are taking a great one now.'

The Legate nodded slowly.

'I suppose,' said Lucius, 'I only wish to know why. Then you may tell me what I must do.'

Caerellius did not answer for a long time. Several times his mouth would half form a word, go still, and then close with it unspoken. Perhaps he had never had to put his desire into words before. Perhaps it was the first time he could truly speak them, to a man such a Lucius, who was soon to die. A man who did not matter.

'You have not been to Rome in a long time, have you?' Caerellius said.

'No,' Lucius answered. 'I spent the last ten years upon the Danubius. And now I am here.'

'So you will have forgotten of what I speak. To stand upon the Palatine, and look upon the seat of the world. To hear the roaring of the crowd answer your speech in the Forum. To smell the blood of the sacrifice in the Temple of Jupiter, and feel all about you the eminence of the gods. For they must be closer to us there than anywhere else.' He looked around, with a faint look of distaste, at the fallen stones about them. 'Do you think men even truly live in a place like this?'

'We are now. You, I, my men. I will keep them all alive, if I can.'

Caerellius shook his head. 'You do not understand. Can we call it life? Scrabbling in the mud and rain, picking at fleas. Fighting over mangy cattle, or petty bloodfeuds. We are beasts, not men, in this place. Such a life means nothing. But in Rome, we live. We may taste of all the joys of the world, before the long dark. And at the very heart of the world, we may reshape it. Nothing matters more than getting back there.' A pitying look, then, as he said: 'All Romans know this, but you have forgotten.'

'They will never take you home?' said Lucius.

'No,' the Legate answered. 'I am like you. Always to be an exile. But unlike you, I shall not accept it.'

'Tell me what you will do.'

Caerellius turned away then, looked out upon the hills that surrounded them, marked with heather and copses of trees, the scudding clouds rolling overhead. Distant, through mist and cloud, a glimpse of the proud grey Wall. A sight that, to Lucius, seemed suddenly beautiful in a way it had not before.

Then Caerellius began to speak again.

'There will be a rising in the north,' he said. 'A great rebellion that will roll across the Wall, that will need many Legions to defeat. And so they shall send them to me.'

'A disgrace to you,' said Lucius. 'They would strip you of your command.'

'After, of course, but they shall send the Legions first. And when the Emperor ceases to cling to life – and it will be soon, I promise you – those Legions will find a better master in me. They will do what Legions always do, in a time of trouble. They shall raise me on their shoulders, and make a god of me. And we shall march to Rome. That is the future that I see.'

Silence, for a time. 'You do not know it will be so,' said Lucius.

'You do not know his son, Commodus,' the Legate answered. 'A fool. Weak as his father is strong. There is a great war coming among the people of Rome – nothing may stop that. I shall win it, with the Legions. And with your Sarmatians too, perhaps.'

Lucius dropped his gaze. For there was hope at those words, hope so sweet and sharp that he knew he must wear it openly on his face. What a terrible weakness it was, his love for his men.

'I want them alive, you see,' Caerellius said, suddenly gentle. 'That is why we are speaking here now.'

'What of Corvus? What prize shall he have?'

'The Wall? The lands around it?' The Legate shrugged. 'Let him have them. I keep my promises, you see. Let them have this whole miserable little island, if his desires go so far. I shall go to Rome.'

'And the Brigantes and the Votadini?' said Lucius. 'The people who live in the shadow of the Wall, who gave up their war spears and trust in our protection. You will feed them to Corvus and the Painted People?'

'There are ancient feuds between all these tribes. They would kill one another whether we are here or not, you know.' Caerellius shook his head, and his horse shifted restlessly beneath him, answering its master's mood. 'But enough of this,' the Legate said. 'We come to the end, and there is no more time.'

'I ask you again,' said Lucius. 'What must I do? To save my people?'

'Your people?' Caerellius answered, a note of disbelief in his voice. 'You truly are lost, aren't you? This is what I offer you.' And the Legate raised his hand, levelled his finger towards the pommel of Lucius's sword. 'You may find your honour in the Roman way, and fall upon that. Free your Sarmatians of their oaths to you, and they shall make their own choices. Some will go to Corvus. Some shall swear to me – they shall ride in a place of honour in my army. For I can give them what you cannot. I can give them what they truly wish for – I can send them home to the steppe, to Sarmatia.'

'I know what their place of honour will be,' Lucius replied. 'A place at the front of every battle. Their blood spilled to spare the Legions.'

'True enough. But more shall go home by my way than by yours. And your Sarmatians shall thank me for the war.'

Lucius said nothing for a time. Silent, he sought another path than the one that the Legate had offered him, even as he saw a patient smile spread across Caerellius's lips. The way a good swordsman will smile on the sparring ground when he knows he has nothing to fear.

'I know what you are thinking,' said the Legate. 'If only you could take a message to your Sarmatians, the others who are scattered across the north. It is true, there are many of them. But in between you and them lie those loyal to me. On either side of you on the Wall, in the lands around us. You are alone out here, Lucius. You may take the quick death of your own sword, or wait for the slow death that Corvus will give you.'

'We Romans have always thought that quick death upon the sword a thing of honour,' said Lucius. 'But the Sarmatians think the slow death the braver choice.'

Caerellius hissed through his teeth. 'Yes,' he said, 'I feared it. I see you are determined to cling to your pride – it will keep you in cold company at night, I think. Perhaps it is your men you hold on to, thinking they are your sworn companions. Your Sacred Band, like the Thebans used to have? They shall abandon you too.'

'It may be so,' Lucius answered. 'But I think there will come a time when you need someone to stand proudly beside you. To give their life for yours. And you will have no gold or favour to bribe them with – what use are such things to a man about to die? You will have to offer them something that is worth more than their lives to them, and I do not think you know what that is.'

And Lucius saluted him then – the quick snap of the arm, the hand upon the heart. For a moment there was a trace of shame upon Caerellius's face, for in that salute was memory of a different kind of Rome, long since forgotten.

Lucius watched him ride away, re-join his bodyguards, head for the south. Alone for a moment, in that circle of stone, his fingers upon the pommel of the sword. A difficult business, to gut oneself with a cavalry sword. It was too long, and the gladius would be better for it. He should have remained a Legionary if that was to be his path. Yet if ever there were a place and a time for it, it was then, in that circle.

But then a man was at his side – Bahadur, reaching out a hand and laying it upon Lucius's sword arm. Lucius's back had been turned to him – some sign, perhaps, even so. A hunch in the shoulder, a nodding of the head, the way a hand slowly, reluctantly, drifted towards a sword.

When he had chosen the men to follow him to the stone circle, Lucius had chosen Bahadur without quite knowing why. But perhaps in his heart, he knew there was some kinship between them, a kinship founded in betrayal. For the older man smiled gently at Lucius then, and what a rare thing that was, these days. And Lucius could see something there, of the man that Kai had once loved as a brother.

'Will you take us home, sir?' said Bahadur.

And in the end, that was all that it took to stay his hand – for a time, at least.

22

All about Arite, it seemed, the world was ending – the omens clustering thick as ravens after a battle, whisperings of curse and rebellion and war to be heard wherever men spoke to one another in the empty streets of the *vicus*. Yet for all of this, Arite knew no fear. Only that impossible sense of luck that comes to a young rider before the charge, the sense of time suspended.

The days she spent once more with horse and spear, taking her place on the practice grounds with the warband. Relearning the arts of killing that she had sought to forget, for all knew that war was coming, and she was still warrior enough to long for a proud death in the rush of battle. And the nights she spent with Kai, a different kind of remembrance, her fingers tracing scars and tattoos, a mapping of a body once so familiar to her. The beautiful relearning of what it was to be loved.

None of it could last, of course. All spells were broken eventually, the stories told, and all memories were, in the end, as dust. And she knew the end was coming when she heard that Lucius had taken his bodyguards, Bahadur among them, and ridden out of the fort. Dressed for war, and yet riding to the south and not the north, to face an enemy of a different kind.

After she heard that they had returned – alive, unbloodied, yet still with the look of defeat about them – she went in search of Bahadur.

She found him marked with dirt and dust from a long day in the saddle, surrounded by his spear brothers as he haggled for a meal beside a smoking cookfire. A clutch about the heart at the sight of him, a fear that lasted only a moment. For when Bahadur saw her, he smiled, waved to her a carefree greeting, strolled over to speak with her with a lightness to his step.

'May I swallow your evil days,' he said as he approached – the old greeting of the steppe.

'Where have you been?' she said.

'Oh, on a parley of sorts.'

'I heard that it was south of the Wall,' she said softly, 'and not to the north. A strange place to parley.'

He offered a shrug. 'North or south,' he said, 'I think there is no difference in the danger now. We have enemies on all sides.'

'Then I am glad to see you safe returned.'

'And I am glad to see you.' Some little warmth in the words, like embers after a winter's fire.

'Bahadur—'

He shook his head. 'There is no need to speak of it. I understand all now, what I have done to you. Too late, but that is the way of the stories is it not?' He paused for a moment, seeming lost in memory. 'You remember the story that Saratos used to tell?' he said. 'Of Balin and Balan?'

She did – the tale of two brothers, whom chance and fate brought to the battlefield against each other. Neither recognised the other until the moment the spears drove home, all for the amusement of the cruel gods. Yet the brothers had died in each other's arms, each swearing his love to the other. A happy tale, the Sarmatians called it, one told to children for them to act out – duelling and dying in a close embrace, lying still for a moment, then springing, laughing, to their feet to do it all over again.

'That is what that story tries to teach us,' Bahadur continued. 'That we shall understand the truth too late.' He hesitated, then said: 'You are happy?'

'I do not know,' she answered.

'Well, that is honest enough.' He looked away, ran a hand through the thick braids of his hair.

'What shall happen now?' she said.

'I am no dream reader, who may tell the future.'

'Yet I think you know something of it, all the same.'

'Perhaps that may be true,' he said. He turned back, a strange tenderness in the way he looked at her. 'You have heard that Laimei is with the Votadini, north of the Wall? You should go there to join her.' He hesitated, then said: 'And you should take Kai with you, too.'

'Why?'

A shaking of the head – sharp and sudden, as a man struck by palsy. Some sworn secret, news too terrible to be spoken of. But he was smiling, even so, a bright and brilliant smile, like a child with a secret.

'Why do you smile?' she said.

'Why do you think?' he answered. 'There is to be no more waiting for me. I am to get what I wish for more than anything else.' And with that, he wandered away into the streets, chuckling merrily to himself, an arm draped companionably across the shoulders of one of his spear brothers. She watched him go, knowing all too well the joy that gave such a lightness to his steps. For her people longed only to be brave – the greatest treasure that they knew. And for the countless boasts that were made by the fire, all knew the way fear struck before the battle. A shock like cold water, that bowed the head and stilled the limbs. And for all the boasting talk and the promises that had been made, there was no courage to be found, nothing to carry a warrior through the battle without shame. It was such a difficult thing, to be brave.

Yet there was one thing that made such courage come easy. She saw it all about her, then, for that half-abandoned *vicus* had the reckless air of a festival. The wine flowing freely, voices lifted in the high, winding songs of the steppe.

The Sarmatians had no place to run to, no chance that they might live beyond the battle, no quarter to be asked or given. And so instead they had that last gift of the gods to doomed men – the hopeless bravery that comes only when death is certain.

It was with a heavy tread that Lucius paced along the walls of the fort. Step after step, over and over again, a man seeking to outpace his destiny. Yet the path of the walls was squared, and soon enough Lucius found himself once more where he began.

As night had fallen, a calm fell too upon the fort, a calm that had followed their return from the circle of stones. No longer the sudden quarrels in the street, the keening of grief echoing out for those who had been lost. No longer the even more frightening sounds that had followed, songs and laughter echoing from the walls. Only a stillness, a waiting.

An end to uncertainty, of jumping at shadows in the dark. No curse or mystery working upon them any more, but an enemy they would soon see and touch. No matter that the enemy was numberless to the north and the south, only that the battle would come soon.

He had hoped to find some clarity of thought, up in this place. To feel the wind upon his skin and smell the smoke upon the air from the cooking fires, and find some way to save his people. Yet every time that he would try to think, his eye would be caught by some sight from the streets below. A band of men weaving drunkenly through the *vicus*, singing the sweet sad songs of the steppe. Another standing alone, tending a horse in the street, stroking its mane and whispering to it like a lover. A young warrior laughing as he tried one perfume after another from a stallholder in the marketplace, casting away a month's wages upon musk and rosewater. The Sarmatians had never seemed so completely full of life, here at the eve of their end.

One more turn about the walls, he promised himself. One more, and then perhaps it would be time for the path that Caerellius had offered to him. A tall cup of unwatered wine to dull the mind, a sword braced against a pillar, a pressing of flesh into iron. Darkness, and freedom.

Yet, at last, something had changed – a figure waiting for him, as he went once more about the walls. A shadow in the darkness, until they both drew close enough to a torch to see one another. And it was no sentry bearing cuirass and spear, no assassin sent by his enemies to the north or the south. In the light of the fire he saw braided hair of gold and silver, the long, proud face of Arite.

'I hope I may be welcome here,' she said.

'I shall have to speak to the sentries,' Lucius answered, 'if they let up women upon the Wall at night.'

'Do not punish them too harshly,' she said. 'I spun a great story of love between us that they believed.'

He could not help but laugh at that. 'They should still know better.'

'They do love you, Lucius,' she said gently. 'They wish for your happiness. There should be no punishment for that.'

Lucius looked away. Out to the north, where, upon the horizon, he could see the flickering sign of a fire. Some hunter of the Votadini, perhaps, sharing a deer carcass with his family, trading stories without a care in the world for the Romans on the Wall. Or a scout of the Painted People, come to watch and wait, to signal to his master when the Sarmatians were starved enough to fight. When none but ghosts watched upon the Wall.

'I thank you for your words,' he said at last. 'You were so kind to me, out upon the steppe.'

'And you have been kind in turn.'

Lucius hesitated. 'Kai would not say so.'

'He has hurt you. I know this.'

'We have hurt each other, it seems.' Lucius shook his head. 'It does not matter. None of it matters now.'

'So Bahadur tells me.' Seeing his expression, Arite smiled gently, and said: 'Oh, do not worry, he has broken no oath of secrecy. But we all know that some disaster is coming. Do not take me for a fool.'

He turned from her then, leaning against the Wall, looking out towards the northlands. 'You did not come to speak of Kai.'

'No, I did not.'

'What then?'

'To talk of what brings you here at night. To stare beyond the Wall, and to think, and to try to find a way out.'

He did not answer for a time. Then: 'What do you know?'

'Only that no one in this fort thinks to live to see another full moon.'

Lucius tilted his head towards the sky then, to see a white half crescent rising through the clouds. 'There will be a great host coming from the north,' he said. 'And there will be no help coming from the south.'

'A simple thing, spoken that way.'

'If only the answer were so simple.' He looked back to her. 'You think that you may have an answer? That you may know something the others do not?'

'Perhaps. For they are all death mad. It is our way – it was my way, too, when I held a spear in the warband. They hear the call of the horns and see the light upon the spears, and can think of nothing else. A beautiful death against impossible odds. They shall die happy.' She tilted her head to the side. 'Is that what you want?'

'Often, your people have called me one of your own,' said Lucius. 'A Sarmatian soul in a Roman body. Perhaps it is a little true, but in this I am unlike your people. I do not want a beautiful death. I want to win.'

She nodded. 'Bahadur says that I should flee to the north. That I should take Kai with me.'

'Will you?'

'No. I do not care to run.' A careful smile. 'I am like you, perhaps. I like to win.'

'But I cannot see how.'

She thought for a time. 'The Legate has betrayed you. If there is no help to come from the south. That is where you went today?'

Lucius nodded.

'A man such as that,' Arite said, 'his word cannot be trusted. Men will not believe in him, the way they believe in you.'

'No,' said Lucius. 'He shall have the leaders – the Prefects, the centurions. But it will be enough, and most of the Legionaries and Auxiliaries will follow wherever there is silver and slaves to be taken.'

'There must be some whose honour will be offended. To have us left here to die, and the Wall broken open.'

'Some. Many, perhaps. But we have no way to give word to them. And would they believe us, if we did?'

'And the Sarmatians? How many of our people are close by?'

'Five hundred near Vindolanda. Five hundred more at Vercovicium. Three thousand more near Eboracum. But we cannot reach them. And it would be death to them, if they abandoned their posts without orders.'

He heard her hiss with frustration. 'You see why our people do not care to be locked up in these stone tombs of yours. Why we care little for rank and command. Would that were upon the steppe…'

'Maddening, is it not? They are so close, yet they might still been in Sarmatia, for all that they can help us.'

Together, they stared out towards the northlands. Arite drew her cloak close about her, blew on her hands as a ward against the cold, or perhaps for luck. She had a look about her that Lucius had seen before, in the eyes of centurions and Legates. Once he had even seen it in the eye of an Emperor.

Plan and strategy weighed and discarded, the cold balancing of lives and chance – the search for victory at any cost. The Sarmatians had lost a great war leader, he thought to himself, when Arite had put up her spear.

'There is some answer, I think,' she said. 'It scratches at the corners of my mind. But I cannot see it yet.'

'You think that the gods mean to make us wait for that answer?'

'Or help us not at all. But we must wait for now. Though I think there is little time left. Very little.' She smiled gently at him. 'Until then, do not think to fall upon your sword.'

He started at that, a guilty gesture that she laughed at. 'It is as obvious as that?' he asked.

'Oh, you are death mad, too, in your own way. But by your own hand, not another's. The Roman way, I have heard it called. Always thinking that to throw yourself upon your sword will make another man's life better.' She looked suddenly serious, reached out and took his hand. Such joy at the simple comfort of the touch – he had not known how lonely he was, until that moment.

'You must live, if you can,' she continued. 'So much rests upon you. We are a shamed and broken people, our names taken by our conqueror. And you are our Great Captain and war leader. If you die, we shall not long outlive you.'

He put his other hand to his heart and nodded, not trusting himself to answer with words. It was only when she turned from him, making slowly for the way down from the Wall, that more words came to him.

'Tell Kai that I forgive him,' said Lucius. 'That I wish him all the happiness in the world.'

He meant the words kindly, but still she flinched as though

struck. 'Bahadur said something similar,' she said. 'But I shall give him your words, and I thank you for them.' And then, she was gone.

Lucius turned back, once more towards the north. To feel the cutting wind upon his face and wait for some word from the gods. Yet a little lighter about the heart, the relief that comes with true words spoken. And the comfort of knowing this – whether the gods spoke to him or kept their silence, whether there would be some miracle to save them or one final ride into darkness and forgetting, he would find out soon enough.

23

In the darkness beyond the Wall, Kai waited.

He was alone, and yet not alone. For he knew his companions were close – two picket lines of sentries, two walls of flesh and blood to guard the great Wall of stone that rose behind him. But he could not see or hear them, for they were spread thin across the hill and the heather. His last sight of his companions had come many hours before, when a man rode past Kai to take his place at the furthest line of sentries. Kai could only trust that they were still out there.

He pulled his cloak close about him, and when he shivered it was not just from the cold. For the Sarmatians had learned to be brave when they hunted in great warbands, when they fought in open fields beneath the light of the sun. But this lonely waiting in the dark was a thing of nightmares to them.

Yet he knew it had to be done, as Lucius ordered. They could not leave themselves unguarded against the horde that was coming from the north. And so night after night they went out and waited, buying time for their commander to think. Waiting for a miracle that would not come.

Kai passed the long cold hours in the only way that he knew how: thinking of Arite, memories that he clasped close in the dark like a treasure jealously guarded. Before their love had been a thing tainted with shame, and now, she had chosen him openly. What lay between her and Bahadur was truly broken, and by Bahadur's doing. He thought about the joy of their loving, and better, the whisperings afterwards, when they lay in each other's arms and spoke simple truth to each other. And though he knew that he should love in the Sarmatian way, that careless kind of love that thought a day of love as good and true as a decade, he knew he could not. His heart was like a Roman's, ever greedy, wishing to build a monument that would endure against all that might destroy it.

A whispering fear still came with those memories – the fear that he was not worthy of the love she gave him, that he would, in the end, be found wanting. And that night, there was something else, too, a cold and creeping sensation that stole over him the longer his watch stretched on.

It was no false fear, no thing of ghostly imaginings – out there beyond the Wall, he had none of the Roman ways of counting the time, no waterclock or hourglass to tell him when his time was over. The wind too high to hear the sounding of horn and drum from the Wall, the clouds too thick above for him to judge the passage of the moon and the stars. Only the nomad's instinct, that same knowledge that guided the birds south before the killing winds came, sent the bear to his cave before the snows fell. He knew it spoke true to him. He knew that the man from the line ahead should have returned by now.

The heavy step of hooves behind him – too heavy to bring any fear with them, for no enemy would move so carelessly in the night. They were accompanied by the familiar rattle and rasp of a Sarmatian scale cuirass, and then by the calling of a password: 'The River,' he heard a voice say in the Sarmatian tongue.

'The Dragon,' Kai answered.

The man sent to relieve him approached, and Kai saw it to be a silver-haired warrior called Saratos.

The older man blew on his hands against the cold, and said: 'You need any further invitation? Get back to the fort.'

'I cannot,' Kai answered, and levelled his spear forward, towards where he knew the second picket line was. 'The man from the next line has not come back.'

'Who is it?'

'Tor, of the Shining Company.'

Saratos hissed through his teeth. 'Tor. Useless bastard. Asleep on his horse, I think, soaked in too much wine. Forget him. Get back.'

'I cannot.'

Even in the darkness, Kai could see the white of teeth, a weary smile on Saratos's face. 'Very well, then. Let us go together and wake him up.' And in spite of the smile and the carefree words, he saw Saratos take the bow from the peak of his saddle, test the weight of the string, for he was one of the few Sarmatians left who still knew the old steppe art of archery.

Together, they went into the dark, their horses taking slow, reluctant steps. Kai and Saratos listening more than seeing, for in the night their ears were of better use to them than their eyes, even with the traitor wind blowing hard all about them. It brought them no sound at all – not the rattle of cuirass or the whicker of a horse or the rustling footfall of a man. It brought them only silence.

On and on they went until it seemed that they must have gone beyond their lines. A shiver of fear settling between one footfall and the next, the same sensation that comes upon a man in the water who suddenly knows himself too far from the shore. But then the wind brought with it a comforting, familiar sound, the gentle whinny of a horse.

Kai chanced a whistle, and following it, he called the password: 'The River.'

And from somewhere ahead, he heard the answering call: 'The Dragon.'

Saratos was grinning at him then, calling out into the night. 'Tor, you stupid bastard. Get back here before…'

But his speech trailed away – a knowledge that followed slow behind the words, the way that thunder follows lightning. For there was something wrong in the way that Tor spoke – a voice like his, and yet not. A lingering upon the words that no true Sarmatian would speak. A mimicry, the way demons spoke with the tongues of men to lure their companions into a trap.

And in that moment, the world held still – a gift from the gods that comes when death is close and the odds are against you, the fair chance offered to the brave. And Kai saw it all.

A red-headed man nocking an arrow to his bow, a trio of spearmen rising from the heather, naked and blue painted. Shapes upon the hillside, mounted men descending and cutting around behind them. He saw too a shadow upon the ground, the shadow of a horse and a man. Tor and his mount, lying still upon the earth.

And he saw something beyond it all, something too great and terrible to truly understand in that moment.

For there was no time to think, only to lead, to go towards

the worst of the danger, those mounted men who had looped behind, and try and cut a way through. The ground seeming to jump and roll beneath them, the tribesmen growing tall and distinct as they raised their bows and set their spears.

But Saratos was answering in kind, arrows loosed in return. One of their warriors fell to the ground screaming, his face curtained in blood, and the line was wavering before them, the shock of the charge as Kai's palms were struck numb as the spear shivered in his hands, felt the stumble of his horse as a man rolled beneath its hooves.

Then they were through, cutting back towards the safety of the Wall. They were almost free – the horses had their wind once more, the ground open ahead of them, the war songs of the northmen falling away behind them. A scatter of arrows through the air, shot almost blind in the half-light, unaimed and trusting only to luck. Yet one still found its mark.

It was a jealous god who guided it – one of the old, nameless gods of the east, the lord of eye and arrow who had few followers left to him. And now that god was calling home the last archer of the steppe, for when Kai turned in the saddle, answering a soft whisper of his name, it was Saratos he saw, pierced through by the arrow.

His eyes wide and dull as a drowning man's, a hand reaching forward, trembling and shaking, all the old warrior's years suddenly falling upon him all at once. Almost graceful as he tipped forward and lay against the neck of his horse, one arm wrapped around it as though in a lover's embrace. The horse stumbling to a halt – mistaking the weight across its back for a command, or perhaps, with the kinship of horse for its master, it had no wish to outlive him.

Kai could not stop. Only press forward and watch long

enough to see the tribesmen gathered about Saratos's horse, to claim their prize in flesh. There might still have been some sign of life – a twitch of the hand, an arm rolling against the face to ward away sight of the killers who gathered there. Then the knives were rising and falling, the horse was screaming into the open air, and Kai did not want to see any more.

He rode until his horse could run no farther, its sides foamed in sweat, breath gasping and rattling in its chest. An old man could have walked them down at that moment, but the land was empty around them, the long loop of the Wall growing tall on the horizon. The fear receding, and only the nausea and weariness that comes after the battle, the weight of shame that settles when a man runs for his life.

But he knew that he would not have to contend with that shame for long. That soon it would be washed away, as all things are, in blood.

For he had given one last look back as they fled, the way those in the old stories, fleeing the Otherworld, were cursed to look back one more time and so doom themselves. Beyond the hunters who had ambushed them, the tribesmen butchering man and horse, Kai had seen something else. The shadows upon the horizon, lurking among the trees, scurrying between the folds in the land. No mere raiding party or band of scouts, but the men of the northlands, gathering in their thousands, to sweep the Romans from the Wall once and for all.

At the gate Kai called the watch word to the sentries, but they hardly seemed to hear him – he could hear the shouts breaking out high, for it seemed they saw the Painted People too. Stumbling with exhaustion, he made his way to the tower and the stairs. For weary as he was, he wished to see the death that came for them.

It had been no trick of the mind, no false alarm. They were there, clear to be seen and making no effort to hide their numbers. The horizon marked with shifting silhouettes, the banners of bone and hide raised high, the Painted People come southwards in numbers not seen for half a hundred years.

And at that moment, he felt a hand settle upon his. No need to look and see whose it was, for he knew it by pattern and scar alone. No wondering as to how she had known where to look for him, for always it was that she seemed to know when he needed her most.

'I wish we had been given more time,' he said to Arite.

'It was time enough,' she answered.

He pulled her close to him, lifted the gold and silver braids of her hair to his lips, and wished that what she said were true.

All around them the horns were blowing, the signal beacons lit. But the horns were swallowed by the wind without any answer echoing back to them; the distant towers to the east and the west remained dark. They were alone there, it seemed.

Then, as if in mocking answer, there was an answer in flame on the plain before them. A great fire, some terrible ritual of the Painted People. For Kai could see his companions there, the sentries lost to the darkness, like bloody guests at a feast. Men and horses raised upon the tall spears, silhouettes against the flames, as the warriors of the northlands made their trophy of war and danced before it.

All across the Wall, Kai could see the Sarmatians staring at that fire. Not with rage or disgust, but a strange kind of longing. For all fire was sacred to their people – the ritual flames that rose high upon the steppe, the little campfires they had gathered around with sworn companions, those victory pyres that had burned after battle. A lifetime for the nomads spent tracing the path from one fire to the next. And now the last point of their journey was lit before them.

A catching of breath beside him, a tightening of her hand against his. And there was no need for her to speak why, for they both saw it then as they looked upon the fire – a vision of how their people might be saved, the two of them of one mind. And how Kai wanted to believe that this was what had brought them together. The pain they had caused, the bonds that had been broken – all of it had been destined and fated so they would stand in this place together and hear the message of the gods.

A close embrace, and he could hear her laughing softly, the breath hot against his ear. A sound not of hope or certainty, but of a fate made uncertain, a destiny called into doubt. The way Kai had once seen a man on the battlefield, cut open and half his blood soaked into the tall grass of the steppe, stagger to his feet and take a dozen more steps before collapsing for the final time. That man had laughed, too, laughed with the joy of choosing one place to die over another. To have, for one last moment, a hand in the shaping of his fate.

'It must be you,' Arite said to him as they broke the embrace. 'You must go to Lucius, and tell him what must be done.'

He nodded, unthinking, for it was the gods who spoke through her, and there was no doubting them. And he was moving along the Wall, pushing past the Sarmatians, towards the tower where the familiar figure stood.

Lucius did not seem to see Kai approach – his gaze fixed

upon the fire, stone-faced, lips moving in some silent prayer of his people. The Roman's mail was bright, for no doubt he had passed the days as many of them had, in polishing and burnishing his arms and armour, the warrior's vain desire to be glorious even in death.

And when Kai took his arm, the Roman recoiled from the touch, a kind of disgusted weariness upon his face. What a cruelty it must have seemed to Lucius, that even in the facing of his death, he would have to look upon Kai again and remember his betrayal.

Kai had to shout to be heard, for here there was no silence. All discipline broken, men calling curses and singing their death songs, or looking to Lucius and shouting for orders that would not come. 'You must burn it all, Lucius,' said Kai.

Empty eyes stared back. It seemed the Roman did not understand.

'Burn the fort, Lucius. Let that be our signal.'

Still, it seemed that Lucius did not see it. For the Roman was lost somewhere in the workings of his mind, the winding paths that a man follows when he believes himself defeated, seeking refuge in memory or tormenting himself with what might have been done to turn his fate aside.

Kai tried once more. 'The gods speak through fire,' he said. And at last, it seemed that Lucius heard him.

For a moment all was as it once had been. The pair of them clinging to one another and laughing, like half-drowned men in sight of land at last.

Not a certainty that they might be saved – barely more than a glimmer of hope. But at the least, one last act of defiance, a spear thrown at the eye of a vengeful god. And in that moment, it seemed as though that might be enough.

24

The barracks went up first – the hay catching fast and crawling up the columns, the tiles sliding and smashing from the roof as the rafters cracked and split. The ladders and staircases that fed the Wall caught next, the flames hidden at first within the stone, then the smoke boiling out and up until the fire broke free and reached up like a beckoning hand into the sky.

From outside the fort, gathered up upon the parade ground, the Sarmatians watched their home burn.

When Lucius had given his orders, there had been no hesitation. It was as if it had been something known in the heart of these people, an unspoken longing that every Sarmatian had felt since they made their home in that tomb of stone that was finally given voice.

And so they had moved at once. Stacks of cloth laid up against the walls and lantern oil poured upon them, flaming brands taken from bread ovens and the blacksmith's fire. A whisper of prayer, a touch of a hand to the heart, and then in a dozen places across the fort, acting as one, the Sarmatians had laid flame to fuel and let the fire burn. For it was how the

Sarmatians had always greeted both life and death. To mark the turning of the seasons, the beginning of a war, the coming of peace – always, there was fire.

From beyond the Wall, the wind brought the words of the Painted People – the war chants rising at first, the hoots and calls of tribes that saw the fire as a sign of their victory. But as it grew higher and higher, the chants weakened, faded, fell to silence. For they must have known then that this could be no accident, no drunkard tipping an oil lantern into a storeroom, no brazier knocked into silk and cloth. This was something deliberate – a portent, a ritual, and a signal.

The gods had cleared the skies for them, leaving none of the rolling cloud that so often masked the stars. For many miles about, as dusk gave way to night, all would see that light marking the sky, their enemies and their friends alike.

For now, the Sarmatians stood alone, five hundred mounted men in row and column, the light of the fire shining upon cuirass and spear. No war cries or death songs rising from them, no sound at all. They were utterly still. An army of statues, or of the dead – that was how they seemed to Lucius, as he looked upon them, and tried to think of what he must say.

They were waiting for him. Still, it seemed, they believed in him. And perhaps they believed enough to hear the truth.

'They will be coming for us soon,' Lucius said at last. 'From the north and south, our enemies. Thousands of them. From the north and the south, our friends too. I cannot speak for their numbers. And I cannot say if any will answer the fire.'

He pointed first to the Wall, and then to the great ditch of the *vallum* behind them. 'Not one step back, our orders are. The Romans will raise us upon crosses if we flee from this place, outnumbered as we are.' In spite of himself, he smiled. 'Though I know that the numbers mean nothing to you.'

At another time, that would have drawn laughter from them, boasts, oaths of heroism. But they remained silent now, for it was death they faced. A holy thing, it was to them. They would go to it bravely, he knew, but they would have to know why.

'I must tell you this,' he said. 'If by some miracle we fight and live to see another dawn, you shall not be given what you have been promised. Twenty-five years you swore to Rome, but she shall not give you your reward. There is no journey home, at the end of all this. You shall never see the steppes of Sarmatia again. That is gone. I promised what I could not give to you.'

Something like a sigh, echoing around from one man to the next. A whisper of noise, but no more than that. Perhaps, in their hearts, they had known this, too.

'And so,' Lucius said, 'the sword oaths you gave bind you no longer. You have a choice.' He nodded towards the Wall. 'Ride carefully and you may slip past the army of the Painted People to the north, carve out a piece of land to call your own. The gates lie burned open, and there are none to stop you.' Lucius tilted his spear down towards the ground. 'Or you may stand here, with me, and fight.'

Still, the silence. The firelight falling upon dulled eyes, the eyes of dead men.

'If you stay, it is twenty-five years' service to liars. A home here at the end of it, in this country. That is all that remains.' Lucius shook his head. 'I thought to build a new Sarmatia here. Perhaps I still can. But I make no more promises of the future. Only an oath I can keep, an oath of war. For there will be a battle here soon. No more than that can I promise. No more than the next day.'

He breathed in deep – the smell of the smoke, the sweat of the horse beneath him, the light rain lifting the scent from heather and bracken. 'I do not choose to run,' he said. 'But what you choose – that is up to you.' Once more, he levelled his spear towards the fire upon the Wall. 'You may go to the north, and be enemies of Rome once more.' He let it sweep down, and score a line across the earth. 'Or you may stand here, with me, and fight.'

Still, the silence held. Yet in that silence, it seemed the Sarmatians spoke without words. The shift of a horse, the creak of armour, the tilt of a spear. A glance from one man to another, a tongue rolling across dry lips, a gloved hand touching a tattoo and remembering the oath that had inspired it. A hundred beats of the heart, perhaps, while the Sarmatians communed in sight and gesture, and decided their fate together.

Then they moved all at once – a single step towards the Wall. Lucius thought it certain that more would follow, enough steps to lead them beyond the border and into the darkness beyond. And there was a sense of relief, then. To know that they might live another day at least. To know they would not die with him.

But it was one step only. And the spears were lifting high, the light of the fire falling upon the iron, and the voices raised, a chant sounded by one and taken up by all. Only two words, repeated again and again.

'Death! Lucius! Death! Lucius!' Not one of the old songs that had led them to war in the east, the chants of iron and gold, the hope of the reward they would receive to honour their bravery. It was a song for their Great Captain, a promise of blood and doom for the old gods. And Lucius was weeping then – not for the loyalty they showed him, but for the madness that he had led them to.

For he was a priest at a dark ritual, the making of a bloodpact. Perhaps this was how the druids at Yns Mon had felt a century before, as the Legion closed all about them, as the smoke of the sacred groves hung thick in the air as they burned, and they led their naked warriors into battle one last time, calling out curses, praying to the gods who would not listen. One final lighting of the fire, before it went out forever.

The battle to come would be no beautiful thing, no place to prove honour and valour. And so what held the Sarmatians there was the joy of the killing, that mad hunger that was the curse of their people, the price that was paid for their bravery. But it was, too, the keeping of a promise. To stand and fight where they had said they would. To stand and die for themselves.

And they were about him then, the rows and columns broken into a swirling mass. All the Roman tenets of rank and discipline forgotten, and there were hands reaching forward to clasp his arm, fingers touching his brow in blessing, men leaning in close to him to laugh and howl like wolves. And he was laughing and howling with them – for here, at least, was something beautiful. The love they felt for one another, with the shadow of death hanging over them. Brothers once more.

Then the horns sounding out, the captains calling them back to ranks. And just as quickly as they had been his brothers, they were his soldiers once again.

He led them beyond the river and into the *vallum*, into the woods. To wait for the enemy to come. And before then, to make their partings and say their farewells.

25

Close to five hundred men watched the fort burn, and listened to Lucius speak. And there among them, silent and unnoticed, was one woman.

For now that Laimei had gone to the northlands beyond the Wall, Arite was the last of the warrior women left among the Sarmatians. The warband was still hollow, the old songs of death only half sung, missing the high voices of the women to make them whole. And so she was there as an emissary, the last child of the Amazons, to bring them what blessing and what counsel she could, to remind them of who they were meant to be. For in that silence that fell after Lucius gave them their choices, she too had a voice without words, as her people decided what it was that they would do.

More keenly than Lucius could possibly know, she felt how close the warband came to abandoning him. How much it cost them to give up that chance of freedom, that promise of the open country to the north. And perhaps it was her presence that swayed them one way rather than another – the last of the Amazons, imploring them to stand, and fight, and die.

Then orders were given, the warband divided under the captains as they split and scattered. And all about her, the clasping of hands, the exchanging of little gifts – all the signs of feuds being settled. For in peace, there were none so proud or quarrelsome as her people, as each day brought another knife fight over a stray insult, another friendship broken for the love of a woman. Yet when the battle was close, all might be forgiven, and all about here she saw men dismounted, tottering around like children in their bowlegged way, smiling and laughing together. She knew there was but a little time left to do what must be done.

She found Bahadur on the fringes of the warband. She knew he would be there, for always he sought the quiet places before a battle, to sit and think and be alone. He did not seem to notice her approach – it was only when she knelt beside him, took his rough, scarred hand into her own, that he at last seemed to see her. A smile for a moment, bright and brilliant, until she gently brought him to his feet and began to lead him through the crowd. He understood what she intended then, and his feet dragged and caught upon the ground, as she led him to where Kai was waiting.

For a time, the two men looked upon each other in silence. Nothing but the light of the stars that made shadows of them both, but still it seemed she could see them both so clearly. Silver in Bahadur's hair, lines of weariness and pain etched into the skin, but lines of old laughter too from the lost days of wine and song. And Kai, the old marks of the clan cut away from his cheeks, younger than Bahadur and yet older all at once. She wondered if they knew how similar they were –

not in the way they looked, but in the little gestures each had learned from the other. A finger brushing across the lips and leaving a smile behind it, the proud toss of the head when they were asked a question they did not like.

'We may be at the end here,' she said. 'There is no more time left. I have loved you both, and hurt you both. And ask that here you make peace.'

'It is much that you ask,' Bahadur said.

'Much,' she said, 'and very little. The lightest of things.'

'I do not know that it is so,' Kai said. 'I have given you much to bear, Bahadur. You have suffered for me, and I am sorry for it.' He hesitated, then said, 'And I know a little of what hurt comes with a broken promise.'

'Yes,' said Bahadur, 'perhaps it is that you do know. The gods taking my revenge for me, do you think?'

Kai made no answer. Distant, the calling of the captains for their men to mount and arm. The moment ebbing and drifting away.

'No,' Bahadur continued, 'I do not think it so. The gods do not take my part. They favour the brave.'

'You have always been brave,' Kai said quietly.

'As have you,' Bahadur answered. 'Yet we would still, I think, call ourselves shamed men. Perhaps in this we are still alike.'

Again, the captains' voices sounding. The rattle of armoured men taking to horse, the restless stamping of the horses themselves.

'It is time,' Arite said. 'Speak it now, or do not speak it at all.'

The silence hung between them a moment longer. Then Kai said, tentatively: 'Though our lives be short...'

'Let our fame be great,' Bahadur answered. He shook his head. 'I suppose there shall be a good song at the end of this day.' He looked towards the Wall, the light of the burning fort playing across his face. 'I do not know if there is any fame to be found here,' he said. 'But it is true. Our lives are short – a few hours more, perhaps. It seems a shame to waste them on hate.'

'It does,' Kai said softly.

'May I swallow your evil days, Kai.'

'And I yours.'

No embrace, not even a joining of hands. A tilt of one head towards another, answered in kind. No friendship, no wound truly closed, but perhaps a truce of sorts. Somewhere close, the ring of metal against metal. Perhaps nothing more than the tap of one spear against another, two friends exchanging the warrior's salute. But Arite chose to think it the chimes that the dream readers sometimes heard, the ghostly signal of watching gods who liked what they saw.

Bahadur turned to Arite, and laid his hand upon hers. 'And now, you must follow the grey road south and east.' He tried to smile. 'Live, and we shall live to come and find you.'

Kai was behind him, not daring to come forward. For what a fragile truce it was between those two men, so fragile that any touch or word that she gave would break it. An open palm facing towards her, lips moving to form silent words that she could not read in the darkness – that was all the farewell they would have.

No answer that she could give him with Bahadur's eyes upon her, and so she gave the nomad's farewell instead – a leap into the saddle, a touch of the heels to the flanks of her horse, a hand raised in the air as she rode away. For what did goodbyes mean to those who did not think beyond the day's end? They would meet again with the dawn or in the Otherlands, and it was not supposed to matter which one of those it was. And yet it did.

Then the road was ringing beneath the hooves of her horse, music to keep her company. Stay on that path for but an hour, and she would be at the gates of Coria. To seek safety within its walls, to wait for the battle to finish – that was what had been asked of her.

But stone walls offered no sense of protection to a nomad, and it was not the way of her people, for the women to wait for the men. Her people knew this to be true above all else – given the choice between two paths, between safety and danger, one must always go towards sword and spear, and choose the iron way.

And so she checked her horse, glanced back towards the fort that burned upon the Wall. Shadows only she saw there, and a shadow she would be to them in return. They would not see the path she chose as she turned her horse from the road.

The hooves fell near silent upon the soft ground, the folds of the land closing about her as she went into the valley, not wishing to offer a silhouette against the skyline. Then she pulled the reins until the horse was still for a moment, listening for the unlikely sound of pursuit. Somewhere distant, the calling of an owl, the rustling of an animal moving through the woodland close by. The trickle of water falling from the leaves of the trees as it began to rain. But nothing more than that.

A moment longer, alone in the dark, as she thought through what she must do. She closed her eyes, and saw the land she would pass through – every turn of the hills, the lines of the river and stream. In her imagined journey, she could reach out a hand to the heather and feel its rough touch against her skin, smell the rich scent of the bracken rising up from the ground.

Then it was time – a calling of that owl the signal she chose to follow, the way that horns had called her to the battle so many times before. And she followed the path she had marked in her mind, invisible to any but her, to the north and to the west. To a place on the Wall, where all would be decided.

'Let us speak together now, you and I,' said Bahadur. 'Truthfully, now that she is gone.'

Kai made no answer at first. For these were the first words that Bahadur had spoken since his wife had ridden from them.

They had been called to their place in the line by a captain, orders given and shared, and the older man had said nothing. Kai had hoped that perhaps it was a companionable, healing kind of silence, the kind they had shared many times before, side by side before a battle, each drawing strength from the other. But now when Bahadur spoke, his voice was soft and hollow, with none of the warmth that it had held before.

'I spoke truthfully before,' Kai answered.

'I did not.'

Kai leaned forward and put his hand to his horse's cheek – even with the barding she wore, she muttered appreciatively, leaned into him, both of them seeking that comfort in touch. 'Then tell me what you must,' he said.

'What will you do?' said Bahadur. 'After the battle?'

'You believe that we shall live through this?'

'Oh, I think that you shall.' A curl of the lip. 'You have always had good fortune, not that you deserve it. They could throw you in the sea and you would come out dry.'

'Bahadur, enough. Say what you must.'

And yet the words took a long time to come. Long moments spent, the wind blowing hard across the plain, until at last, Bahadur spoke again.

'I thought there could be peace between us,' he said. 'Perhaps there could have been. If only…' A rattle of armour, as Bahadur shook his head. 'But it cannot be.'

'I understand.'

'No. You do not.' Bahadur turned his head, and in the darkness Kai could only see his eyes – alive with pain, running with tears. 'It is no thing of jealousy. Or at least, not just that.'

'Then what?'

'It is that I am the better man than you.'

Kai nodded slowly. 'I have never doubted that, Bahadur. You have no need to prove such a thing to me.'

'And so you think she may be content with you?' said Bahadur. 'That she may love you? Knowing the kind of man that you are. Knowing it as we both do.'

Once more, the whisper of the gods. The secret words that Kai spoke to himself in the night, and here they were, from Bahadur's lips. A man who knew him better than any other, better than Kai knew himself. For always it was that Bahadur had seemed to see the truth of things. He had always known how to judge the word of a man, to see in the heart of captain and chieftain and know if they were worthy.

'You know this,' Bahadur said, 'Do you not?'

'Perhaps,' Kai answered. 'I cannot say.'

'But I can. For I know her better than you ever will.'

'I see her with me,' Kai said. 'Alive, as I have not seen her in a long time. I see her joyful.'

'Aye, I see it too,' said Bahadur. 'For a time, it may be so. Until she knows you as I do. As Lucius does. And then you shall break her.' A long pause. Then: 'The way you have broken me. You break us all in the end.'

'What would you have me do, then?'

'Set her free of you. In this battle, or after. Have courage, and set her free. For she is caught by you, the way some men are by wine. And it will destroy her, in the end. *You* shall destroy her. This I know.'

'I love you as a brother, Bahadur,' said Kai. 'Nothing you say may change that.'

And there, at last, was doubt in Bahadur, a break in the guard. He was there once more – a man as gentle to those he loved as he was fierce to his enemies, a man who would gift away all he had and ask nothing in return, a hero of love and song. Then Bahadur drew away, and once more, he wore his mask of pain, those cold narrow eyes that looked out upon the world and saw nothing beautiful there.

'What is the love of such a man to me?' said Bahadur.

What could have been done with more time? Perhaps nothing. Perhaps everything. Yet there was no time left. Soft whistles, passing down the line. More whispers, saying what all could now see.

The enemy was upon the Wall.

26

It was the world inverted, the law of the borderlands turned upon its head. For now it was Painted People holding the Wall, masters of their domain, and the Sarmatians looking toward it with hungry eyes. And with his people, Lucius watched and waited, to see what the tribes of the north would do with their prize.

The sky began to redden with the coming dawn, and the war chants of the Painted People grew softer, discordant. The blood fever leaving them, perhaps. Or it might be that Corvus the Deserter, knowing that the Romans had conquered more with stone and mortar than they had with the sword, was begging his war chiefs to be satisfied with what they had taken.

For the Painted People had but to hold their ground. There was nothing that the Sarmatian cavalry could do against fort and wall. A single last charge, useless and glorious – that would be all that was left to the Sarmatians. Beating their blades dull against the stone of the Wall, the way the heroes of the old stories, knowing their doom was upon them, sometimes chose to wage impossible battles against mountain and sky and sea.

But the land beyond must have called to those people of the north. Open and unguarded, the forbidden country that they had dreamed of for half a hundred years. A people who lived by raid and feud with that great hunting run denied them for so long. And perhaps it was that the Painted People felt an evil in the stone of the Wall, peopled as it was by the ghosts of the Romans who had broken their people, cut their country in two, murdered their gods. And so the shadows began to move beyond the Wall, through the smoking gates of the fort, spilling out upon the open ground beyond.

A stirring beside Lucius in the ditch of the *vallum*. The restless movement of men and horses, as eager to flee as to fight. Anything but to sit and watch death come towards them.

'Wait,' Lucius said to them. For the timing must be perfect.

The Painted People were beginning to grow in confidence. The wind brought the sound of screamed orders, the captains and the war chiefs trying to keep the tribes as one, but they were beginning to scatter, dispersing into bands of hunters and raiders. The open land calling to them, the glory of the hunt, the prizes they would win and take home.

'Wait,' Lucius said again.

The sky a little lighter – dawn, perhaps, though none could tell with the clouds so thick upon the horizon. Lucius was waiting for an omen, for he knew they were beyond the world of drill and tactics now. He needed the magic that Mor had spoken of, and nothing else would do.

A shadow among the Painted People. A giant it seemed at first, a creature from myth and omen, before it shifted and became hauntingly familiar. A tall man on a Roman horse – Corvus the Deserter. The omen, come at last. The beginning, and the end.

There was no need to wait any longer – no need to speak the order. For the Sarmatians saw what he saw, thought what he thought. And as one, they rose from the ditch of the *vallum*. As one, they put their horses to the charge.

A moment of perfect silence, utter stillness. That last gift of the gods, offered to those about to go to battle. To hold the world in place and make a life stretch out just a little longer. One last moment to think of a lover, to hold a particular memory close like a sacred treasure, before the hooves rolled like thunder beneath them, the war banners drinking the wind and screaming it back into the sky. With the world falling past Lucius, in the half-light of dawn there was no telling how many others were about him. There might have been ten thousand following him, or he might have been riding alone.

Then the rattle of the lances tilting down, and before him the first hunting party of the Painted People gathering together, trying to form the lines and set the spears, aping the tactics of the Romans they so hated. But they did not have the time or the will to do it – a startling jolt that numbed Lucius's hands, the trip and stumble of his horse as it stamped a man's life away, and then they were through, the scattered dead left behind them.

A moment to rein in his horse, to bring the Sarmatians close about him once more. A moment too for the Painted People to see how few they faced. For there were only fifty men and horses behind Lucius, and the men of the north were rallying together, the war songs singing out once more.

But there were other horns blowing, echoing and ringing back from the high Wall before them. The Sarmatian calls of war that had led them on the hunt for hundreds of years, and it was from valley and forest and the heather they came, in scattered bands of men and horses that encircled the Painted People. The gamble that Lucius had made, to break apart his already outnumbered company, to hope that the shadows of the dawn might make five hundred seem as five thousand. That a circle about the Painted People, no matter how thinly drawn, might be enough to break them.

Then once more the world was a stream of colour and light surging past Lucius, before him a forest of spears set against the charge. If the line of the Painted People held, the Sarmatians would be destroyed, impaled on the spears or thrown by their bucking horses, swarmed on the ground and hacked to pieces. And in that charge, the Sarmatians asking a question of those men of the north. Did they trust the man beside them? Did they love them, in the way that the Sarmatians loved one another?

The spears shivered, trees in a storm. Then scattering and breaking all at once – as if ordered to, commanded by man or god to throw down their weapons at the same instant. And the cavalry of the Sarmatians plunged into them and through them, swimmers to the sea.

This time, there was no silence. The deafening sounds of war all about him, the rending of metal and flesh, the high-pitched shrieks of men and horse dying. Locked in the close confines of his helm, the world was reduced to the reach of Lucius's spear, and when that was broken, his sword. There was only the careful, patient work of killing, over and over again.

He did not know how long it was, a moment or a lifetime, until there were no more of the Painted People within the reach of his sword. Only the Sarmatians, wearing blood like warpaint, grinning and wild-eyed with joy. The northmen had drawn back, the war chants ringing shrill and hollow as the Painted People scattered into the familiar bands of clan and tribe. No will to advance on the Sarmatians it seemed, even as they stood and shrieked curses and insults.

The question had been asked, and answered – the Painted People did not have the courage to stand against them. If the Sarmatians were to charge again and again, they would break their enemies one time after another. Lucius knew this to be true, yet still he felt, settling upon him, the sweet sadness of defeat.

For he could hear the gasping breath of the horses, see the white foam dripping and falling from their lips, feel the weariness of the steps his own mount took beneath him. For that was what would kill them, at the last. Not sword and spear, but aching lungs and trembling legs. When the horses could no longer run, that would be the end of them all, and it would come soon enough.

Lucius looked to the horizon, and found it empty. No Sarmatians come from Coria or Vindolanda. No sign of the Legion marching from Eboracum. The great signal fire they had made of the fort had come to nothing.

Now the time to retreat – all that he had learned of the art of horse and spear told him this. His mount almost spent, his people outnumbered. Yet he knew retreat offered nothing but a slow death on the cross, the deserter's fate. And there was still one chance left to them.

He lifted his sword up high, the sword that had killed a Sarmatian king far to the east. The sword that bore a charm of victory, or so his warriors believed. And he led them not to the south but to the north – to the most dangerous place of all, between the Painted People and the Wall.

The Sarmatian horns blowing, the high songs ringing in the air. Half songs sounding out, missing the voices of the women, but still there was no mistaking them for what they were – songs of victory, of death to their enemies. And Lucius could see the fear rolling through the Painted People like a wave as they saw the Sarmatians take their place beside the Wall. That cursed place of stone, guarded now by monsters of iron and bone, who did not seem to fear, who did not seem to die.

One charge, perhaps, was all that their horses had left. It might be all that it would take.

The sword flashing high above once more, the Sarmatians lined up behind him, the order ready to be given. But then there was a sound ringing out high above the songs of his men, a roaring, terrible voice that spoke in all languages and none. The voice of Corvus the Deserter, calling in Latin, calling in the tongue of Marcomanni, in all the languages of the Painted People of the north. And Lucius could see him then, riding back and forth across the line of his warriors. And wherever that man moved, a mad bravery seemed to follow him. The spears were steady once more.

Too late, Lucius signalled the charge. For once, he had waited a moment too long.

Arrows flew forward, thrown spears arced through the air, and before him he saw the Sarmatian horses were stumbling, lamed through the chinks in the armour. Horses went to the ground, the line falling, failing, breaking. The wet crunch as his horse went over one of his own men, and their charge cut in two – half the Sarmatians trapped behind the fallen horses, a few others pressing on, a hundred men who did not know themselves to be alone. And Lucius could see it all then – the

Painted People setting their spears firm against the charge, believing once more in their victory. The horses breaking away from that thicket of iron, bucking and throwing their riders.

And he saw too, who had led that last charge. He saw Kai, his horse cut and bloodied, turning to try and lead his men back. He saw the spear cut through the air, saw it take Kai's horse in the side. And he saw the man who had once been his friend go flying and falling towards the hungry earth, and lie still once more.

27

The taste of earth and blood in his mouth. Half his vision struck to blackness, and the other touched with stars. Kai had been weightless a moment before, as they had seemed to fly into the charge on horseback – now it seemed to take all the strength he had simply to stand, the cuirass of horn and iron trying to drag him back to the ground as though he were crawling up from deep beneath the soil, from his own grave.

His horse had carried him far before it had fallen, and the Painted People seemed in no hurry to cross the ground to reach him. He could hear the Sarmatians, calling to him, screaming at him to come back to the line. He could hear Lucius's voice above all of the others, and felt a longing to answer the call.

But there was something he had seen a moment before, as he lay on his back with the world inverted. A dead horse with markings that he could not place at first, a rider beneath it who seemed familiar. And like those heroes of the old tales he could not help but look back one more time.

It was Bahadur's horse he saw. Bahadur, lying beneath it, unmoving.

Kai pulled the helm from his head with a trembling hand, felt the sharp touch of the sun against his eyes, took a shaking breath in that came out steady. The world bright and beautiful about him, as he looked on it clearly for the last time.

No strength to run, and so he walked, limping steps that dragged and caught on the tussocks as he waited for a thrown spear or arrow to find him, the Painted People to come forward like a wave from the sea and drag him down.

But they waited. For Kai knew, with that strange intimacy that comes upon the battlefield, that those men were weary, impossibly weary. For they were at the time where broken men will clutch and lean against their enemies, gasping for breath and weeping with pain, before they try to kill each other once more. Moments before he had smelled the rotten scent of their sweat, seen them grey-faced and panting, leaning upon their spears with the utter exhaustion that only comes upon men in battle.

And perhaps it was more than weariness which held them back. Perhaps it was that they understood this particular kind of bravery, and they respected it. For they were watching a man go to die with his friend.

Bahadur was pinned beneath the horse, lying as still as the dead. But when Kai leaned down beside him, pulled off a glove and held his hand to Bahadur's lips, he felt the breath there like a kiss of the wind rolling across the steppe. He saw those eyes open, narrow slits that stared at him, silent and questioning.

Kai knew what had to be done, yet he did not wish to do it. He wanted only to wait there forever beside his friend, for Bahadur to know that he had come back. But he could hear the calling of horn and drum, the rattle of the spears. There was so little time left. And with the last of his strength, he pushed and dragged the horse from Bahadur, a man trying to move a mountain, until he could look at what lay beneath.

The hot taste of bile in his throat, his vision swimming and tilting with nausea. For what he saw were legs folded at impossible angles, the hips rolled flat against the earth, flesh opened, the white of bone daubed red.

But Bahadur did not flinch at the sight. He looked down upon himself in the strangely calm way men often contemplated their mortal wounds. A whole life spent cowering in the shadow of death, fearing that the slightest wound would fester, nightmares of the sudden invasion of iron into flesh, the winter fever that would steal in unseen and take a life away. And now the waiting was over, and even the certainty of death might offer some comfort to the fearful.

A hand reaching out, trembling in the air, and Kai searched the grass for the thing to fill it. Nearby, a broken sword, the best weapon that Kai could find, and he gently placed the hilt in Bahadur's hand. A weapon for him to carry into the afterlife, to prove to those who waited for him that he died as a warrior should. Nothing, it was said among the Sarmatians, mattered more than that.

But the weapon was falling upon the ground, and the shaking hand reaching out once more. And upon Bahadur's face was the weary and patient expression of a father waiting for a son to understand.

Kai clasped Bahadur's hand in both of his own, rocked back and forth as though he were trying to lull a child to sleep. And Bahadur looked up at him, still and serious, the way only the very old and newborns look, those who stand on the threshold of life and death.

They were together once more, and all was as it should be.

All about them, the sounds of war had fallen to near silence, as the Painted People and the Sarmatians gathered their strength for the last time. No rattle of spear and shield or whisper of arrow, no ring of iron or splintering of wood, no heavy tread of horse or man. Only the soft music of the voices – the slow, sweet death songs of the Sarmatians, the victory music of the northmen. Even exhausted as they all were, with lungs of fire and mouths that tasted of iron and sand, they still found the strength to sing.

And then somehow, above it all, other voices joined them.

For Kai heard it then – a song that spoke of childhood upon the steppe, of great journeys across the plain. Of cattle raid and feud. Of war, and victory. It was the song of the women of the steppe.

And they were coming through the broken gates of the Wall. The warriors of Votadini, the skin painted blue and their spears burnished bright. And there, leading them forward, leading them in song, were Laimei and Arite.

Few they were – they should have been too few to make a difference. And yet a change was upon the Sarmatians, and on the Painted People too.

Kai held Bahadur close to him, whispered to him softly. 'The women have come, Bahadur. To fight for us, and for you.'

Once more, the trembling fingers reaching to Kai, beckoning him close. And even as the horses shook the ground like thunder, even as the iron sang and the killing began once more, Kai did nothing more than lay his ear to Bahadur's lips, and wait for him to speak.

★

Half a lifetime it had been since Arite had ridden in a battle, and yet it was all so familiar. The hot taste of metal in a dry mouth, the way time seemed to move all at once or not at all. The fear that was a cousin to madness, that grew stronger and stronger until the very last moment, when it became something unfeeling that could be mistaken for bravery. It might have been but a day before that she had gone to battle, as though the twenty years had been nothing but a passing dream.

It had been a hard night of riding to bring her to that place. Through the abandoned gate of a milecastle to the west, then out into a strange land with only rumours to guide her, those words describing rivers and hills that she had heard Kai and Bahadur both repeat to themselves like a prayer that might keep them safe. And she had found the Votadini gathered solemnly at a tree near a river, the holy place where great choices of their people were made. They were staring at the great fire on the Wall as an omen from the gods that they could not decipher, and when she arrived, it seemed that she was their sign, their answer to the riddle. A messenger telling them to fight and die in the shadow of the Wall.

Once, she had fought dressed in the horn and scale of her people, a great tall lance in her hand, in a warband of a thousand horses and men. Now she had a near lame horse under her, nothing but a round leather shield to protect her, a half sized hunting spear, and two hundred men of the Votadini. Yet with her was Laimei – and such a champion might make all of the difference.

Their charge was a stumbling thing upon horses ridden almost lame, but still there was strength and weight behind it. Like a river flowing beyond its banks in the flood season, that moves slow and yet may sweep entire villages with it – that was how they struck the Painted People.

The battle fever came, the white touch upon her vision, a dull silence. For killing was a thing of forgetting for her, something seen in glimpses between the pain. Like the work of birthing a child – a thing of agony and gasping breath, of summoning strength from some deep and secret place to do the impossible.

How long it was before a break in the battle, she did not know. But like a dreamer waking, she came back to herself. Her arms aching and bruised, splinters driven deep into the hand that held the spear, her shield hacked and battered half to pieces. The taste of dust in her mouth. A wound upon her thigh, the flesh cut open and bleeding but no white of bone, and no pain, not yet. And as she looked about her, at the Sarmatians and the Votadini, it seemed as though it would not be enough, that all they had done would come to nothing.

For there were so few of them left, now, and before them the Painted People still held their line, through a stubborn exhaustion more than anything else. Too tired to run, they had gone to that most dangerous place of the mind, a place beyond fear and pain, too weary to think one's own life worth saving. But still strength enough to kill.

She found herself beside Lucius – his armour hacked and sword blunted, but the blood he wore belonged all to others, it seemed. And in that brief moment they had left, they leaned against each other, the way lovers sometimes rode together out upon the steppe. Each of them dreaming for a moment, in that strange embrace, of the ones that they had lost.

For as she looked about the warband for Bahadur and Kai,

she could not see them. And some part of her knew that if they still lived, they would have found their way to her. There was a lightness then, to think that she would join them soon, that she would see her lost children too, in the fields without end beneath a golden sky in the Otherlands.

She saw that Lucius could not give the order he must. That he could not tell his people to ride to their deaths. And so, with what remained of her strength, she lifted her bloody spear high and prepared to lead them forward.

As if in answer, a sound rang in the distance. The sound of trumpets, echoing from beyond the hills and against the walls.

There was fear at first to hear them. For a hundred years or more, that sound had brought war and death to the Sarmatians. But now, it might save them.

For the eagles were in the sky, the golden eagles of the Legion – she saw them first, cresting over the turn of the hills. Then she heard the heavy tread of the Romans on the march, the ringing sound of nailed boots upon metalled roads, six thousand feet stamping the ground at once. And at last, they were there – the thin cruel spears, the iron gleaming upon helm and cuirass, the tall shields like a walking fortress.

Still, there was no relief to see the Romans. For centuries her people had learned to fear them, and even now, in that place, there was no telling what their arrival might mean. Perhaps Caerellius had bought them all, or spun some story of Sarmatian rebellion. Perhaps they were here to merely watch the Painted People work, to be certain that Lucius and his Sarmatians died there, in that place.

But beside them, she saw something else.

Again, she saw the banners first. The open-mouthed

dragons, the painted wolves, the hunting falcons of the steppe that danced in the sky as though they quarrelled with the eagles of the Legion. And then they were there, upon the great tall horses, dressed in armour of horn and iron and bone – the Sarmatians, the nomads of the open plain, the children of the sun and the wolf.

From Eboracum and Coria and Vindolanda they had come in their thousands, summoned by the fire, summoned by omens.

And she and Lucius clung to each other, laughing and weeping and singing once more. For they knew then, beyond all doubt, that they were saved.

28

It had begun like a tale from the old stories – with fire and omens, a stand of few against many. But it ended with no glorious charge, nor the bloodshed of a rout. It ended with a shambling retreat, an exhausted truce between men who had no strength left to fight each other.

Lucius watched as the Painted People staggered through the burned gates of the fort and Wall, passing within a few spear lengths of those Sarmatians who remained. They moved close enough for Lucius to see the glassy eyes of broken men and their lips moving in wordless prayers or oaths of vengeance, for they had no breath left to curse or sing. But even the Sarmatians, who worshipped warriors above all else, did not raise their spears again even though their enemies were close enough to touch. Exhausted, they clung to their saddles as shipwrecked men cling to wreckage, wishing only for the battle to be over.

If they had seen Corvus the Deserter, Lucius knew that they would have had to try to fight – a clawing, desperate battle of defeated men. But for better or worse, there was no sign of him among the Painted People who moved like a band of walking corpses through the gates. And at last, when they were all gone to the north, it was time to count the dead.

Arite had remained beside him, unflinching. For she had seemed fearless a moment before, a blind courage written upon her face, a steady hand upon the spear as she watched the Painted People go. But now they were gone, she was hunched over in the saddle like a woman twice her age, her skin so grey he thought her badly wounded at first. And in her eyes, when she looked at him, there was a silent question.

'There,' Lucius said, and it seemed to take all his strength to point the way, to the tattered and bloody tussocks where he had last seen Kai and Bahadur. 'That is where I saw them fall.'

She nodded absently, as though he had pointed the way to a river or stream, a decent path through a forest or towards a mountain pass, and not towards the men that she had loved. And she set her horse stumbling forward, to see what waited there for her.

He should have followed to face the sight with her. That much he owed to her. That much he owed to Kai. But he knew that she had the courage to look and he did not.

A hand upon his shoulder. Mor of the Votadini was there, that merry light gone from his eyes. For in that moment, perhaps, there was a brotherhood between them. The look of those who have led men to their deaths, over and over again. Those who have lived, but left something of themselves behind with every battle that they fought.

'Magic, you see?' Mor said. 'It was as I said it would be.'

'Magic, you call it,' Lucius answered. 'I call it spearmen and cavalry, in the right place at the right time.'

'True enough. But the magic is in what brought us here.'

'A foolish Roman thing, you said. To come and fight for a land that is not yours.'

A smile then, and the light returning to the chieftain's eyes. 'Yes,' he said, 'it is a foolish thing to fight for another's land. But to fight beside a man such as you – that is the way of the Votadini. A way that has served us poorly, it is true. It is why we scratch a living north of the Wall, a broken and beaten people, for we choose to fight when we should not.' A bark of a laugh. 'But is there any other way to live?'

'No,' Lucius said, 'there is not. And that was what changed your mind? To fight beside me?'

Mor nodded. 'And more than that, to fight by women such as you have. It was they that brought us here, after all.'

For in the distance, they could both see Laimei – cut and bloodied, all the signs of weariness upon her too. Yet she alone seemed as though she had fight left in her, sat tall in the saddle with her spear held high, stalking back and forth across the line.

'Like something out of the old stories, she is,' said Mor. 'Does she never tire of the killing?'

'Not yet, at least,' Lucius answered. 'You still think to win her as your wife?'

'I would not wish such a dull fate for her. Besides, I think that she is married to a god of war. Our Morrigan, perhaps, or your Mars. I would not wish to face such a bloody rival for her love.'

'That is true.' Lucius reached up and ran a hand through his sweat-soaked hair, feeling the fingers tremble against his skin. 'You have my gratitude, for all that you have done. Will you feast with me tonight?' He tried a laugh, and found it came out hollow. 'After all, you have hosted me twice already. Will you join me?'

'I thank you. I would like to drink good wine with you, my brother.' Mor paused, his eyes straying towards the marching Legion. 'But my people go now, back beyond the Wall. I do not think I care to stay for *them* to arrive.'

'Why? You have fought beside Rome. You shall be well rewarded for it.'

A cryptic smile from the chieftain. 'We shall see. The Romans like to say of my people that we are foolish, little more than animals. That we cannot control ourselves, or think beyond the moment that we are living in. That we learn nothing of what you have to teach us. But we have always found that it is the Romans who have very short memories.'

Once more, a touch upon the shoulder. And a strange knowing settling upon Lucius, that the feast would never come, and no wine would they share beside the fire.

Mor spoke again, and said: 'Be brave, Lucius of the Wall. Bear of the North I name you. A terror to your enemies, and your friends, too, perhaps.'

There was so much more to be asked. A lifetime they could have spent learning from one another. But there was a howling cry, rising from where Arite had gone, the cry of grief and mourning. As if in answer, the trumpets calling once more, the Legion offering its greeting, saluting a great victory.

Lucius turned his horse towards the south, towards the Legion. For he knew that, in spite of all the blood they had spilled that day, there was one more enemy left for him to confront. And so he stirred his horse forward, to face that enemy alone.

*

There should have been no telling them from any of the dead that lay strewn across the battlefield. All about Arite were dead Sarmatians lying still upon the ground, dressed in their cuirasses of iron and horn, skin painted in earth and blood. Only their wounds made them distinct from one another – those with their chests caved flat by the press of horse and men, those with the thighs carved open and their feet painted red by blood, those folded over and clutching at the arrows and spears that pierced them through.

But Kai and Bahadur she would have known anywhere. The particular curve of Bahadur's shoulders, like a bow drawn taut. The way that Kai's hair, when matted with sweat or dirt, always fell towards the left. By these and a dozen other secrets of the body, she knew them, and by something else besides – of all the fallen upon the field, it was only those two who lay in one another's arms.

She had seen that embrace many times before, back upon the steppe, on those beautiful, lazy days at the height of summer, when there was nothing to do but doze in the sun and keep half an eye upon the wandering herd. Before the wars had come, and the feud that had broken their friendship to pieces. Before she had broken it.

A moment where she tried to understand what she was seeing, to accept what had been lost. And then a shifting upon the ground, as one of those figures began to move.

One hand pushing against the earth to lift himself upright – trembling and shaking, a newborn foal struggling to rise. And even as Kai's eyes met hers and blinked slowly, there was hope, mad and wild, that Bahadur might live too. If there was one miracle that had kept Kai alive, why should there not be two? But it was a hope that lasted no more than one breath, a single beat of the heart. For the movement of one only showed the stillness of the other – life made death unmistakeable.

Kai looked up to her, waiting for her to speak. And all she could think to say was: 'You were with him?'

A fading, in Kai, to hear those words. They must not have been what he had hoped for. 'Yes,' he said. 'Bahadur was not alone.'

'Yes he was,' she said. 'Without me, he always felt alone.' Pain, then, quick and cold like iron into skin, but she breathed it away. 'Did he speak to you?' she said.

Kai did not reply for a time. Then: 'He tried. But he could not.'

She nodded absently. And then she knelt beside them, and looked upon her husband for the last time.

A strange kind of calm settled upon her, a cousin to the battle fever. A sharpness to the air she breathed, as though there were little slivers of metal in the air, each breath seeming to cut against her lungs. The madness was close, and she did not know that she would survive it. So many upon the steppe were broken by grief, sitting and starving or finding some other way to die. She had buried all of her children – now, she would bury him too.

But she had felt it before, mourned for him when she thought he was dead. And perhaps, in the end, that was what had parted them, more than anything else, the wound made that would not close. And perhaps she would not grieve for him again. Why mourn for one who had courted death like a lover, the way that he had? Why mourn again, when that grieving had been done once before?

An evil thought then, scratching at her mind – if a god had offered her a dark bargain before the battle, had promised to save Kai or Bahadur, is this what she would have chosen? Did she make such a choice without knowing, in those early hours before dawn, before the battle? Perhaps some hidden part of her mind did such a thing, and a god heard her. Perhaps this was her doing.

And there was grief at that, for what she had already lost and had not known. The songs that would not be sung again. The touch of his hand upon hers. The way that, around a campfire, he might make one feel as though there were nothing beyond the reach of the firelight, that she was a world in herself. The way he once had of making the broken pieces of a life come together once more, until he had been broken himself and found no one able to help him heal.

A sound in the air, then – a tearing, echoing scream. Some miserable soul grieving nearby, she thought, until she paused to breathe, felt the heat and pain in her own throat.

And she let the madness come, and sweep over her like a wave. A grateful drowning in her pain.

29

They came on the sword straight road – the marching Legion, the eagles high above, the sun falling upon mail and cuirass. And Lucius went alone to greet them, as though he were one of those heroes from the stories they told by firelight and beneath the stars, those men and women who made their place by a ford or bridge or mountain valley, and fought alone against an army.

Always before, he had looked upon the Legion with pride, a kind of belonging. Now, as Lucius saw them, he felt something of the fear that generations of barbarians must have known. To hear the fell tread of six thousand feet, and know that it was death that came marching towards him.

A bark of orders and a sounding of trumpets, and the Legion fell still. A single man rode forward from their ranks, a champion to face Lucius – their Legate, Caerellius Priscus. His armour unmarked and sword still bright, yet he had the merry glow of the victor about him. He called a greeting to Lucius, and when the Legate rode forward it seemed for a moment as though he would draw close enough to offer the warrior's clasp of one arm into another. But something in

Lucius must have given him pause – a shift of a shoulder, the tightening of a hand upon a sword. And, just for a moment, there was fear upon Caerellius's face. How long had it been, since that man had looked at one willing to kill him? And so instead he kept a careful distance, and waited for Lucius to speak.

'Why did you bring them?' Lucius said at last.

'Would you believe me if I told you I had a change of heart?'

'No.'

'Good,' said Caerellius. 'You are no fool. But we know this already.' And the Legate cast his gaze towards the fort upon the Wall, the fire-blackened stone and the smoke still rising. 'A clever idea, to burn the fort. There are some things stronger than the word of men up here, or the promise of gold. Your Sarmatians would have mutinied in their thousands, if we had not let them ride to that fire in the sky. You knew how to set them in motion in a way that I could not stop. But I am glad that you did.'

'Glad?'

'Of course,' said Caerellius. 'The day is ours. It is a famous victory for your people to sing of.'

'The fort is burned,' said Lucius, 'and half my men are dead.'

'Yet I think that they shall still sing of it. Don't you?'

'Yes, they will.' And perhaps that was the worst wound of all – that he had led his men to death, and they would thank him for it. Lucius's vision swam for a moment, the world shifting and tilting, until he breathed hard enough to put it steady once more. 'What happens now?' said Lucius.

'To you?'

'To them. To my people.'

The Legate shrugged, as though it were a trifling matter they spoke of. 'You are the victor today. So, let us ask that question once again – tell me the future that you see?'

At once, Lucius answered: 'Your head upon a spear, outside my fort.' And Caerellius grinned at him, as though Lucius had made a fine joke.

'That is one future,' he said, 'though I do not think it shall come to pass. There are better futures for both of us.' The Legate turned, and gestured to the ranks of men behind him. 'We fight together. I am here. The Sixth Legion are here. This is a victory we may share.'

'They are here only because you could not keep them away. I have a mind to tell them.'

'You could tell them, if you would like to. Do you think that they would believe you?'

'No.' Suddenly Lucius was weary – impossibly, terribly weary. Perhaps he could still have found strength to lift his sword and lead a charge, if he had to. But this game of politics had him beaten. 'Why are you smiling?' he said. 'You shall have no Legions sent by Rome, no men to make you Emperor.'

'You must think me reckless,' the Legate answered, 'to wager my life upon a single throw of the dice. Perhaps I will, when the time comes. But not yet. For there are many ways to win the favour of Rome. We have drawn the barbarians here, broken their people. The old enemies of Rome, those who lurk beyond the Wall, are defeated. And this is only the beginning.'

It was then that Lucius understood. 'A war beyond the Wall,' he said.

'Yes, of course. After Teutoburg, the Legions shall not march beyond the Rhenus. They did not march past the Danubius, even when your Sarmatians were broken before them. But here is a border that may still be crossed, where we may still win glory. The kind of war your Sarmatians love. Not the restless guarding of a line across a map, but the glory of battle – that shall be our gift to them, yours and mine.'

'This is the future you see?' said Lucius.

'Yes. And I hope you see it with me.' The Legate looked Lucius up and down, and said: 'You shall rest a few days. Then we shall burn them out and hunt them down, leave blackened ground all the way to the old Antonine wall. And perhaps we shall go beyond it, this time.'

'There are allies of ours,' Lucius said, 'north of the Wall. The Votadini. They fought with us today. If we burn their lands, they shall never forgive us.'

'There are no allies north of the Wall,' the Legate said flatly.

'And if I kill you now?'

Caerellius gave a little shrug. 'A moment of satisfaction, perhaps. Then you shall be cut down by my men, and your Sarmatians crucified as traitors.'

'They would trade their lives for yours in a moment.'

'I have no doubt of that. But you shall not.' An open palm swept across the horizon, as though offering that land up as a gift. 'You shall be a great man, Lucius. To the Sarmatians, and to the Romans. For you shall have my place in Eboracum, as Legate of the North. Your charge shall not be a single fort on the Wall, but the Wall itself. All the Sarmatians at your command, and under your protection.'

Lucius let his eyes drift along the long line of the Wall – a proud mark of an Empire, a monument of greed. His gaze came to rest at last on the smouldering remains of Cilurnum, the great offering he had made in fire, in the hope that the gods would give him a way to save his people.

'What of the fort?' he said.

'We shall rebuild it,' Caerellius answered. 'We always do. It is good to keep the Legions busy. They fall idle, otherwise, into drink and gambling.' And even without looking at him, Lucius could hear the smile in the Legate's voice. 'Once again, you have done me a fine favour without meaning to.'

Lucius looked back at him then, and laid his hand upon the hilt of his sword. And Caerellius turned away. A deliberate carelessness – a challenge, a mockery.

Revenge was there to be taken – the Sarmatian way, to settle things with the blade no matter what the cost. And even if they hung his men from the crosses for it, they would not blame Lucius. They would sing to him, and laugh, too, even as they died.

But he let the grip go slack, the blood already spilled running and dripping against his fingers. He watched the Legate go, and in the silence, in the stillness, he made his bargain.

As the day had begun, so it ended, with fire upon the open plain. But the burning of the fort had been a beacon for the living. These were fires for the dead.

First, they burned the Painted People. The Sarmatians would have left them for the crows and the wolves, but the Legion, ever fearful of disease, busied themselves with gathering the corpses together – a crude mound of the dead that was soon aflame.

The Sarmatians they laid into the great ditch of the *vallum*. There had been five hundred living at the dawn of the day, and more than half that number now lay together in that grave. Once they had covered the dead with earth, the Sarmatians gathered wood and kindling to lay on top of it. Soon, it would be ablaze, with a sword thrust into the earth at the centre of the fire. For the Sarmatians did not burn their dead, but made that fire above their graves as a sign to the gods who watched above, so that they might gather the brave warriors and take them to the Otherlands.

But it was not the time to burn it yet, to send those souls into the next world. For those Sarmatians that were left went wandering across the battlefield, searching not for the corpses of their friends, but for their ghosts.

For the divide between worlds drew thin at the time of killing, and not just for those who had been lost that day. You might catch a glimpse of a lover killed in a feud, a child lost to the winter fever, a father whom the wasting sickness had taken ten years before. Many there had been, back upon the steppe, who had sought out every feud and battle they could fight in, just for one more chance to see those that they had lost.

Like the others, Kai went alone through the bloodied grass and torn earth. The Sarmatians were a people who kept no secrets, for whom every act was shared, who did nothing alone – nothing except for this. For in the twilight after a battle, if you looked to the rivers and the trees and the grass, you would sometimes find the faces of the dead looking back. If you listened to the wind, you might hear the whispering of a voice that had long fallen silent. But only if you went alone.

Each step Kai took was a thing of pain, but he paid it no mind. He limped and stumbled through heather and bracken, mouthing silent words that he knew the dead would hear, hoping against hope to feel an unseen touch of a ghost against his skin. And he searched for his father in the bark of a tree, the mother he had never known in the curling smoke that twisted through the sky. And Bahadur, above all – he clung to the hope that one last time, Bahadur would speak with him and tell him what to do.

And in the end, he did not find any of the dead that he sought. But he did find one of the living.

Perhaps this wandering was a ritual of the Romans, too. For Kai could see Lucius alone in the field, his movements those of a man drunk on grief. And when they looked upon each other, it seemed as though neither of them knew for certain whether they looked upon the living or the dead.

Only through touch would they know – a testing, hesitant embrace. And once they were certain of each other, that their hands gripped firm flesh and not an empty shade from the spirit world, Lucius said: 'Can there be peace between us? Can it be as it once was?'

And without any more being spoken, they sat together on the ground. There was something boyish to Lucius, Kai thought, as the Roman sat cross-legged upon the earth, leaned back and closed his eyes against the dying sun. For all the marks of age and war that were written upon his skin, still there was a glimpse of the child he had once been – Kai could see him as a lanky young boy, charging around a courtyard with a stick for a sword, dreaming of heroism and valour. Now, thirty years later, the boy was there once more. And when he spoke, they were the words of a child, too, a child to whom forgiveness means everything.

'I do not know if we have accomplished anything today,'

Lucius said. 'For all the men killed, I do not know what has been changed, what good may come of it. But perhaps we have earned a chance to forget.'

Kai made no answer for a time. For he knew that he had to speak the truth, that nothing mattered more than that. But that he could not speak all of the truth.

'I do not know that all things may be forgotten,' Kai said at last, 'but what hurt we have done each other, let that be forgotten.' Kai looked down at his hands, deep scored with blood and earth. 'I placed too much upon you. You were to be our Great Captain and my brother. You were to lead us to glory and see us home, back to the steppe. I gave up my clan, and thought you could replace them all. It was more than any man could do.'

'I made those promises freely,' Lucius said. 'I believed that I could do it.'

'I believed that you could, too. I know that you tried. But there is no shame that you could not.' Kai hesitated, and looked towards the distant pyre. He could see the Sarmatians cease their wanderings, could see them gathering there. The time of ghosts was almost over, it seemed.

'I saw you lead that charge,' Lucius said. 'It was bravely done.'

'Brave, perhaps. Foolish, and it did no good. It was Arite and Laimei who broke them.'

'The coming of the Legion, I think. That was why they ran.'

And against all odds, Kai felt a smile touch his lips. 'Let us say it was you, then. You were the one who brought us this victory.'

'It does not feel like a victory.'

'They rarely do, at the time. But later, I think, you shall be proud of what you have done here today.'

'Later…' And that word seemed to act like a spell upon the Roman – the years came tumbling back, the war weariness lay upon him. 'This is but the beginning, and not the end,' Lucius said. 'There will be a war beyond the Wall. We shall burn and raid and drive them north. That is the bargain I have made. The Legate shall have his glorious war, and my Sarmatians shall live.'

'Laimei is in the north,' said Kai. 'Mor. Those who saved us.'

'I know. They have always seemed to know before we marched to the north before. I hope they shall escape us.'

'Lucius—' But Kai did not get to speak any more.

'I shall need you at my side,' said Lucius, 'for what is to come. I do not think that I can do it alone.'

'I understand.' A longing, then, to reach out to Lucius, to offer the Roman the comfort that he asked for. But Kai knew that he could not do it. 'I say again, be proud of what you have done today,' said Kai. 'No matter what follows it.'

Perhaps the old stories of the Sarmatians were true, and it was in blood and fire that the broken bonds between men might be remade. For the pyre was being lit before them, the smoke rising high up into the sky and twisting up towards the stars. Into the places where gods and heroes lived, and looked down upon those who remained below. Watching with pity, and with love.

Once more, the brotherhood between them. But Kai knew it would not last for long.

Where Bahadur was among the dead, Arite could not tell.

Kai had helped her carry her husband to the grave, laid

him there among his companions. She had watched him, as the earth began to fall upon the grave, as all about her men gathered wood for the pyre. But she had looked away – only for a moment, at some tearing sound of grief that one man made for another, and when she turned back once more, she could not find the place where Bahadur had been. Only a moment and he was gone, lost in the sea of the numberless dead.

Still, she waited. She did not go walking in the field of ghosts, there was no need. She could feel him there beside her, so long as she stood still. She could hear him, if she closed her eyes and listened.

The madness of grief had left her for now. Only a hard hollow remained behind – another weight to carry, that itself might be enough to break her. For it seemed sometimes that this was what remained to her in life. Not to feel the peace of love or that wild magic of kinship that was found about the campfires or upon the travels across the open steppe, not to feel anything that gave joy to her life. Simply to carry the weight of her grief, to move slower and slower as she dragged it with her, until she received the burden that would break her.

It seemed at first that the time had come, as the flames were lit, the smoke and the heat rising from the pyre. All that she had loved seeming to take the air with that fire, and only the ashes of life remaining behind for her to taste.

Then she saw the sword silhouetted at the heart of the flames, a symbol that had spoken the same message to her people for hundreds of years – a command to fight, to be brave. And all about her, the Sarmatians were there, the hands linking and joining together, Kai to one side of her and Lucius at the other. Together, they closed the circle around the fire.

There was no ritual speaking, no chants or song, for their music was for the living and not the dead. There were only whispers in the dark, fragments of speech and stories, as those about the fire were compelled to speak as though by the ghosts from the world beyond, sharing tales of those they had lost. *Do you remember when he... He told me once that... He was always...*

And she joined them, sharing all the secrets that she and Bahadur had learned together, just as beside her, she heard Kai and Lucius speak their stories. A pride grew in her then, a strength to bear the grief, that she had known and loved such a man. It was a gift that could not be taken away from her.

The time of her breaking might still come, and it might come soon, but not yet. For she knew once more the sweet gift of her people – to be glad of what was there, and not to think of tomorrow. She knew herself part of the many, and knew that for all that she had lost, she was not alone.

The fire was burned to ashes, carrying the dead away. Only the living remained behind, together.

She saw the Sarmatians look towards Lucius, expecting him to tell them what must be done. But it seemed that he had no commands to give – not tonight. Tomorrow they would be soldiers of Rome once more, bound to the commands of ambitious, ruthless men, kept in line by whip and blade, bought with silver and bound by the oaths they had given. For one night alone they had earned their freedom.

And so they wandered to the horses, pulling blankets and furs from the saddlebags. For they would not sleep in the burned barracks, those smoking tombs of stone, but out beneath the open sky in the old, familiar way of their people. Sharing wine and swapping stories of the dead, sleeping beside fires and beneath the stars, they might dream their way back to the steppe they would not see again.

Arite led Kai by the hand to some quiet part of the open plain, watched him test the ground with a probing foot with a nomad's simple chivalry, seeking for her the most comfortable place to lay her head. And he cast the blanket down on some dry flat piece of ground, and gathered her to him.

Her head was upon his chest, and she felt his hands gently trace the loops and braids of her hair. They did not speak, did no more than hold one another close, match their breaths together, and think of the long road that had brought them to this place, perhaps to stay for the rest of their lives. And as she began to slip into sleep, into that place where the world of the waking warps and bends to the impossible desires of the heart, she made her prayer for the future.

Just as sleep took her, there was some answer made in flesh. Not the answer she had hoped for, but an answer nonetheless that she felt deep within, a sensation familiar but almost forgotten – the quickening of life beneath the skin, the first, impossible sense of a child. And she fell asleep smiling, with a secret she would keep until the morning.

30

It was in the deepest part of the night, when Kai woke once more.

He had hoped against hope that he would sleep through until the dawn, battle weary as he was. That he would see the rising sun, feel the yoke of Rome descend upon him, and have all his choices taken away again. But the restless gods had woken him, to see if he would keep the promise he had made.

He slipped from Arite's arms, silent as a thief – another hope then, that perhaps she would wake, and see him, and stop him. But still she slept, dreaming with a smile upon her lips. A dream of Bahadur, no doubt.

There was grief to look upon her – grief for a life that might have been. He could hear it calling to him, the years of quiet joy they might find together. And then, when there was silver in his hair and he was free of his debt to Rome, that they might ride free from this place, nomads once more.

But there are things that call more strongly than life and love and joy. For still, he could hear a voice – Bahadur's voice.

He remembered once more the battlefield. The ground shaking with the passage of the cavalry, the war songs sounding out. And Kai embracing his dying friend, Bahadur's last breaths hot against his ear. The words spoken, there at the last.

'Arite,' Bahadur had said. 'Promise me.'

And Kai had remembered what his friend had said before. That Arite would be broken by her love. That Kai would have to set her free. 'Yes. I swear it.'

Bahadur had made as if to speak again, fear suddenly written upon his face as though he wished to unspeak the words. But there were no more breaths left to take. Only a bubble of blood breaking upon the lips, a tremor that Kai felt as if in his own body. The rattling sigh of the dead.

The cold air blowing down from the north brought Kai back to himself. Summer was gone, the harvest was taken, the heather was purpling upon the hills. A long winter ahead – a hard winter, no doubt, in a country such as this one.

Within him, the nomad's restlessness that came with the browning of leaves and the call of the cold wind. The longing to find a place for the winter, a fire to sit beside, good company to keep. That foolish hope that, at the end of the journey, one would be made whole again. The foolish hope that was sometimes true.

And so he began to move, surefooted in the darkness, to where the horses had gathered. His own mount lay slain on the battlefield, and he would have to trust to fate, that one would let him ride. Most were wary of him, a stranger in the night, for they were raised to be killers of men, to trust only one who courted them carefully and patiently, to serve that warrior and no other. But there was a soft whickering call, the syncopated tread of hooves on soft earth, as one of the horses came forward.

Perhaps she had lost her master in the battle, and sought anew that strange, particular love that exists between horse and rider, each completing the heart of the other. And there must have been something about Kai that she recognised – in step or breath or touch, the horse recognised the promise of freedom. Her black eyes shining in the darkness, a tremble of excitement rippling across her flanks like a wave across the surface of the sea.

Soon he was riding alongside the Wall, and from time to time reaching out towards it, feeling the rough touch of the stone, the smooth kiss of the mortar beneath his fingers. Such a little thing, that border seemed now. He fancied that if he were to press a little harder against it he would feel it crumble beneath his fingers, dissolve to dust in the air.

He came to a milecastle with the torches still dark, still abandoned from the day before. Tomorrow it would be ruled once more by the ways of Rome, the ways of the hourglass and the watch word, the fires always lit, the eyes always watching. But for now, for one night alone, it was empty. And he passed through it and into the land beyond.

Alien stars above him, yet he found his way from them, let them whisper their stories and guide him in the darkness. A strange land too, but he had the nomad's instincts, the shape of the hills and the turns of the river marked deep in his mind after but a single journey through it. And so he ventured into the night until in the distance, he saw another fire. And in the air, he could hear what must have been the victory songs of the Votadini.

The chieftain's hall once more before him, the dancers silhouetted before the flames. And when he came closer, he saw that the chieftain's hall *was* the fire – the roof fully ablaze, the walls crawling with smoke. All about, he could see wagons packed and the herds corralled, a sight so familiar that his heart ached to see it. A people ready to move, gathered for a long journey.

He saw Mor, laughing and dancing before the burning wreckage of his home, his light steps those of a man half his age. The men and women all about him, the warpaint running from their skin, the horn cups of heather beer passed round and round and round again.

And she was there too – Laimei, sat cross-legged beside the fire. All about her, the men and the women of the tribe made their celebration, but she did not join them. As always, she was apart, and alone. Staring into the fire, lost in thoughts of her own.

But she saw him then – he must have been nothing but a shadow in the darkness, and yet it seemed she knew him at once. Disbelief written on her face at first. Perhaps she thought he had come from the spirit world, or that her mind had finally broken, the way all heroes lost themselves at the end of their stories, and that she saw some phantom riding in. And whether she thought him a ghost or not, she mounted up and came to meet him.

Their horses called to one another, the whicker and mutter of old companions meeting once again. Kai saw that his sister did believe then, for like all their people, she trusted the wisdom of horses above all else.

He expected no welcome from her. A cold nod, perhaps, a curt greeting spoken. Nothing more than a word to the others to make him welcome at the fire, or perhaps not even that. Perhaps she would mark him as an enemy and an outsider, and they would offer him only death.

But she seemed strangely hesitant. With a spear in her hand she had always moved without doubt, the champion's faith in fate and the watchful presence of the gods. Yet now, without a weapon, she sat hunched in the saddle, fingers toying with the reins.

He led his horse beside hers, let them come nose to tail. And she was reaching for him then, placing her hands upon him. He knew what to do, for he had done it many times before – back upon the steppe, back when they had been children without a mother, when they had only each other for comfort. He put his arms about her, rested his head in the hollow of her neck, and let her hold him close.

They were together once more – the long feud between them cast into the fire and burning away to nothing. Only on this night could it have happened, this night between the worlds of the living and the dead, and at last Kai understood what had truly guided him to that place. He had ridden north to set Arite free of him, to keep his promise to Bahadur. He had ridden north because he could not stand to fight against his sister in the wars that were to come. But above all he had ridden north in the hope that he might be forgiven.

They dismounted together, joined the tribe in the steps of the dance. And at a distance, there could be no telling one shadow from another as they moved about the fire. From further still, no sense of where one of them began and the others ended. One people together, forged by the fire.

And in the morning, when the fire was burned to embers, they had vanished from that place as if they had never been there. Gone to the north, venturing to lands that they had never seen, seeking their home.

Historical Note

This is a work of fiction. Relatively little is known for certain about the Sarmatians, a primarily nomadic people with no written record of their own left behind and a minimal archaeological footprint. What we do know of them is pieced together from written Greek and Roman sources such as Strabo, Cassius Dio, Ovid, and Herodotus, as well as the archaeological finds that survive (mostly from grave sites). So what we have is limited in scope and unreliable in nature – frustrating for the historian, but exciting for the novelist (and, I hope, the reader).

We do know that there was a war with the Roman Empire in AD 175 or so, a battle upon the frozen Danube, and eventually a peace settlement which sent thousands of Sarmatian heavy cavalry to the north of Britain. Much more than that remains mysterious, but the Sarmatians are pleasingly connected to many myths, ranging from that of the Amazon warrior women to that of our own King Arthur.

If you'd like to read further, I recommend *The Sarmatians* (Tadeusz Sulimirski, 1970) and *Sarmatians* (Eszter Istvánovits and Valéria Kulcsár, 2017) as excellent summaries of the archaeological and written record, and *Tales of the Narts* (John Colarusso and Tamirlan Salbiev, 2016), and *From Scythia to Camelot* (C. Scott Littleton and Linda Malcor, 2000) for more on the mythological links.

Acknowledgements

Every book is the work of so many people.

As always, my agent Caroline Wood has been a wonder – a champion for all of my books, with a keen eye for story and tremendous good humour and encouragement through every setback. The team at Head of Zeus have given their all bringing this book to the world, especially Nic Cheetham for getting the project going in the first place, Clare Gordon and Greg Rees for steering this book through its development, Peter Salmon for saving my blushes in the copyedit and Nicola Bigwood in the proofs, and Mark Swan for yet another gorgeous cover.

I receive continuous inspiration and support from my colleagues and students at the Warwick Writing programme. I owe more to my parents than I can ever put into words. Huge thanks are also due to my friends for their good company (often through a screen) during the very strange Covid years – I'd like to thank Kate, Paddy, Lucy, Ness, Tom, Lynsey and Dan in particular for all the good times that we've shared; we made it through with lots of Zoom, lots of D&D, and too many press-ups (I'll always remember 'Eye of the Tiger'...).

These are books about companionship and courage, and so who better to dedicate this book to than to Sara? My love, your courage inspires me every day – I can only hope for many more adventures (and more Prosecco and sushi) in the years to come.

About the Author

TIM LEACH is a graduate of the Warwick Writing Programme, where he now teaches as an Assistant Professor. His debut novel, *The Last King of Lydia*, was shortlisted for the Dylan Thomas Prize, and his first Sarmatian Trilogy novel, *A Winter War*, was shortlisted for the Historical Writers' Association Gold Crown Award.

Follow Tim on @TimLeachWriter